CHICKEN ABOUT LOVE

KACI LANE

Copyright © 2021 by Kaci Lane

All rights reserved.

This is a work of fiction. Names, characters, organizations, places, events and incidents are either products of the author's imagination or are used fictitiously. Any resemblance to actual persons, living or dead, or actual events is purely coincidental.

No part of this work may be reproduced, or stored in a retrieval system, or transmitted in any form by any means without written permission from the author.

For my daughter, Blakely.

You were my inspiration for Taylor, from the cuteness and sass to the "huggy" hugs.

I love you!

AUTHOR NOTE

Chicken about Love is the second book in the Bama Boys Sweet RomCom Series. All books can be read on their own, but if you'd like to read from the beginning, check out *Hunting for Love.*

If you want to keep up with all my books and get updates about opportunities to receive Advanced Reader Copies as well as backstories on my content, join my newsletter.

Happy reading!
Kaci :)

CHICKEN ABOUT LOVE

CHAPTER ONE

Hannah

I'm unemployed, recently divorced, and living with my parents. I have nowhere to go but up. At least, that's the motto I've adopted lately to help me put on a brave face for my daughter.

My stomach buckles as I unplug my flat iron and run another layer of lip gloss across my bottom lip, then smack my mouth. I need to stop. Any more dusty-rose tint on my lips and I may as well apply for a job as a rodeo clown.

I put a hand to my swirling stomach and check my appearance in the mirror. That'll do. I want to make a good impression, but this is a job interview for the last teller window at Smart Money Credit Union, not an audition for *The Bachelor*.

Though thanks to my ex-husband, I've endured enough drama to win an Emmy.

I puff up my cheeks and exhale a foggy circle into my

vanity mirror. Then I step into my heels, grab my purse, and head for the door. My mom offered to take my daughter shopping for school before registering her for kindergarten. I'm hoping moving back here and finding a job will make for a positive change in both our lives.

There's no way I could afford to keep living in Birmingham without Dalton's help. And I'd rather lie in the woods and let chiggers eat me alive than depend on him.

I pull my purse over my shoulder and open the front door to my parents' farmhouse. Skip meets me on the front porch, fluffy tail wagging. I bend down and pet his head.

My mood lifts temporarily at his joyful, slobbery face framed by the morning sun glistening on the fresh dew in the fields. I've missed this view. It's the one thing my high-brow neighborhood in Homewood couldn't offer. I mean, I could've bought a dog. But you can't buy hayfields in Birmingham.

I lock the door behind me and walk to my car. Thanks to my stay-at-home mom days, I barely have any miles on my Jetta. Which makes it all the more disheartening when I notice that my front tire is flat.

My pulse races as my daddy's lectures on how to change a flat funnel through my brain. I pop open the trunk and pull up the latch hiding the spare tire. My eyes widen when I stare down at an empty hole. Where's the tire?

Just great.

Daddy's at work, my mom is in Tuscaloosa with Taylor, and I haven't exactly built any new or old relationships in the two weeks I've been back. Instead, I've laid low with my daughter, applied to the few and far between jobs in town, and tried to steer clear of anyone over fifty not in my family. Small-town folks love to fix up single young adults, and I've caught wind that a few grandmas have their eye on me for less-than-eligible bachelors.

CHICKEN ABOUT LOVE

My underarms start to perspire from both the summer humidity and my slight panic attack. *Think, Hannah.*

I check my phone. There's no time to call someone for a ride—old friend, gossiping granny, out-of-town Uber. As I scan the house nervously, my eyes fall on Daddy's rusty old Ford parked by his shop.

I slam the trunk of my car shut and bolt toward the truck best I can in my heels. The door creaks when I open it. I squeal as a grasshopper bounces onto my skirt before hitting the ground. After a deep breath, I gain the courage to stick my hand in the ash tray. Sure enough, the keys are still there.

I dust off the vinyl seat and plop my purse down before climbing in myself. With a silent prayer and a jiggle to the ignition, it cranks. I exhale and jerk the stick shift into first gear. Maybe the air will kick on in a minute.

My stomach knots with every inch of gravel I travel, as I pray to God that Big Red doesn't break down. I scoot forward to unstick my sweaty legs from the seat. By now, I'm sure the air conditioner doesn't work, so I roll down the windows a few inches.

Some of my hair starts blowing out of the open space, but it's either have a few messy strands or show up covered head to toe in sweat. I hold my arms out from my sides to hopefully not leave pit stains on my white blouse, then blow a string of tangled hair from my view.

I turn onto the main road into town and shift gears. When I lift my foot off the clutch, I roll my ankle in tiny circles. I don't mind driving with a clutch, but holding in Big Red's requires a leg routine fit for Crossfit.

Before I shift gears again, I kick off my heel. Maybe I can stomp the pedal in better flat footed. That would've worked, had my shoe not fallen underneath the clutch. I bend down for a second to move it, then jerk my head up when a horn honks.

I'm now on the opposite side of the road, driving head first toward a poultry truck. I spin the oversized steering wheel with all the gusto of the Titanic's ship captain in an effort to change lanes. Unfortunately, I'm not quick enough, and the bed of my truck clips the front of the chicken truck. I skid across the road and roll over on my side in the ditch.

I release my foot from the gas pedal and thank God that the one thing working on this truck is my seat belt. White bits of fluff swirl down from the sky in front of me. For a brief moment, I think I'm dying. But a strong stench and some irritated clucks prove that what I'd mistaken for angel wings are actually chicken feathers.

The white feathering descends from in front of my windshield, giving way to a crime scene of chickens scampering around the road and a truck driver whose face is redder than today's heat index.

Uh-oh. I just played chicken with a chicken truck. And I didn't win.

My hands tremble as I fumble around to unbuckle my seat belt. It takes longer than usual to get upright thanks to all the tension in my body. I equally blame the wreck, pushing the clutch and gear shift, and propping my arms out to try and avoid pit stains.

At this point, pit stains are the least of my worries.

By now, the sun is beaming down, but it could be post-wreck jitters making me sweat like a hog.

The truck driver sticks a phone in his front overalls pocket and marches toward me. I swallow. I need to call the bank and explain that I can't make it on time due to hitting hundreds of chickens.

I've never been so thankful for manual windows. After cranking my passenger window down, I climb out and adjust my skirt. I glance around the road, as I'm not brave enough to make eye contact with the bearded man approaching me.

Chickens meander around, scrounging for food. A slight breeze whiffs a poopy stench up my nose. I hope that's the chickens and not me.

Dusty work boots enter my peripheral vision, and I slowly lift my eyes. The man strokes his long gray beard and squeezes his bushy eyebrows into a point. "Do you realize what you've done?"

Isn't it obvious? "I've made myself late for a job interview."

He crosses his arms and scowls. "You wrecked no tellings how much money in chickens."

"I'm sorry."

"Can you not drive?"

Big Red in the blazing heat? Apparently not. I sigh. "Sir, I'm sorry. My shoe got stuck on the clutch."

He surveys the one stiletto still on my right foot. "Well, if you'd wear some decent shoes instead of those black carpenter's nails."

If my eyes weren't so dry from the heat, I might could squeeze out some fake tears. But I'm so over crying—fake or real. I've cried enough in the last year since Dalton left me to refill my daddy's fishing pond ten times over. And it's a big pond.

"I'm sorry. I really am. I tried to correct it and miss your truck. I wouldn't be in this old truck if my car hadn't had a flat with no spare." I motion back toward Big Red. "And it looks like this ride has more than a flat tire." I frown, then turn back to the chicken-truck driver. "Excuse me a minute."

I hobble back to my truck, practically fall inside, and dig for my phone to call the bank. The old chicken dude yells behind me in a gruff yet snappy tone, "Well, I called my boss. And the sheriff."

Oh fun. And I thought moving back to Apple Cart would make things simple.

Tanner

I fill my favorite coffee mug most of the way and top it off with caramel creamer from the Pig. Our card game ran a little late last night, and I still haven't recovered. How pathetic. I stayed up all weekend during my college years. Five years later, and I'm yawning by midnight.

Of course, I didn't sign up for any classes before ten in college. Getting to work by eight has knocked me off my preferred timeline.

I nod and greet coworkers while maneuvering down the hallway toward my office. Mondays make up most of my in-office time, as I have to catch up on any calls and emails from the weekend.

Much like my younger self, the chicken business never sleeps.

I flip on my office lights and settle into the well-worn chair behind my desk. Not that I've worn it out, since I spend most of my workday in the truck. According to the secretary, the older man who sat in this chair before me tasted a lot of our products.

My office phone blinks red, alerting me of a voicemail. More like three voicemails, all recorded within the last twenty minutes. I scrunch my brow and punch the button to hear my messages. Most likely an issue at one of the poultry houses I inspect.

Gary's voice growls across the speakers. He's one of the company's most trusted drivers, which makes it all the more surprising to hear he's wrecked. I click a pen on my desk and jot down his location. Then I listen to the next two messages to make sure I don't miss any information.

Nope. Same ole griping Gary, except with more colorful language. Ms. Ethel sticks her head in my door on her way down the hallway and frowns. I shrug and turn off the message. I'm not the one cursing some person who can't drive a pickup. It's all Gary.

Besides, Ethel should be retired by now. Anyone who requires a walker to move from her desk to the filing cabinet should transition to a rocking chair on a porch, in my opinion. Rumor has it she sticks around to stay in everybody's business.

I pick up the receiver and give Gary a call to let him know I'll be right there. Today's inspections will just have to wait. I've got a wreck to see about first.

I chug what's left of my coffee and shiver at the burning sensation in my throat. Then I head out of my office, nodding at Ms. Ethel as I pass. Yes, she's still within earshot of my doorway. Maybe she got an earful and can go about the rest of her day.

Dozens of responses spin in my mind as I rush to my truck. Gary mentioned in his last message that he's also contacted the "blankety blank blank" sheriff. Not that Bradley needs any help with Gary, but I'd like to be there when it all goes down.

I hop in my truck and head for the highway, popping my knuckles one by one. Luckily, it doesn't take me long to get to the scene of the crime. And it wasn't hard to spot. Even a blind man on a galloping horse could see it.

A million white feathers scatter across the asphalt with our full-grown broilers clucking along the road. Bradley beat me to the scene, which is understandable, since he has a blue light and all. His lights are flashing, and he's set out cones around the wreckage.

I park nearby and get out. Several people shoot me a disgusted face as they turn in the road to take a forced detour. Like working for Top Chick makes me responsible for this. Well, I guess it kinda does, whether it's my fault or not. I jog up to Gary, Bradley, and a pretty blonde with tangled hair.

The closer I get, the better view I have of the woman. And she is hotter than the Alabama asphalt in July. How I'd love to run my fingers through her tangled hair.

"Tanner!"

And all it takes is Gary's grumpy voice to shake me from that daydream. "Yes?"

"Can you believe this mess?"

I shake my head. I'd like to say I can't, but when it comes to chickens, I've pretty much seen it all. "We'll get it taken care of."

Gary starts mumbling obscenities, so I turn my attention to Bradley.

"Hey, big dog." Bradley tips his tan cowboy hat at me. "I'll take Gary's report now and get him out of your hair. I've already taken Miss Abner's." He winks at the girl.

She barely lifts the corner of her lips, then stares at the ground. I'm no shrink, but I get the hint that she doesn't care for Bradley's flirting after having a wreck.

I take a step in her direction and half smile. "Hey, is that your truck?" I nod toward the old red Ford flipped on its side.

"It's my daddy's, but I had a flat on my car this morning, so . . ." She sighs, then lifts her head.

My mouth drops open when her eyes meet mine. "Hannah?"

Her eyes widen and she nods. "And you're Tanner?"

"Yeah." I chuckle. "Well, look what the cat drug in."

She blushes and tries to smooth out her hair. Bad choice

of words on my part. But I'm stunned. I haven't seen her since high school. She was a year behind me in school, dating the biggest jerk on the football team. And I don't just think that because he rarely threw me the ball.

After an awkward pause, her shoulders relax and she smiles the slightest bit. "My shoe got stuck beneath the clutch, and I bent down to get it, then looked up as I was headed toward the truck."

I smile and bite back a laugh. "Man, that sounds scary."

She nods. "At least I had a legitimate excuse to not make my job interview."

"You have a job interview?"

"*Had*. I'm not sure they'll want to see me now. It was at the bank in town."

"Hold on, Hannah." I raise a finger and give her another smile. She returns the gesture, assuring me that I don't have the same creeper effect on her as Bradley.

I jog over to Gary. Bradley is busy scribbling notes. Gary turns his attention to me. "It's not my fault, you can ask Bradley."

I nod. "I know. Can you still drive the truck?"

"Yeah, I believe so."

"Okay, if its drivable, then go ahead and load what chickens you can and take it to the warehouse once Bradley clears you to leave. I'll call and have people there to help you with it and the chickens."

Gary nods. "Thanks, Tanner."

"Sure thing." I make a quick call to our plant manager on my way back to Hannah. Then I call the bank. I don't care for the branch manager, but I tolerate him for business. And even though he didn't grow up here, I've known him long enough to call in a quick favor for a friend.

Our call ends as I'm walking up to Hannah. I drop my phone in my back pocket and raise my eyes to her. "That was

Samuel from the bank. I explained the situation and told him I'll drive you in for your interview."

Her brown eyes bug. "Really?"

"Yeah. Someone with a higher pay grade than me is going to come clean up this mess. I've just got the unfortunate job of breaking the news to the chicken farmer." I wince. That should make for a fun Monday.

"I'm sorry."

I shake my hand in front of my face. "No, I didn't mean it like that. This was a freak accident." I glance around at the feathers blowing by our feet.

Hannah smiles when I turn back to her.

"If you're ready . . ." I motion toward my truck.

"I just need my purse."

"'Kay." I head toward my truck and wait for her to join me. I haven't seen her in town in years, and I'm not quite sure where she's been all this time. But I hadn't much thought about it, either, since she spent our high school years glued to Dalton Abner.

Abner. Didn't Bradley call her Mrs. Abner?

A few minutes pass, and I notice her hoisted over the window to her truck. Her front half is inside the window, and her back half—uh, let's just say it's a nice view. I rush over to her, trying my best not to gawk at her toned legs dangling over the side of the truck.

"Need help?"

She shimmies down the side of the truck and groans at the rust stain down her white shirt. "Ugh, I'm trying to avoid falling again."

If I were my grandma, I'd bless her heart right about now. "Allow me." I leap inside the open window and retrieve her purse from where it fell against the windshield. Then I climb out and hand it to her.

She blushes, bringing attention to her wide eyes and pink lips. "Thanks."

"No problem." I wipe my hands on my Carhartts and roll up my sleeves to my elbows. I seriously need to hit the weights if that made me sweat.

Hannah smiles again and brushes her hair to the side, revealing a flushed collar bone. I'm beginning to think she's the reason I'm sweating. We walk together to my truck. When she gets in, I glance at her hands. No rings. Interesting.

Not that I'm interested in her in that way. I just always check. Because what single twenty-seven-year-old man doesn't? Probably Bradley. Or Dalton.

I clear my throat and pop my knuckles before cranking the truck. Not a fan of silence, I attempt to make small talk. "Do you have someone to get your truck?"

"Yeah, Bradley called a tow truck. Thanks again for the ride, and for making sure I still have an interview."

"You're welcome." I glance her way and smile.

She smiles back, then flips the air vent toward her face and closes her eyes. "It feels amazing in here."

I laugh. "I take it you've been out in the sun a while?"

"Not too long. But Big Red doesn't have air conditioning."

I laugh again. She sounds like my grandpa, naming old vehicles. "On a day like today, that's got to be rough." I turn the air so cold that little frost balls bounce our way.

"So far, you've been the only good part of my day."

I grip the steering wheel tighter and force myself to focus on the road. I could easily say the same for her, and it's barely past nine a.m.

CHAPTER TWO

Hannah

I haven't seen Tanner Nash since high school. He played football with Dalton and was a year ahead of us in school. That's all I remember about him, aside from him getting in trouble for playing pranks.

But today, this prankster is my knight in shining armor. He's the sole reason I'm pulling up to the bank with dry armpits. Or that I'm pulling up to the bank at all.

As Tanner parks in front of the brick building, I take a deep breath and rummage through my purse for lip gloss. I need this job. I haven't heard back from the community college, which is the only other place needing help. Well, unless I count the Help Wanted sign I spotted in Wisteria. But I'm already in enough of a life slump without slinging dishes at Waffle House.

"If you want, I'll wait here, then drive you home."

I smack my lips together and face Tanner. "Don't you have to work?"

He shrugs. "Yeah, but I was about to check emails and stuff when I got Gary's call. I'll do that on my phone while you interview, then take an early lunch before making my rounds."

My freshly glossed lips tug upward. He doesn't have to do this for me, and I start to tell him that. Then I talk myself down, since I don't recall any Uber drivers near Apple Cart. Instead, I look in the sideview mirror and tussle my hair to try and make my windblown look seem intentional.

"You look great."

My fingers tingle as I pull them through a tangle. I know he's just being nice, but the compliment hits me extra thick since nobody's said such to me since . . . my divorce. Unless you count the sheriff's flirty faces at the wreck scene. I scrunch my nose at the only memory I have of Bradley Manning. He led the Wisteria team to beat us in the playoffs my senior year.

"You all right, Hannah?"

I snap my head toward Tanner. "Yeah, just nervous."

"You'll be fine." He smiles wider than before, revealing dimples so deep that my cheeks warm.

"Thanks." I drop my lip gloss in my purse and clutch it close to my chest as I climb out of his truck.

I step onto the sidewalk and open the front door to the bank without looking back. I'll save his compliment for a much-needed confidence boost and leave it at that. What I need now isn't a man, but a job.

My heels click across the tile floor as I make my way toward the office hallway. Before I get to the door I was told to enter, a tall blonde woman pops in front of me. She's wearing a teal pencil skirt and really cute leopard-print shoes. If a Barbie came to life, it would be her.

"Can I help you?" Her eyes trail me up and down, then land on my hair. She scrunches her mouth either in disgust or a failed effort to hide her amusement.

"I'm Hannah, and I have an interview with Samuel."

"You mean Mr. Covington?"

I transfer my purse to my shoulder to give my hands a break from white knuckling it. Then regret the move when I remember the rust stain down my blouse. "Yes, Samuel Covington."

"I'll let *Mr.* Covington know you're here." She raises a thin eyebrow as she overenunciates his name. Then she sashays toward the door and gives it a rhythmic knock before sticking her head inside. "Sam, there's a girl here for an interview."

I busy myself dusting at a dirty spot at the bottom of my shirt. When she returns, a guy with sandy hair and an expensive suit follows her. He smiles and extends his hand. "Samuel Covington."

"It's nice to meet you, Mr. Covington, I'm Hannah." I shake his hand.

"Please, call me Samuel."

The woman with the cute shoes, whose name I still don't know, lets out a slight huff and hurries toward the lobby. Samuel shakes his head. "Ashley's our head teller. She can take her job a little too seriously at times."

"That's a good quality." I give him a nervous smile.

"Indeed it is. Now, let's discuss your qualifications, Mrs. Abner. Or is it Miss?"

I swallow. "It's Miss." I'm still not used to not being a Miss, even though my divorce was final almost a year ago. As much as I can't stand Dalton right now, I also kept his name. I assumed it would make things easier for Taylor.

Samuel smirks and motions toward the open door. "Please, follow me."

We go inside his office, which could easily double as a golf museum. Samuel sits behind his desk, and I lower myself onto one of the royal-blue armchairs in front of it and drop my purse by my feet. I'm amazed at how something that appears so sophisticated can also be incredibly comfortable.

"So, Hannah." Samuel clears his throat and glances down at a sheet of paper.

I lean forward enough to see that he's printed out the resume I emailed a few weeks prior.

"You're from Apple Cart."

"Yes." I straighten and lift the corners of my mouth.

"Your background check proved you're an upstanding citizen, but it looks like you don't have a lot of workplace experience . . ."

My temples throb as his voice trails off. Here we go. I swallow the lump forming in my throat before explaining. "I got married in college, and soon after, I got pregnant with my daughter. I took some time off to have our baby, then my husband went to law school and made good money so I decided to stay home."

"And now you want to enter the workforce."

My throat closes up slightly as I try and read his expression. Is that a good or bad thing that I want to work now? Or more like I *need* to work, as I refuse to live off my parents and become a total small-town cliché.

Somehow, I find my voice. "Yes. My daughter starts school this year, and we just moved in with my parents. Temporarily, until we get settled back in town."

Samuel nods. "I admire someone who stays with their children. My mom never worked outside the home." His face curves into a smile.

I return his smile and start to relax for the first time since going to sleep last night.

"A teller position doesn't require a college degree, and

most of its learned on the job. But I can see you have a lot of organizational skills that will help." He scans my resume top to bottom.

"Yes. I was very active in my sorority and then in Junior League once I stopped college." I feign another smile. "Stopped college" sounds lame, but I refuse to use the word "quit."

So much of my life has been defined by quitting or giving up on things. School, marriage, making it on my own in a big city. Regardless if I quit something, I draw the line at admitting it out loud.

Samuel stays quiet as he continues scanning my resume. After an awkwardly long pause, he glances back at me and smirks. "So when can you start?"

This time, my smile is real. I relax my shoulders and send silent thanks to the man upstairs. For the first time since waiting tables in high school, I'll have my own paycheck.

"Whenever you need me."

"That's what we like to hear." Samuel stands, and I reach for my purse, then stand as well.

I follow him into the hallway. He turns toward me as we cross the lobby. "During office hours tomorrow, swing by to fill out the necessary paperwork. If you have extra time, we can discuss a schedule for training."

"Thanks."

"Come on, I'll take you to meet Glenda. She handles the paperwork."

We step behind the swinging door to the teller station. Ashley's oval-shaped eyes are narrowed on me as we maneuver toward a back room. I go through the motions of meeting Glenda and letting her copy my license for the paperwork. All the while, I try and ignore the sense that Ashley doesn't want me here.

It's most likely my insecurities messing with my head.

Why would she have something against me? She doesn't know me.

I thank Glenda once she hands me my license and exit through the lobby, with Samuel matching my steps. He opens the large glass door, blasting us with sunlight. "I'm glad you made it in, Hannah. I look forward to us working together."

"Thanks again for rescheduling my interview."

"Of course." Samuel extends his hand, and I shake it again. He lingers a beat longer this time before releasing his grip.

I blink into the sun and head for Tanner's truck. When I open the passenger door, he sits up straight in his seat. "How'd it go?"

I grin. "I got the job."

"Great. I knew this day had to get better."

I laugh as I climb inside. "Pretty much everything's better than hitting hundreds of chickens with no air conditioning."

Tanner's face goes serious. "That's where you're wrong."

"Oh?"

"All our chicken trucks have air conditioning." He chuckles at his own corny joke.

I roll my eyes and shut the door. At least someone can find the humor in my mistakes.

Tanner

I turn down the long gravel drive where Hannah told me she lives. A familiarity lingers when a white farmhouse appears at the bottom of the hill. Her family hosted a football barbecue once when we were in school. Probably since Hannah was a cheerleader, or because she dated our obnoxious quarterback.

"Didn't this used to be your parents' house?"

"Still is. Taylor and I are staying here until I find my own place."

"Oh. That makes sense." I shut my mouth before I ask anything that might cross a line. She mentioned moving back and having a daughter named Taylor. She hasn't mentioned Dalton.

I'm no genius, but all signs point to Hannah splitting with him. And while I hate to hear of anyone's marriage failing, I can only imagine she's better off without that nut job.

I park in front of the garage, right beside a small Volkswagen car. "Well, I see the flat."

She lets out a heavy sigh. "Yes. The wonderful start to this adventure."

I laugh. "Mind if I take a look at it?"

She shakes her head. "You don't have to. You've already done so much. Besides, Daddy can check it out when he gets home."

"Nah. He's already got the Ford to worry with. It won't take me but a minute." I open my door and get out. An active Border Collie bounds toward me. "Hey, buddy."

Hannah gets out with her purse. "Skip, leave him alone."

"Ah, he's fine. I love dogs." I make kissing sounds and rustle the guy behind the ears. He barks and wags his tail ninety to nothing.

Hannah smiles and shakes her head. "You're sure you don't mind fooling with my tire?"

"Absolutely not." When I stand, the dog bounds off in the opposite direction. I go to the tire and assess the damage. Hannah comes over and leans against the door of her car. Putting toned calves beside my face. I scoot a little closer to

CHICKEN ABOUT LOVE

the tire, trying to ignore the way her smooth skin glistens in the sunlight.

I don't see any obvious holes in the tire, so it must be a leak. "Hey, does your daughter like to play with bubbles?"

"Bubbles?"

I force my eyes toward her face rather than her legs, which isn't a bad view either. "Yeah. Like a bottle of bubbles you blow."

"Yeah."

"Can I borrow some?"

Hannah shrugs. "Sure." She disappears through the garage door, and I watch her legs every step of the way. Then I chastise myself for doing so. She's here to try and make a fresh start after spending the best years of her life with an idiot. And she's a mom. She doesn't need me ogling her.

She returns a minute later with a purple bottle. "Here you go."

"Thanks." I take the bottle from her and try not to focus on the softness of her hand when it brushes against my fingers. Then I perform the little magic trick my daddy taught us about finding a prick in a tire. I rub the bubble wand over the area I think has a leak and wait for a bubble to blow.

"There's your leak." I turn back to Hannah. My necks heats up when my face lands within inches of hers. I was too busy concentrating on the tire leak—and on not staring at her legs—to realize she'd bent down beside me.

"That's so cool."

"I can't take credit. My daddy owns the rights to this trick." I stand and reseal the bubbles. "Got any Fix-A-Flat?"

"Uh, we can look in the shop. Daddy keeps stuff like that on a shelf."

"'Kay." I follow her through the side door of a nearby metal building. A shelf at the far end is lined with bottles of this and that for all kinds of loosening and tightening of things. Two bottles of Fix-A-Flat sit on the end. "Ah-ha. Here we go."

I grab a bottle and head back into the sunlight. Hannah stays a step behind me. I glance at our shadows dancing beside us on the gravel drive. Even in heels, she's a good bit shorter than me. I've never stood this close to her until today.

Back at the car, I go through the motions of patching the small hole. "Do you have an air compressor?"

"Yes, but it's heavy." She heads back toward the shop and motions for me to follow.

A few minutes later, I have the air compressor hooked to an extension cord and rolled out onto the lawn. I blow up the tire, then put everything away. "You should be good to go. At least for a while." I lift my mouth into a grin.

"Thank you, Tanner. Let me pay for you for all your trouble today."

I lift a hand. "No, not at all. I like helping people. Besides, you broke up the monotony in my daily routine."

She smiles, causing her brown eyes to twinkle in the sun. "At least let me feed you. I know it's near lunchtime now."

I waver my head. "I don't want to impose, but I'm not one to turn down food."

"Okay." Her face lights up again, sending a tingle down my spine. Then she heads for the house, and I follow her up the porch and inside. "What do you like?"

"I'm not picky. Something quick that isn't much trouble. A sandwich is fine."

"How about a grilled cheese?"

"Yeah." I sit down at the kitchen counter as she bends to open a cabinet.

I swallow the heat rising in my throat and force my eyes away from her skirt tightening around her thighs. She's an old acquaintance going through a tough time. Not someone

I need to hit on. I keep my head lowered, studying the tile countertop until I hear noise near the stove.

When I raise my eyes, she's in the refrigerator. "Do you want sweet tea, a Coke, water?"

"Tea's fine." I glance around the kitchen, which is decorated in roosters. That would drive my sister crazy. She hates animal themes, which I think is hilarious. I purchased one of those huge cow-face pictures for my rental house just to bug her.

The rustle of something landing on the counter catches my attention. I stare down at an assortment of cheese crackers, chips, and fruit snacks in individual packages. "Pick whatever you like. Thanks to Taylor, we have plenty of snacks on hand."

"Sweet." I snatch a bag of cheese puffs with cartoons on the front. "I'll have the Marshall puffs."

Hannah raises an eyebrow. "You know your *Paw Patrol* characters?"

I grin. "Isn't that a rite of passage for every good uncle?"

She smiles. "I bet you're a fun uncle."

I shrug. "I try." My brother's kids are five and two, so they're really just getting to a fun age where I can aggravate them and teach them to aggravate their parents.

A few minutes pass, then Hannah brings over the grilled cheese sandwiches and two glasses of tea. I follow her eyes toward the back porch. "If you want, we can eat on the patio. It's cooled."

"Sounds good."

I hold open the back door and Hannah passes me. Her head bobbles beneath my nose, sending a honey scent my way. My insides flip a bit, but I blame it on hunger pains and not the good-looking woman with honey-scented, tangled hair.

We sit in rocking chairs facing the back field. Several

large oak trees populate the space between round bales of hay. "Y'all have a great view."

"Thanks. That's one of the things I missed most when I lived in Birmingham."

"I bet." I take a bite of my sandwich, then swallow. "How'd you end up in Birmingham, if you don't mind me asking?"

"Dalton and I both went there for college." Hannah rolls her eyes. "Well, he went to play football, and I followed like a fangirl."

"Don't say that. You went to college too."

Hannah takes a sip of her drink, then frowns. "I didn't finish."

"So? A lot of people don't finish college."

She stares at her feet and rocks her chair. "We got married during college, and I got pregnant pretty quickly. Then after Taylor was born, I never went back."

"There's nothing wrong with that. Neither of my parents went to college."

"A lot of people say that, but I can't help wishing I'd kept going."

She glances up, and I study her face. A subtle sadness hangs beneath her beauty. I can see it in her eyes. Like she doesn't quite feel she measures up. As the unofficial black sheep of my family, I totally get that. But Hannah shouldn't feel that way.

"I'm no expert on anything. Well, except for maybe chicken crap." Hannah laughs, and I join her before continuing. "But I think one thing all successful people have in common is that they keep going when life gets tough. You moving here and starting a good life for Taylor and doing all you could today to find a job . . . that takes some perseverance."

I feel my lips curl as the worry starts to drain from her

face. "So what if you stopped going to school for a while? You can go back later if you want. You didn't stop being a mom, and you didn't stop trying. That's what matters."

Hannah reaches over the small table between us and touches my forearm. "Tanner, thank you for everything today. Especially just now. I needed to hear that more than you'll ever know."

I smile and attempt to downplay the firestorm that started when she rested her soft hand on my bare arm. But I've never been the best at taming my wandering mind. The only thing holding me back from dipping her over the rocking chair and kissing her like my life depends on it is her complicated situation.

CHAPTER THREE

Hannah

"Mommy!" Taylor's voice jolts me out of my trance. I spin around and pause the playlist on my phone, then wipe my hands on a nearby towel.

"Hey, love." I squat to her level and open my arms.

"Huggy!" She leaps into my lap, temporarily knocking the breath out of me. "What are you cooking?"

"Mac and cheese, and chicken."

"Yummy." Taylor tosses her head around and exaggerates sniffing the air.

I snicker. If she's this dramatic at age five, I can only imagine how she'll be at fifteen.

"You didn't have to cook," Mama calls from the archway to the kitchen.

"You've had Taylor all day. It's the least I could do."

She gives me a tired smile. "Thank you. It smells delicious." She walks up and strokes Taylor's blonde head. "We had a full day, but a fun day."

Taylor nods enthusiastically, not the least bit tired like us adults. "Nana took me to Chuck E. Cheese's."

I widen my eyes at Mama. "Wow. No wonder Nana's tired."

Mama grins. "It was a compromise for her being so patient while I went to Target."

I nod. There's no question where I learned my parenting skills.

"How did your interview go?"

I wash my hands to continue cooking, then wipe them dry. "I got the job."

"Wonderful."

"Yeah, I need to stop in tomorrow and fill out paperwork. He's going to give me a schedule then."

"That's good. The Covington boy?"

I nod and start breading chicken tenders. "Yeah, Samuel Covington. I've never seen him before."

Mama sits at the kitchen table, and Taylor climbs on her lap. "His family bought the bank a few years back. They own several chains of Smart Money Credit Unions and put him over this one."

"Oh." That makes sense. I know just about everyone in this town my age. Except for him and Ashley, who seems like a real peach. I clinch my teeth and focus on supper. No use pitting her against me until we've had time to work together.

After breading the chicken and putting it in the oven, I join them at the table. "What did you think about school, Taylor?"

"The room isn't very pink."

Mama and I exchange glances, then I fight back a laugh. "It isn't going to look like your room. You need all the colors at school."

Taylor throws her head back and sighs. "Then why are all the chairs red?"

I frown at Mama. "Was I ever this high maintenance?"

"Do you really want me to answer that?" Mama pats Taylor on the head as she squirms out of her lap and runs into the living room.

"No." I smile and go check on my Crockpot, then open a can of beans. Unlike my mom, I use canned green beans. Not ideal, but Taylor eats them and I haven't mastered cooking the rubbery texture out of the fresh-cut ones.

"I'm glad you had a good day."

I laugh under my breath as I dump the beans in a pan. "It's much better now."

"Something happen after the interview?"

I flip the stove eye to medium heat and sit in front of Mama. "More like before. I went outside to a flat tire."

Mama's bottom jaw drops. "It didn't look flat when I drove up."

"It's patched now. But I had to drive Big Red to my interview."

"Big Red?" Mama cranes her neck to see out the window. "Where is he now?"

I twist my lips. "You noticed my tires but didn't notice the truck being gone?"

She shrugs. "I had my hands full with all the stuff I bought Taylor."

I can only imagine what she bought. "Unfortunately, Big Red is with Kyle. He towed him away."

"Towed him away?" Mama's voice goes up an octave as she stands to get a closer look at the shop. I'm not sure why, since I literally just told her the truck wasn't there.

"Yeah, I had a wreck on my way to the bank."

"A wreck!" She rushes to my side and braces her hands on my shoulders, then touches my face. "Are you okay?"

CHICKEN ABOUT LOVE

"Yes, Mama. Just a little sore around my sides and under my arms."

She pulls me in for a hug and squeezes me close, which coincidentally does nothing to sooth my sore ribcage. I give in and hug her back, knowing its necessary before she'll let go.

Sure enough, after one tight squeeze, she releases me. "Why didn't you tell me that as soon as I walked in the door?"

I lift my shoulders. "I don't know. It's a bit embarrassing."

"How is a wreck embarrassing?"

I push my thumbnail cuticle back with my index finger. "I hit a chicken truck."

"A chicken truck? Like a KFC supplier?"

I laugh. "No, these chickens were still alive."

Mama covers her mouth and gasps.

"It's fine, really. The truck could still drive, although the driver had a few choice words for me."

"Oh, sweetie, I'm so sorry."

I raise my hand. "No really, I'm fine. I managed to get to my interview, and it all worked out. Big Red is the real casualty."

"So how did you get to your interview? Uber?"

I blink. "Apple Cart has Uber now?"

"Hannah, everyone does Uber. We only have one driver, though—Earl Ed Mayberry."

I click my tongue. Where have I heard that name. "Oh." I raise my eyebrows high enough to hurt my forehead. "Isn't that the Wisteria guy who went to jail for stealing mail?"

"Yes. But he's out now and doing quite well for himself."

"Well good for him."

We both turn to heavy footsteps coming down the hallway. As soon as Daddy appears in the doorway, Taylor leaps into his arms. "PawPaw!"

"Ahhh, my girl." He picks her up and plants about a dozen kisses across her face. She giggles as he lowers her to the floor. "Did one of y'all move Big Red?"

Mama cuts her eyes at me and grimaces. I shake my head before turning to Daddy. "He's at Tolbert Auto."

"Why?"

I lick my lips, trying out words in my head. There's no way to sugarcoat what happened, so I go for broke. "I wrecked him."

"You what?"

"Now, Darrell." Mama steps toward Daddy and places a hand on his chest to calm him.

"My tire was flat, and I didn't have a spare. I had to get to my interview and Big Red was just sitting there. So I got in and drove toward town. Halfway down Highway 7, my heel hung on the clutch. I reached down to unstick it, and when I looked up, a chicken truck was headed toward me. Or more like I was headed toward it. I swerved, but my back end hit the truck, and I flipped it in the ditch." I suck in air and release it slowly after spilling my guts in record time. Mama's eyes are now the size of half dollars, as they've widened with every new detail.

Daddy's jaw unclenches. "Okay . . . You don't look hurt."

"I'm not, and I'm super sorry about Big Red. I'll pay for the damages."

Daddy's whiskered jaw turns up into a smile. "It's fine, really. I'm actually impressed you cranked the old boy and made it into town."

I slump my shoulders like someone dropping a hundred-pound dumbbell to the ground. Tears come out of nowhere. As soon as they hit my cheeks, Mama wraps me in a hug. I cry a few seconds into her shirt before pulling back.

She wipes a stray hair out of my eyes. "Hannah, it's fine. Big Red is the least of our concerns."

I shake my head and break free from her arms, then sit on a nearby bar stool. "It's not Big Red." I look at Mama, then Daddy. "It's everything. My whole life. Six years ago, I was in a sorority, making straight A's and dating a college football player. Now I'm a divorced single parent and college dropout who's living with her parents and relieved to get a job at the credit union so I won't have to flip bacon at Waffle House."

"Honey." Mama puts her hands on my shoulders and rubs them gently. Her warm hands soothe me momentarily, but can't compete with my feeling like a total loser.

"I'm one of those people I always made fun of that peaked in high school. I may as well change my social media profile to a picture of myself as Apple Sauce Queen."

Daddy straddles the stool beside me and looks me in the eye. "Hannah, you are not a failure, and you have not even began to accomplish all you're going to."

"You mean that?" I ask, because Daddy always talks as if I hung the moon, and because I could use a good pep talk.

Daddy nods. "Dalton is an idiot, and one day, he'll regret what he's done."

I scan the room for Taylor, hoping she's not hearing all this. Daddy can use some choice language when it comes to Dalton. Luckily, she's no longer in the kitchen.

I close my eyelids, sending stray tears down my cheeks. After wiping both eyes with the heel of my hand, I look at Daddy. "All I ever wanted was a full life. A family of my own, a good job. A nice home. I had all that except the job. That is, until . . ."

I let my voice trail off and sigh. It's been a year, and I'm still not sure what hurts worse—the fact that Dalton cheated on me or that he didn't want to try and work things out.

Daddy pats my knee, while Mama continues rubbing my shoulders. It's like I'm Deontay Wilder and they're nursing me back to health after a knockout. Given the events of the day, that's pretty accurate.

The oven dings. I stand and slide past the two people always in my fighting corner. As I remove the pan of chicken from the oven, I take slight satisfaction in cooking what could've killed me today.

It's a small victory, but I'll take it.

Tanner

I chew the last bite of my barbecue sandwich and put my blinker on to turn at the bank. I prefer the chicken to pulled pork at Big Butts, but I don't like to eat chicken while I'm working. Something about it seems unethical.

Thanks to Gary's tirade yesterday, I spent half the day dealing with misplaced chickens and talking to the farmer who'd supplied the load. We didn't lose as many as I'd expected, but Gary was still a handle. My boss was understanding, which helped calm Gary down a bit. Gary complained that maybe he should go back to driving a log truck, and I silently prayed he would.

Today has been filled with catching up on my visits to houses I missed yesterday. However, I prefer that to dealing with Gary another minute. And I don't regret any amount of time I spent helping Hannah. The moment I spotted her standing next to Bradley in a sea of feathers, covered in sweat and fear, I knew I had to do something.

I park near the entrance and grab the envelope of money off my dash. As soon as I enter the glass doors, my first stop is always the sucker bucket at the welcome table. The blue raspberry is my favorite.

I pop the sucker in my mouth on my way to the front and stick the wrapper in my pocket. Right away, I spot Hannah at the far end . . . with Samuel hovering over her like a dog guarding its food.

The temptation to roll my eyes is strong, but I resist. Instead, I plop the envelope on the counter in front of them. Both turn their attention to me.

Hannah's honey scent is overpowered by whatever cologne Samuel is wearing. I cough at the thickness hitting me like, for lack of better words, an eighteen-wheeler full of chickens.

"I need to deposit this into Top Chick Foods's account."

Samuel straightens, finally giving Hannah some air. "This window is closed. We're in training."

Hannah smiles sheepishly as if silently apologizing. A smooth voice calls from my right, "Tanner, I'll take care of you."

Ashley waves when I turn that direction. I glance back at Hannah and smile around my sucker before going to the first window. Ashley's still waving when I walk up, bulky bracelets clanking together on her slim arm.

"Whatcha need, Tanner? You know I'm always available."

I bite down on my sucker, trying to decipher the meaning behind her last statement. Nah, I'd rather not. I'll stick to random dates with out-of-towners.

I drop the envelope on the counter like I'm unloading a dead deer. "I need this money deposited into the business account for Top Chick Foods. The account slip should be in there." I nod, not wanting to pull out the slip myself and risk Ashley hooking onto my hand with her ridiculously long nails.

Nothing against well-dressed, good-looking women, but

there's nothing practical about having extra-long nails or wearing that many bracelets.

As she shuffles through the stack of money and taps on her keyboard, I lean back to check what's going on with Hannah. Samuel is giving her very hands-on training. I bite my sucker in half and exhale though my nostrils. Just because I work with all men and geriatric Ethel doesn't mean I can't tell that's not professional.

"Okay, Tanner." Ashley calls my attention back to her. "Is there anything else I can do for you?" She leans her elbows on the counter and bats her eyelashes. I force my eyes away from the cleavage I'm certain she meant for me to see.

I crunch the last piece of my sucker, then hold out the soggy stick. "Can you throw this away?"

She straightens and pinches the end of the stick between two fingers. "Of course."

"Thanks," I murmur as I turn toward the exit. When I reach the front table, I look back once more at Hannah. Samuel has backed off some, but he's still all up in her business. Both of them stare at the computer screen, oblivious to me.

I push open the front door, and a surge of summer heat hits my face. It's much needed to clear my head from thinking about Samuel hovering over Hannah.

His little weaseling way got me all worked up. Hannah's been through enough lately without having her boss cozy up to her under the ruse of training.

I climb in my truck and stare one last time at the bank before backing out of the parking lot. If her situation were different, I might hit on Hannah myself. Heck, I know I would. She's even hotter than she was in high school, especially without Dalton's ugly arm around her.

But she doesn't need anyone pawing after her right now. Besides, I'm not exactly the best candidate for her. Hannah needs someone who can help with Taylor, not someone who still goes to college parties on occasion and buys random things on eBay to annoy his sister.

What she needs right now is a good friend. And despite the way my neck starts to sweat every time I get near her, I need to be her friend and nothing more.

CHAPTER FOUR

Hannah

I plop down on the couch and kick off my heels. Taylor bolts across the room and hops in my lap with a thud. She weighs maybe forty pounds but lands like a linebacker. I huff and wrap an arm around her back.

"Mommy, you were gone so long."

A tsunami of mom guilt washes over me. She's been with me every day since birth. "I'm sorry, baby. The training took the rest of the day. I didn't think I'd be gone that long."

She pokes out her bottom lip. I pull her to my chest and sigh. "You had Nana here. Besides, you'll be in school soon, so you won't miss me as much."

"But I'll miss my toys."

"It'll be fine." I close my eyes and stroke her golden hair, happy for a moment of peace. I've spent a lot of days corralling Taylor around and running extravagant events for

Junior League, but none have exhausted me like dealing with the public.

Not to mention the fact that Ashley was less than happy to train me and Samuel was all too eager to step in her place. It'll all work out, though, when I get a paycheck. Tanner stopping by was some nice comic relief. I enjoyed watching Ashley unsuccessfully woo him a little too much.

I kiss Taylor's temple and move her to the couch cushion beside me. "I'm going to see if Nana needs me." I stand and stretch, then make my way into the kitchen. Mama stands over a pot on the stove, stirring. "Do you need any help?"

She turns and peers over her reading glasses. "No, I'm just mashing potatoes to go with the roast."

My stomach growls. I've gone longer than ever without sushi, but Mama's meals make up for it and then some.

"How was it today?"

I lean against the counter beside her. "A lot to take in."

"What's the plan for work?"

"He wants me to come in half a day tomorrow like I did today, then actually start all day Friday. If that's not good with you, then—"

Mama sets her spoon on a plate beside the stove. "I'm happy to keep Taylor. This is what I wanted in retirement, to spoil grandbabies and go shopping. Your dad will want me to keep her, too, since I'm less likely to go shopping."

"Thanks." I slump back against the counter, relieved to hear that. Leaving Taylor with a sitter isn't something I want to do unless necessary. She's already jittery about her dad leaving us.

Us. I shudder. Whether Dalton wants to admit it or not, that's what he did. He may think he left just me, but he hasn't exactly reached out to Taylor much in the past year.

My phone rings. I push myself off the counter and retrieve it from my purse in the living room. Taylor is on the big area rug, brushing a plastic pony's mane. I stand beside her and answer the call.

"Hello?"

"Is this Hannah Abner?"

"Yes."

"This is Kyle from Tolbert Auto. I'm afraid your truck is totaled."

My shoulders sink, and I sigh heavily.

"I'm sorry."

"No, it's fine. I'll tell my dad. It's his truck."

"Okay, he can call me at this number when he decides what he wants to do with it."

"Thanks." I hang up and save the number into my contacts.

Taylor hums by my legs as she brushes her pony's tail.

"Hey, Taylor, I've got to find PawPaw. You want to play outside?"

"Yes." She hops to her feet and grins. I tap the end of her button nose.

We stroll onto the front porch together, and I lift my hand to shade my eyes. The sun won't set for a few hours, but it's lowered below the eaves of the house.

"Skip." Taylor giggles as he bounds up the steps and wags his tail. She pats his back and grins.

"I'm going to find PawPaw. Make sure you stay near the house."

"Okay," she answers through a giggle as Skip paws her leg.

My heart warms knowing we get to live in such a beautiful area where she can run free. Even though our old neighborhood was safe, I still had to worry about her getting close to the road or wandering into a stranger's yard.

I leave Taylor with Skip and cross the front yard. Sure enough, Daddy is near his shop. I tap my phone against my hand as I play out scenarios in my mind. Big Red was on his last tire, for sure, but that doesn't make me feel any less guilty about wrecking him.

"Daddy."

"Hey, Hannah." He twists toward me, still keeping a hand on the lawnmower he's working on.

"I'm afraid I've got some unfortunate news."

"If Dalton's done something else . . ." The muscle in his jaw twitches as his eyes narrow.

"No, nothing like that." My nerves unbuckle knowing Daddy will leap to my defense if need be. "Big Red is totaled. Kyle from the mechanic place said you can call him to talk about it."

"Well, I figured as much." He stands and transfers the grease from his hands to his jeans. "Better that than any other ride around here. And you came out unscathed. That's what matters."

I fall toward him and wrap my arms around his waist. Daddy has always been my hero, and all I ever wanted was someone like him for a husband and father to my children. Instead, I naively chose Dalton.

Daddy hugs his arms around me, but holds out his hands. "Darlin', I've got grease on me."

I shake my head. "I don't care. Thank you for taking care of us."

He taps my back lightly. "Always."

I pull back and smile at him before dropping my arms.

He returns my smile and nods toward my car. "You did a good job patching your tire."

"Tanner did that. I didn't even think of patching it. I was going to wait for you to get home."

Daddy rubs his jaw and chuckles. "Did he do this before or after he took you to the interview?"

"After." I fold my arms and stare at the ground. "He actually stayed at the bank while I interviewed, then brought me back here."

"Then fixed the flat."

I glance back at Daddy. "Yes, sir."

"You know, back when y'all were growing up, I thought he'd never amount to much. He turned out pretty well."

My lips lift as I replay the day with Tanner. I can thank him for having a job right now and for saving Daddy time working on my car. I really should repay him with something more than a grilled cheese.

"Tanner helps out a lot of people around town when they need it."

"How so?" I turn to face Daddy, who's now back on the ground, tinkering with the lawnmower.

"He's good about running random errands for people like Ms. Ethel, and he's helped Jack out a lot whenever he's been overworked at the lodge."

"That's good."

"Yeah." Daddy grunts as he turns a wrench, then drops it. "I get the feeling he wants to look tougher than he is."

I laugh. "Typical for a lot of guys I know."

Daddy grins. "I don't know what you're talking about."

We both laugh a second, then Skip interrupts us by pouncing on Daddy.

"Hey, boy." He rubs the dog's head.

Taylor runs up to me and hugs my legs. I hug her small shoulders. "What do you want to play?"

She looks up and taps her chin with her finger as if thinking. "Hmm, swing me?"

"Yes, ma'am."

She takes my hand and leads me to the swing set Daddy built some twenty years ago. I pull my hair back with the hair tie on my wrist and circle behind the swing.

I pull the swing back and let Taylor go, giving her a big

push when she sails back to me. She pumps her little legs best she can, but relies on me to send her higher. My chest tightens at the realization that she depends on me for everything, and only me. Of course, I have my parents to help. However, I would prefer her dad's family play a part in her life as well.

His entire family now lives in Birmingham, and once he filed for divorce, even his parents snubbed me. Not that they ever really welcomed me into their family in the first place. To them, I was the high school girlfriend whom they'd assumed he'd shake loose at college. Instead, we'd married against their wishes.

Looking back, I wish they'd gotten their wish.

The one upside to our young marriage and to wasting ten years of my life with Dalton is Taylor. I push her small frame higher and admire the sun dipping behind Daddy's shop in the distance. I have my parents, I have Taylor, and I didn't die in the chicken-truck wreck. Oh, and I have an actual adult job that doesn't involve fast food.

Even if I stay single the rest of my life, as long as Taylor and I are together, I will have everything I need.

Tanner

We used to play cards every Thursday night like clockwork. Now we play whenever we can. Sunday nights, random evenings during the week, or Friday nights, like tonight. That is, when Jack's not in Atlanta with Bianca.

I wish they'd hurry up and get married so she would move here. She's cramping our style.

I scratch my head and stare at the cards as Jonah tosses them my way. Jack's busy texting Bianca. He bought a cell service booster just to contact her easier. Love makes a man do strange things, I guess. Not like I would know.

"Is Bianca gonna let you play with us whenever after y'all marry?"

Dang, Jonah just read my mind. Jack glances up from his phone for a second and shrugs. Jonah shakes his head at me. I frown. Playing poker with two people wouldn't be much fun at all. Maybe we should learn chess or take up cornhole.

I refocus on my hand and try not to doom our guy time before necessary. Bianca's cool. Maybe we could teach her to play with us.

"Maybe we need to recruit more players," Jonah says.

That's where I draw the line. I'm a friendly enough guy, but I can get kinda cliquish when it comes to hanging out.

"Let's not put the cart before the horse. Jack's not married yet."

Jonah fans out his own cards in his palm and moves some around. "I'm just sayin'. Michael or Kyle might be a good option."

"Uh, no."

"What's wrong with them?" Jonah says this as if these guys are our best friends we know so well.

"Michael married that chick from the casino. He'd probably take us to the cleaners every game, and Kyle's a traitor."

Jack sets his phone down—finally—and shakes his head. "When are you gonna let that go about Kyle? We've all been out of high school forever."

I palm the back of my neck with my free hand and narrow my eyes. Jack didn't play football, so he has no idea the extent of Kyle's betrayal. He grew up at the edge of Apple Cart and went to school with us until his junior year. Then he transferred to Wisteria because their team was on fire back then. They beat us for the championship that year.

Jack's heard my spiel before, so I come up with a more neutral rebuttal. "Can we not just keep it us three, at least for now? That is, unless the old gun guys come back in town."

Jack laughs. "I'll have to tell them your nickname."

I nod. "Go ahead. They won't mind. Ronnie and I are tight."

"Sure you are," Jonah says.

I ignore Jonah and lay out my cards. I'll let my hand speak for itself.

Ronald and Macon just built a sporting goods store on the interstate that backs up to the hunting lodge. Every time they swing by to check on it, they stay at Jack's. Ronald is my favorite. He's like a fifty-year-old bachelor who hunts for a living. Talk about living high on the hog.

Jonah lays out his hand next and casually comments, "Samuel mentioned something about liking poker one day."

"The banker?" Jack lays out his cards and takes our chips. Maybe my hand wasn't so great.

"Yeah." Jonah collects the cards and reshuffles them.

I gag at his confirmation of my worst fear.

Jack reaches for the open Doritos in front of me and examines the bag. "Are these bad?"

"No, the chips are good. Samuel's bad."

"What do you have against Samuel?"

I balk. They can't be serious right now. First, the welder married to a card shark, then Kyle. I can handle those, but Samuel?

"Do you guys even know Samuel?"

They exchange a look and shake their heads. Jack turns to me. "You don't know him either."

Heat rises in my face. "I know enough."

"What's that mean?" Jonah asks, while trying something

fancy with the cards. It doesn't work. He spills them all over the table.

I smirk at his mess before I continue. "I was at the bank the other day, and he was hovering over Hannah like Ronald does a plate of deer poppers."

"I find that hard to believe." Jack crosses his arms in protest.

He would say that. Jack thinks his precious deer-meat jalapeños trump everything. "All I know is the girl just moved back after getting divorced. The last thing she needs is some sleazy dude dressed like a used-car salesman barking up her tree."

Jonah laughs.

"What?"

"Just you. Badmouthing someone for hovering over a girl."

"What?" My voice squeaks as my temper flares up a bit.

Jack looks me straight in the eye. "If I recall correctly, you got in Bianca's personal space the first time you saw her."

"It's not like you two were together yet. And it's not like some hot blonde lands in Apple Cart every day."

"Kind of like Hannah?" Jack cocks his head to challenge me.

I try to speak, but my voice cracks.

Jonah starts chanting, "Tanner likes Hannah."

One immature act deserves another, so I wipe my hand across the cards he just stacked, spreading them across the table again. Then I laugh like a cartoon villain.

"And for the record, I do not like Hannah. I mean, she's all right, but I don't like her in that way. I just helped save her is all."

"Save her?" Jack rolls his eyes and snatches a handful of chips from the bag.

"Yeah. Y'all heard about Gary wrecking the chicken truck, right?"

Jack shakes his head while chewing Doritos.

"Carol told me." Jonah laughs. "She said Gary was maaaad."

"Yeah, well. Gary's always mad, and my sister exaggerates." I turn to Jack. "And I'm sure y'all can read all about it in next week's paper. Becki already called me for a quote."

Both of them break into obnoxious laughter. After Jack catches his breath, he says, "I hope you make the front page."

"It's summertime. So unless Bradley busts a drug deal in the next day or two, I'm quite certain it will." Our county paper considers high school sports the most timely news. Followed closely by any major arrests or extreme weather. Then there's whatever's left.

"Hey, what about Bradley?" Jonah's face is sincere, and I doubt he's gotten better at faking. His poker face is practically nonexistent. I want to slap him.

Instead, I take the higher road and join Jack in yelling, "No!"

"Okay." Jonah shakes his head and gathers the remainder of the cards. *Again.* Hahaha. He hugs them toward himself, out of my reach.

Jack eats another handful of chips, then stares at Jonah. "Do you really want to hear about Bradley Manning's glory days every time we play poker?"

Jonah clicks his tongue and lifts a shoulder. "I guess not."

"I certainly do not." I take the cards being dealt to me and give Jack an approving nod.

"Back to Hannah." Jack raises a brow. I sigh. Here we go. "How did you save her exactly? Was she flogged by a mass of chickens? Or was it Gary?"

"Haha. No, she wrecked her daddy's pickup into our truck. That made her late for a job interview at the bank.

With Samuel." I say his name like I'm the announcer at Wimbledon, then I continue before either of these idiots can comment on it. "I drove her to her interview, then home."

"Are you talking about Darrell's black truck or the red one?"

"The old red one."

Jack wrinkles his forehead. "Why would she drive that to town?"

"Everyone else was gone in their vehicles and hers had a flat. I patched her tire when we got back to her house."

"Wait, so you drove her all around town, then fixed her tire?" Jonah's mouth twitches as if he's fighting back a smile.

"Yeah."

Jack and Jonah exchange a smirk.

"What?"

"You sure went out of your way to help her," Jonah answers.

"I help people all the time. I rotate Ms. Ethel's tires on the regular. And I help you out a lot, my friend." I point to Jack.

He nods. "True, but I think the point Jonah's trying to make is you dropped everything on a work day and spent a lot of time helping Hannah."

I scratch my head as if I can dig up an excuse. When one conjures up, I snap my fingers. "What about when I drove Bianca to the airport for you?"

"Can you honestly say you didn't hit on her?"

I scowl. "I didn't know you two had a thing yet."

"And weren't you headed toward a chicken house past the airport that day anyway?" Jonah's smirk grows like the Grinch's smile.

"Where do you get all this intel?"

"Carolina."

I throw my head back. "I've seriously got to quit talking to my sister."

Jonah shrugs. "It's a boring drive to and from Auburn. A lot comes up on the way."

I toss my cards on the table and stare at my so-called best friends. "You two are worse than Ms. Ethel and Mrs. Maudy. We may as well transition to playing bridge."

CHAPTER FIVE

Hannah

To my knowledge, none of the banks in Birmingham opened on Saturdays. At least our bank didn't. I was skeptical as to why Smart Money Credit Union is open a half day on Saturdays, until my first Saturday at work.

All kinds of people stopped by to deposit money, retrieve statements, and cash checks. Samuel explained that a lot of people don't have time to come by during their lunch break, and most don't do online banking. The combination of stubbornness against online anything for the older generation and the lack of Wi-Fi in most of Apple Cart made it unpopular.

By noon, my fingertips ached from shuffling bills and typing in account numbers. I really don't see how Ashley does it with those super-long nails.

Samuel locks the front doors and flips the sign to Closed. All that's left to do is count down my drawer. I pull my hair back into a low bun and stretch my fingers. A few more shuffles through cash, and I can rest my hands for a while.

I count every bill and coin three times to make triple sure I get it right. Then I lift the drawer to retrieve the checks underneath. I'll count them several times as well.

Wait. There's another stack of cash to the left under my drawer. How could I miss that? I set the checks aside and grab the stack. As soon as I do, the overhead lights flash and a deafening alarm blares. I cover my ears as my heart pounds. People come out of their offices and question one another, while staring at the lights.

Ashley rushes over to my station and picks up the cash I pulled from beneath the drawer. She pops the blue rubber band holding it together and rolls her eyes.

"False alarm. New girl pulled the bait money."

A collective groan competes for attention with the siren. Samuel rushes over and puts a hand on my shoulder. "It's fine, Hannah. Rookie mistake."

I remove my hands from my ears and turn to him and Ashley. "What does she mean by bait money?"

Ashley speaks loudly, and I'm not sure if it's to override the alarm or to embarrass me. Maybe both. "It's the money we set aside in every drawer to toss out to anyone robbing the bank." She thumbs the tips of the bills with her witchlike nail. "These bills are marked so we can track them. Under every drawer is a stack with a blue rubber band. We're supposed to know not to pull it unless necessary, because it's sitting on a switch that contacts the police station."

She glares at Samuel. "I can't believe you didn't tell her about this."

He snarls. "This wouldn't have been an issue if you had trained her like you're supposed to. I'm the bank president, not a teller."

"Branch president," she corrects with a raised brow.

They continue bickering. Between them and the siren, my migraine is growing by the minute. I close my eyes until someone yells, interrupting their feud.

"Sheriff! Everyone remain calm."

It's Bradley. He's pointing a gun and stepping sideways like an army man on a PlayStation battlefield. Half the people roll their eyes, and several go back to their offices. Most stick around, as I'm sure this is the most exciting event to ever unfold at Smart Money Credit Union. Or at least the Apple Cart branch.

Samuel steps through the swinging half-door beside my station. "False alarm."

"Oh." Bradley lowers his gun and exchanges it for a radio. "Release all alarms at Smart Money. Kill code green. I repeat, release all alarms."

Like magic, the lights instantly quit blinking and the alarm stops. I haven't been so amazed since Elsa lifted her arms at Disney and Cinderella's castle immediately froze.

Bradley clips his radio on his belt and steps toward Samuel. "So, dude, what happened?"

"We had a teller accidentally pull the bait money and trip the wire."

Bradley nods.

"Accidentally?" Ashley snarls her nose at me.

"Yes. She wasn't properly informed," Samuel snaps back, then straightens his tie and turns back to Bradley.

"If you guys are good here, I've got a meth lab to sniff out in Wisteria."

Samuel glares back at Ashley. "We're good."

She buttons her bright pink lips before forcing a smile.

"Okay, then, big dog. Holler if you need me." Bradley tips his hat and leaves much calmer than he came.

I sigh and lean against the wall of my station. Samuel

stands at my window and frowns. "I'm sorry about all that. I should've thought to tell you about the bait money."

I shake my head. "No, it's fine. Like you said, a rookie mistake."

Samuel smiles and clasps his hands together. "Say, if you don't have lunch plans, you can join me. It'll be on the company dime as a celebration of surviving your first work week."

I jerk as Ashley rushes past me, knocking my side with her bony elbow. "Uh." What am I supposed to say in this situation? I don't have plans, but he's my boss. Then again, he's *my boss*. He has to mean it in a professional way to be nice, right? And I can't say no to a polite offer from my boss. Can I?

"I won't accept no for an answer." Samuel opens his palms as if presenting me with something, or begging. "That is, unless you have plans."

I shake my head. "No plans."

"Great. Do you like Mary's?"

"Of course." I have no trouble answering this time. Mary's is my favorite local spot, and I love Mary as much as the food, if not more. I once filled in for a waitress during the summer when she broke her leg jumping off a bridge. True story, and the number-one reason I never accept a dare that involves Broken Bridge.

"Let's get your money sorted out, then." Samuel lifts a hand. "But not the bait money."

"Right." I nod, and place the stack of cash with the rubber band back in its hiding place.

Samuel leans across the counter and helps me organize all the actual money taken in that day as I finish listing it all on my daily report. Then he takes the checks to the back to be sent to the corporate branch, along with my sheet. I take my bag of cash from the day to the vault, where Ashley is waiting.

She stands at the door, accepting a bag from another teller. Once our coworker walks toward the door, Ashley and I are the only ones left standing in the lobby. Everyone else went home shortly after Bradley left.

She snatches my bag and huffs. "I know your game."

"Excuse me?"

"The little game you're trying to play on Samuel. The whole, 'I'm an innocent single mom who needs to catch a break.'"

I wrinkle my brow and swallow the anger welling up inside me. She has no idea what I've been through or how wrong she is about me. After grinding my teeth until I fear I'll need veneers, I calm down enough to answer rationally.

"Ashley, I am a single mom, and for a while, I felt like I couldn't catch a break. But I'm not playing a game. I needed a good job, which we both know are few and far between in Apple Cart for someone who hasn't finished college or any other kind of trade school. Samuel is nothing more than my boss, and that's all he ever will be. Whatever you think about me is wrong. I don't understand why you can't give me a fair shake. All I'm doing is what's best for my daughter and me. And furthermore, my life doesn't concern you."

With that, I make sure to bump her on my way toward the door. My elbows aren't as bony as hers, but I hit her fake boob hard enough to hopefully puncture the silicone.

I hear her seethe as I continue toward the front exit. When I reach the front table near the door, Samuel meets me from the hallway.

"Ready to go to lunch?"

"Absolutely." I twist my head enough to watch Ashley's reaction. With one hand folded into her chest, her face sours as if she won a lemon-sucking contest.

Samuel opens the door, and I walk out, both proud and disappointed in myself for playing the mean girl for once.

Tanner

"So you're headed back tomorrow?"

"Yep." Carolina sips her Diet Coke through a straw.

Jonah asks about one of her friends, and they fall into a conversation about some party. I glaze over as the menu takes precedence over their conversation.

Mary's Diner is one of those places where you pretty much know what you're gonna get, but you still want to look over the menu. Just in case she's added something new. Strangely, she never lists the daily hot-bar items on the menu. They're always changing, so people know to walk by and look before they order.

"Tanner, would you want to go with me?" Jonah says.

"Huh?" I lift my head to both him and Carolina staring at me.

"The rodeo next weekend. Carol said we could stay at her place since I'm leasing my trailer this summer."

I sigh. "Maybe."

I'm at the point in my life where I need to stop hanging out at college parties. However, that's getting harder to do now that Jack's tied down and Jonah is immersed in college life. Besides, it's hard to beat a good trip to Auburn.

That's my excuse. The real reason is I don't want to buddy up to Kyle, or Bradley, or Michael, or his fat cousin who used to steal my Adam Sandler DVDs and made us lose our

Netflix account. And I sure don't want nothing to do with Samuel.

Well, butter my biscuit. No sooner than his name crosses my mind does that devil walk through the door. Hair slicked back like snake oil, high-dollar suit pressed like prom night. My nostrils flare when he steps to the side and Hannah enters.

I cross my fingers under the table and hope this is some sort of bank lunch. Ashley and the other suits will step in any minute. Right?

Wrong.

Pretty boy struts to a booth adjacent to our table with Hannah by his side. Between Jonah and Carolina's heads, I have a clear view of Samuel's face.

"Tanner, what's wrong?"

My sister's voice comes out muffled, like I'm underwater. My ears pound with heat from holding in my rage. It's obviously bad enough to have affected my hearing. "Tan?" She snaps her fingers in my face.

I blink. "Yeah?"

Jonah follows my eyes and turns around. So does Carol.

"Oh." Jonah faces forward again and grins. "I know what's going on."

"What?" Carolina's brows come to a point over her tiny nose.

"He's jealous." Jonah says this in a sing-songy way, not unlike the way he chanted last weekend during poker.

I clear my throat. "I'm not jealous. I just don't like the way he is around her."

"Ah." Carol slips her hand on my arm. "You are jealous."

I slap her hand off. "No, I'm not."

"Sounds like it to me." She bats her eyes and smiles.

"No."

"Kids. Am I gonna have to get your daddy?" Jonah interrupts.

The waitress comes over to get our order, momentarily offering me an escape from these two meddling imbeciles.

Jonah orders, then Carol. I get a burger and fries. At least I think I do. It's hard to focus when slick-haired Sam's over there making bedroom eyes at Hannah.

I can't see her face, but I hope it's awful. *Give him the meanest, most rejecting face you got, girl. You're so out of his league.*

"Tanner?" Carol practically yells in my face.

"Huh?"

She motions toward the young waitress, who smiles before speaking. "Would you like your onions on the side?"

"Sure, thanks." I fan the paper menu for her to grab, then lean my elbows on the table.

As soon as the waitress walks away, Carolina glances at Samuel and Hannah, then me. "Why don't you go talk to her?"

"No, it's nothing like that."

"You're not acting like it's nothing."

"Come on, sis. You know I'm not looking to date anyone." I fumble with the folds of my sleeve to give me something to do . . . besides punch Samuel in the face.

Carolina almost chokes on her Coke. "You're *always* looking to date someone."

"Not seriously."

"Which means he'd take Hannah seriously." Jonah winks at me. Maybe I should punch him instead of Samuel.

I shake my head and stare at the vinyl tablecloth. "You guys can think what y'all want. All I know is she had a rough time last Monday morning." I raise my eyes enough to see Carol and Jonah, but not enough to see Mr. Samuel Covington the Third badgering Hannah. "And anyone who spent their entire adult life with Dalton Abner deserves a freakin' medal. Not to have some trust-fund tool paw all over her at work."

My sister gives me sappy puppy-dog eyes, and Jonah ceases his teasing, which is his way of showing sympathy. I doubt I did anything to convince them I'm not jealous, but at least they're taking me seriously for now.

I take a back seat to their school chitchat for a few more minutes, chiming in now and again to pretend I'm not thinking of Hannah. In the time it takes me to nervously rip a straw paper to shreds and pretend it's Samuel's head, the waitress brings out our food. I have a cheeseburger with onion rings on the side. I guess I misunderstood her earlier question. Given the state of my mind right now, I'm lucky I didn't order an actual plate of onions.

As soon as she heads toward the kitchen, Jonah says a quick prayer. He and Carolina start eating, but my appetite isn't there. I force myself to bite into my burger. It's good, as always. A rock covered in ketchup could come out of Mary's kitchen, and I'd still try it.

I somehow manage to fall into their conversation about the upcoming rodeo. Carol goes on about her summer classes and teases Jonah for taking the summer off, saying he'll fall behind. He argues that he's making the mature choice of saving in rent and making money by helping Jack and working some at their family's hardware store. I swear, those two sound more like an old married couple than friends.

Only a few bites of my burger remain. The waitress comes by with a tray. She sets it on the table beside us and hands Carol a new Coke, then refills mine and Jonah's teas from a pitcher. Then she crosses the floor and sets a huge plate of cheesy fries between Samuel and Hannah.

I have nothing against cheesy fries. Heck, I love cheesy fries. If I'd been thinking clearly, I'd have ordered those instead of onion rings. But the idea of Hannah sharing cheesy fries with Samuel makes me want to puke.

My mind wanders to his soft, slimy hands grazing casually over hers while they reach for the same fry, *Lady and The Tramp* style. I've never shook his hand, but I imagine they're soft and slimy, since he doesn't work like a real man and he applies so much hair gel. What else could they feel like?

But I have felt Hannah's hands. They're soft and tiny and comforting. Hands that he doesn't deserve to graze.

I can't even see their hands thanks to my sister's puffy ponytail, but what I imagine them doing sickens my stomach. I chug the rest of my tea and stand.

"Lunch is on me, collegiates. I gotta run." I pull a five from my wallet and stick it between the salt and pepper shakers, where the waitress can't miss it.

Carolina swallows a bite of her sandwich and widens her eyes. "What about me?"

I nod to Jonah. "Catch a ride with him. You guys ride together all the time anyway."

Jonah turns to Carol. "I'll drop you off when we're finished. He's being weird again."

"Weird? Again?" The again hits me harder than the weird.

"You've been weird ever since the whole 'Hannah and the chicken truck' incident. But it's cool." He fans a hand my way. "Go do whatever it is you need to do."

"Thanks." I sigh and walk to the register to pay. It takes every ounce of willpower I have to not glance at Samuel and Hannah's table. Not to say hi, not to acknowledge them, and certainly not to check their hands.

Because if I do, the "whatever it is" Jonah referred to me needing to do wouldn't work out well for Samuel.

CHAPTER SIX

Hannah

Going to church in Apple Cart is nothing like going to church in Birmingham. A large gravel lot replaces the parking deck lined with spaces. A familiar brick building with a steeple replaces the more modern buildings better suited for a warehouse. And there's a good chance everyone inside will know my name.

I grip Taylor's tiny hand as we stroll toward the church. The loose gravel crunches beneath our dress shoes, matching the crunching inside my stomach as we approach the front steps.

It's not unusual for me to visit Apple Cart Baptist a few times a year—Mother's Day, Father's Day, possibly Easter—to be with my parents. But this will be the first time since Taylor was born that I haven't come with Dalton.

I'm not naive enough to think that everyone in the county hasn't already heard of my divorce and then some.

But that doesn't make going to church and facing prying old women any easier.

We climb the brick steps together and cross the front porch. I reach for the door handle, but a man's hand beats me to it. A familiar hand. My eyes follow his jacketed arm up to Samuel's face.

I flinch. Not that I should be surprised. He would be the only one in Apple Cart to wear a seersucker suit in such heat when it's not Easter. Or the only guy at all over age six to wear seersucker in Apple Cart on any occasion.

"Allow me." He opens the door and gives me his usual smug grin. I've worked with him just long enough to realize it's a confident face that says, "I have money."

He drops his face toward Taylor. "This must be Miss Taylor. So pretty like her mother."

Taylor presses against my hip and dips her chin shyly.

"She's a little shy." I feign a smile and lie through my teeth. She is anything but shy. However, she is a good judge of character. Well, except when it comes to her daddy.

"Say, why don't I take the two of you to lunch after service?"

My limbs tingle like I've stepped in an ant bed. How did he jump from meeting Taylor the first time to wanting to take me to lunch . . . again? "Thanks, we appreciate it, really, but we already planned to eat with my parents."

There. That's not a total lie, I guess. I did plan on going back to my parents' house after church, which would constitute eating with my parents. Who cares if it may mean nothing more than eating turkey sandwiches on the back deck? I so prefer that to another game of "grab the fry before Samuel touches my hand" at Mary's.

"Oh, okay." Samuel grins and opens the door wider. He fans a hand out like someone on a game show revealing the prize. "Ladies first."

Fisting Taylor's hand tightly, I march past him. I make a beeline toward the large wooden sanctuary doors. Taylor struggles to keep up as I pull her along. "Why are we walking so fast, Mommy?"

"We don't want to be late for church," I say in my fakest southern-belle voice.

Not good. I've technically lied three times before we even entered the sanctuary. Any minute now, a rooster will crow, calling me out on my sins. And that isn't too far-fetched, given the number of hobby farms here in town.

Voices ring out beside us, and I turn to throngs of people coming down the hallway. Most likely a Sunday school class has let out. *Dang it.* I planned on sneaking in the back before anyone spotted me. Maybe Samuel jinxed us.

As if right on cue, Mrs. Maudy and Ms. Ethel head my way, leaving Mrs. Maudy's husband behind. I turn around in search of a new escape route. Instead, I face Samuel, smug expression across his face. I sigh.

The ladies rush up to me. At least, best they can, as Ms. Ethel's tennis-ball-bottomed walker and Mrs. Maudy's bad hip slow them down considerably. By some miracle, Samuel passes us and enters the sanctuary before they make it over. I want to enter, too, but I'd rather face the grapevine gossip train than be seen entering with Samuel. He'd no doubt sit with us, which would start even more rumors.

"It's so good to have you back, Hannah. Are you here with Samuel?" Wow, Ms. Ethel wasted no time on that one.

"No, ma'am. Just me and Taylor." I give my daughter's hand a gentle squeeze, and she smiles.

"Pretty girl, here you go." Ms. Ethel reaches in a pouch attached to her walker and pulls out a peppermint. The old-school soft, square kind.

"Thank you." Taylor takes it and drops my hand to fumble with the wrapper.

CHICKEN ABOUT LOVE

Mrs. Maudy pushes her glasses up the bridge of her nose and scans me like I'm a recipe with gluten-free ingredients. "If you're not with Samuel, you should really meet my grandson."

And here we go. I force a pleasant face, but can't convert it into an actual smile. I glance around the lobby, hoping my parents' Sunday school class will get out soon. So far, nobody under seventy has left the hallway.

"You know, you could also go to that singles' Sunday school class here." Ms. Ethel nods. "I tried it for a while after Ervil passed."

A nervous laugh escapes me as I picture myself sitting among a bunch of college kids home for the weekend and widows and widowers, as I seriously doubt the few singles my age in town would attend such a class. They probably avoid Sunday school the same as me.

As if right on cue, Tanner walks in with Jack and who I assume is his fiancée, Bianca. I wave my hand to get his attention. Once he spots me, my insides heat up.

Why did I do that?

Because I'm desperate for someone to ward off these matchmaking grannies. Someone other than Samuel.

My cheeks rise another ten degrees for every step Tanner takes toward us. Mrs. Maudy is overselling her grandson, Kyle—the same one who hauled off Big Red. She suddenly hushes when Tanner stops by my side. I relax my shoulders, happy for the weirdness I feel if it will keep her mouth shut.

"Morning, ladies." He smiles widely, his dimples on full display.

Both of them return his smile, then glance at me with questioning eyes. Desperate to no longer have them bless my poor, divorced, single-mom heart, I link my free arm through Tanner's. Mrs. Maudy's eyes widen behind her thick frames.

Tanner meets my eyes for a second and smirks, then

turns back to them. "Did you ladies enjoy Sunday school this morning?"

Both nod and mutter their agreements. Yet, their expressions are a mixed bag of confusion and curiosity. Mrs. Maudy opens her mouth to ask something, when her husband taps her on the shoulder.

He hands her a Bible big as a college textbook. "Maudy, quit talking and come on. You know how I get if someone gets my seat."

"Oh, all right, Hubert, keep your pants on." She hugs her Bible to her chest as if it weighs twenty pounds. Which it might. Then she shuffles off behind Hubert.

Ms. Ethel pats Tanner on the arm and winks at him as she follows her friend.

I sigh and drop my arm from Tanner's.

He lifts an eyebrow at me. "What was that?"

"I'll tell you in a minute." We file into the sanctuary, and I lock eyes with Samuel once more. He scoots down on his pew as if making room for us. I panic momentarily and grab Tanner's hand. It's a little calloused, but the warmth and thickness of it comforts me. Like a child needing someone to accompany her across a busy street.

I use him to accompany me through a sea of busybodies. I offer Samuel a closed-lipped smile and walk slow enough to make sure he sees me holding Tanner's hand. Then I shuffle Taylor and Tanner into a pew near the back. Once we sit down, I let out a long breath.

"Are you all right?" he whispers in my ear.

I nod, and Taylor leans up to get a good look at him. "Who are you?"

"I'm Tanner. You must be Taylor."

She nods and grins.

Tanner holds out his fist for her to bump. "Thanks for letting me borrow your bubbles the other day."

"Bubbles?" Taylor wrinkles her nose in confusion.

"Yeah, I used your purple bubbles to fix your mom's tire."

"Really?"

"Yes. It's a magic trick."

"Ooh, can you teach me?"

"Sure. But I really hope I don't have to use your mom's tire to do it."

I laugh. "Me too."

"Are you mommy's friend?"

He half smiles my way. "Yes, I am."

I smile back, then scan the congregation. A lot of eyes are on us, but it could be so much worse. I could be sitting by Samuel, or still be listening to Maudy go on about her grandson's stats.

"Thanks for saving me again," I whisper so that only Tanner can hear.

He gives me a questioning face, so I nod toward the front where the older ladies sit.

"Gotcha." He nods, then cuts his eyes toward Samuel.

"And from him too," I add.

Tanner laughs. "I'm happy to be your knight in shining armor any time."

A chill seeps down my spine. He has no idea I thought that very thing the day he carted me around to my interview and fixed my flat.

"Nana." Taylor's voice brings me back to the present. My parents slide into her end of the pew. Tanner and I move down to make room.

Tanner nods and smiles at them, as the piano player strikes the first few keys. We all stand, giving me a better view of everyone in front of us. Samuel twists back toward us a time or two, as do about half a dozen other people. Mostly old and female, but still, enough to spark a forest fire of rumors.

I'd prefer people not think I'm dating Tanner. I'd rather them *know* I'm not dating anyone, nor interested in anyone. However, I can imagine many worse fates than pretending to date Tanner Nash.

Tanner

Brother Johnny dismisses everyone, and people spring to their feet as if he's pulled a fire alarm. Every Sunday, it's like a race to beat the Methodist congregation to Mary's for lunch. I usually hang back, content to go home and eat a frozen pizza. I don't like fighting crowds. Sometimes, I go to Jack's to eat deer poppers and run a few rounds through our rifles. But I don't want to interfere on his and Bianca's time together before she has to leave for Atlanta.

After most of the older people and young families have made it out the door, Mr. Richards leans across Taylor and extends his hand. "Thanks for taking care of Hannah's car last week, and Hannah."

I give his hand a firm shake. "Yes, sir. Glad I could help. Sorry I couldn't do anything for your pickup."

He clicks his tongue and cocks his head. "It's fine. Big Red had seen his best days already."

I chuckle at the memory of the truck turned sideways in a ditch, with chicken feathers stuck to the windshield. "I should say so."

"Tanner, why don't you come over to the house and let me cook you lunch," Mrs. Richards offers with a smile.

I look at Hannah, hoping she'll answer for me. I don't

want to decline her mom's hospitality, but I also don't want to accept unless Hannah's okay with it.

Hannah smiles at me, and I nod.

"Sounds better than the Piggly Wiggly pepperoni pizza in my freezer."

Mrs. Richards smiles wider. "Good."

We file out of the pew and into the hallway. A few people linger, talking or trying to wrangle in kids. I'm sure my parents are long gone. They tend to sit up front and leave out the side door to get first crack at Mrs. Mary's Sunday hot bar. Considering this is one of the few weekends they're home from their summer RV adventures, they're most definitely at Mary's.

We say our goodbyes to Brother Johnny and his wife, then head toward our separate vehicles in the parking lot. Hannah tugs my sleeve when she stops at her car. "Don't feel like you have to come unless you want to."

I search her eyes for a straight answer. The dark chocolate ovals make me start to melt, so I drop my gaze to the gravel and ask her plainly, "What do *you* want me to do?"

She's quiet until I look at her again. "Whatever you want. You did great warding off Samuel and the Golden Girls. Don't think you need to come, unless you want to, of course."

I kick at a few rocks, then stick my hands in my pockets. "I meant what I said about the Piggly Wiggly pizza."

She laughs. "Mama is a good cook."

I tilt my head toward Taylor, who's spinning beside her mom to make her dress go out like a bell. "What do you think, Taylor?"

She stops mid-spin and looks up. "I want you to come teach me the magic bubble trick."

I smile, then glance at Hannah and shrug. "I guess I gotta come, then, huh?"

"Yes!" Taylor lifts her arms and jumps before resuming her spinning.

"All right, you know the way." Hannah shoots me a smile before opening the back door for Taylor.

I continue toward my truck, a slight twitch in my chest from Hannah's smile. She's always been a beautiful girl and is an even more beautiful woman. And she's always been one of those girls who smiles a lot, at everyone. But something was different in her smile just then. Not with her mouth but her eyes. They locked on my face and glistened in a way I've never noticed before. A way that communicated maybe she saw something in me other than an easy buffer from the Apple Cart gossip train or sleazy Sam.

"Tanner."

I look up to see Jack and Bianca standing between my truck and his. I'd assumed they were long gone by now.

"What's up?"

"You bailed on us at church."

I shrug, the back of my neck heating up from more than the noonday sun. "I got to talking to Hannah and didn't see where y'all guys sat."

"Uh-huh." Jack gives me a goofy, lopsided smirk.

"You want to join us for lunch?" Bianca points to Jack's truck. "We're going to pick up some barbecue and go back to Jack's."

"Nah, you two enjoy your time. I'll catch Jack later this week." I nod and climb into my truck, leaving them to get in Jack's.

I didn't dare add that I'd committed to Sunday lunch at the Richardses' place. That would lead to Jack texting Jonah and Jonah texting my sister. I swear, my generation is as bad as all the old folks around here. Must be something inbred in small-town people to spread stuff.

I pretend to check stuff on my phone as I wait for Jack to

back out of the parking lot and leave. Better to let him get toward Big Butts before I leave. That way, he can't catch on to me going the same direction as Hannah, which is opposite of the house I rent downtown.

A ping of guilt hits me as I pull onto the main street. I could try and explain helping Hannah ward off the gossip brigade and slick-haired Samuel, but that would just lead to Jack teasing me. Ah, who cares what people think?

I've spent too much of my life trying to please my parents or smooth things over with apologies for being myself. I like Hannah, and I can see us becoming good friends. With Jack joined at the hip to Hotlanta and Jonah at Auburn most of the time, I could use a good friend too.

The farther I drive out of town, the more I contemplate all Hannah has to offer me as a friend. Then I add the fact that I've saved her a few times since she's been back. We make a good team. A downright attractive team, might I add.

Come to think of it, if I ever feel the need to fake off the old ladies in town or turn away another stage-three clinger after a date gone wrong, I'll consider being seen around town with Hannah. She's pleasant company . . . and excellent arm candy.

CHAPTER SEVEN

Hannah

"Lunch was great, Mrs. Richards."

"Thank you, Tanner." Mama smiles as he hands her his empty plate.

She grilled pork chops and whipped up some vegetables. Thanks to marrying young and being a mom, I cook a lot too. But I haven't yet managed to toss together restaurant-worthy meals on the fly like Mama. I'm hoping and praying it's in my DNA and will show up eventually.

"Would anyone like some cobbler?"

"Oh, yeah." Tanner's eyes light up like Skip's whenever we wield a treat in the air. He looks at me and licks his lips.

My own lips tingle, and I'm not sure why. I press them together and stand, taking my own plate to the sink. "I'll get us some," I say to Mama. I pull the cobbler from the refrigerator and spoon servings onto two small plates.

"Make that three," Daddy says behind me.

I do as I'm told and heat them a few minutes in the microwave.

"Hannah and Taylor made this last night."

I feel my face blush as Mama pats my back. She's bragged on every little thing I've done since coming home, from getting the bank job to making cobbler. She may mean well, but it kind of makes me feel like a kid again. I feign a slight smile when she faces me, then open the microwave.

Daddy grabs his plate, and I retrieve mine and Tanner's, then get some spoons. Taylor meets me halfway to the table. "Can we play outside?"

I look at Tanner. "Want to eat on the porch again?"

"Yeah." He stands and takes his plate. "Thanks."

Taylor snatches both my and Tanner's free hands and leads us outside. A weird déjà vu washes over me. She used to grab onto Dalton and me the same way. I shake my head to shake my thoughts and sit in a rocking chair. Tanner sits in the one beside me, evoking a more pleasant déjà vu.

Taylor slings open the screen door and hurries down the steps. Skip meets her with a tail wag and a hop. She pulls her arms to her chest as a shield from his overpowering love, then pets him once he calms down some. I laugh, watching her.

"She reminds me of my niece."

"Oh yeah?" I turn to see Tanner watching her. His jaw is strong, his dimples set with a smile that reaches his eyes. His short, wavy hair is combed in place today, rather than curled up around the rim of a cap.

I take a bite of my cobbler, more to wet my mouth than from hunger. He's handsome, no doubt, but so is Dalton, and a lot of other guys I know. Tanner, however, has an upbeat quality that makes him a breath of fresh air to be around.

He turns fully toward me, his eyes happy and full. "Yeah,

Carrie's a ball of energy and never stays in one place too long."

Oh, right. I'd asked about his niece. I blink to reset my mind on our conversation rather than detailing his profile like a courtroom reporter.

"That's your brother's daughter?" Stupid question, as his only other sibling is younger and still single. Hey, whatever keeps my mind from lingering on the thickness of his lips.

Why am I checking out his lips? I fan my face with my hand. I can't decide if it's Tanner making my face flush or the sheer fact that I haven't spent this much time with any man in over a year. Well, unless you count my daddy, which I don't.

"Yeah. They have her and Jacob, who's two."

I nod and take another bite of my cobbler. Tanner's is nearly gone, which I take as a compliment. Since I did in fact make it, as Mama so nonchalantly pointed out.

"I guess that's why you knew how to talk to Taylor."

"What do you mean?"

I spoon a scoop of peachy gel, then shrug. "Samuel came up to us at church before you walked in and she acted standoffish. Very uncharacteristic of her."

He faces the field again. "I don't think it's her fault. He can have that effect on people."

I laugh so hard that I almost choke on my cobbler. Tanner smirks at me. "What? You don't agree?"

I stare at my plate, all too sure I'm blushing by now. "He is a little different in some ways, but I probably shouldn't talk about my boss."

I lift my eyes enough to catch Tanner smiling, dimples on full display. My heart beats a little faster, so I turn my attention to Taylor and the dog chasing one another in the yard.

"You know, the other day at Mary's, I thought you two were on a date."

I shake my head and snarl. "No. That was more of a 'I'd had a bad day at work and he wanted to be nice since I'm new' lunch."

"Bad day, huh? I can't imagine it being any worse than the wreck day."

"It wasn't. More like a bad last hour at work."

"What happened?"

I swallow and pick at my nails, embarrassed to say aloud what I did. "There's this money in our drawers for emergencies like robberies and such."

"Oh, the bait money."

"Yeah, how did you know?"

"Full disclosure, I once went to a Kenny Chesney concert with Ashley."

"Oh, how did that go?"

Tanner rubs his jaw. "Let's see, halfway to Birmingham, I regretted accepting her invitation, but stayed the entire night because she bought the tickets."

"Is that why she acted so eager to help you with your deposit?"

He nods slowly. "I made it very clear I didn't need or want her help in any form, but she doesn't always get the message."

I half smile. "Funny, I can't seem to get her to help me with anything. Which is part of what led me to pulling the bait money when counting down my drawer."

Tanner's eyes widen. "You didn't."

I nod, biting my bottom lip.

"Did Bradley come?"

"Oh yes, gun drawn, ready to take someone down."

Tanner beats his fists on the armrests of the rocker. "Noooo! Why do I miss all the good stuff around here?"

I laugh and he joins me. "Then Ashley and Samuel argued about who should've taught me not to do that. Finally, Bradley left, along with everyone else. Samuel felt bad for me and took me to lunch."

Tanner stops laughing. "Wish I'd have known. I'd have taken you to dinner."

The seriousness in his voice sends a heat throughout my body. Is he flirting with me? I try and ignore it and continue making small talk. "I didn't know you were at Mary's that day until I saw you go to the register."

"Yeah, I was with Jonah and my sister. We had a table near the back."

"Sorry I didn't say hi when you passed."

He winces. "No, that's on me. I saw you guys come in, so I should have spoken." He looks at me. "Honestly, I don't care too much for Samuel."

"Good to know it wasn't me." My words come out a little playful, but it's too late to take them back. The way he smiles communicates he picked up on my tone.

My face heats up again, so I start rocking to try and catch some air.

"So next Sunday, or any Sunday, if you ever need me to run interference . . ."

"You're welcome to sit with us anytime." I lift my plate of half-eaten cobbler. "And eat with us anytime."

"Don't tell me that. You have no idea how much I eat."

I laugh. "It's fine, really. I've enjoyed having a friend here."

His smile morphs from playful to genuine. "Me too. I think we make a good team."

I return the smile, then look back at Taylor. Maybe it's the low-key atmosphere or the way I've spilled my guts to him recently, but Tanner starts to open up about himself.

"I understand your need to ward people off. My mom

likes to mention to me that my brother was married with a kid by my age."

I frown. Being an only child, my parents never compared me to a sibling. That must put a lot of pressure on him.

He cracks his knuckles and continues. "I've dated a lot, but never anyone I could see myself marrying."

"I think you're smart to wait. If I'd have waited, I wouldn't be in the mess I'm in today."

"But you might not have Taylor either." He smiles and lifts his brows.

"True." My heart warms as I glance at Taylor playing, then back at Tanner.

"But the whole 'everyone wanting to set you up' thing does get old. Maybe they'll lay off of you after you've lived here a while."

"Doubtful." I roll my eyes and sigh. "Ms. Ethel suggested I try the singles Sunday school class at church."

Tanner belts out a huge chuckle, making me laugh too. "You don't want to do that. Unless, of course, you're in the market for a sugar daddy. Nobody our age messes with that class."

"That's what I was afraid of."

He grins through his laughter. "Just stick with me on the back pew."

"Sounds like a plan."

Tanner's face straightens, and he stares ahead. He's unusually quiet for several beats before facing me again. A mischievous smirk crosses his face. "You know, there might be a way to get all the grannies in town off our backs and shut my mom up, at least temporarily."

I prop my elbow on the armrest and lean toward him. "Do tell."

"Now, this is a crazy idea I just had, so don't judge."

I shake my head.

"'Kay. What do you think about me and you pretending to date?"

I open my eyes so wide I can feel the bridge of my nose stretching. "You and me, in a fake relationship?"

"Never mind. I'm sorry." Tanner wipes his hands over his face as if embarrassed by the idea. "You have Taylor, and I shouldn't—"

Before he can talk me down any more, I blurt out, "That's not a bad idea."

He drops his hands and tilts his head. "It isn't?"

I shrug. "I mean, you bring up a good point with Taylor. Obviously for her sake and ours, we wouldn't want to show affection. However, I think being seen in public, at church or other places in Apple Cart, might solve a lot of our problems."

"Exactly." He turns toward me, face full of excitement. "If all the old women and my mom think I have a girlfriend, then I can live my life peacefully for a while."

"And I can reclaim my life here without having to worry about people nosing in my personal business." Or worry about Samuel asking me to lunch, hopefully.

"I like it, Abner." Tanner extends his hand. "Shake on it?"

I put my hand in his and give it a firm shake. We keep shaking for several seconds longer than necessary, as I wait for him to let go. He must be doing the same, because we're still shaking when I hear Taylor.

"Are you guys arm wrestling?" I drop my hand and blush. A rush of electricity jolts from my arm as soon as it leaves contact with Tanner.

Thankfully, Tanner breaks the awkward silence. "We were actually about to come teach you the bubble trick."

"Cool." Taylor jumps and claps her hands.

Tanner winks at me before standing and following the

excited little girl down the porch. I watch them run toward the garage for her bubbles, wondering what I've agreed to.

Hannah

"Chicken truck, had lunch, started reminiscing about high school . . ." I take a break from talking to myself to sip my water bottle.

Before I get to work, I have to get all my ducks in a row —or should I say chickens in a row—about how Tanner and I started dating. Although we started fake dating yesterday afternoon with a handshake, our agreed upon story starts with the truth of how we met again.

Instead of eating a grilled cheese on my back porch, we decided to say he took me on a celebratory picnic after I got my new job. Not totally a lie. More like more elegantly put. After lunch, a conversation led to planning to get together again. This is also the truth—for the most part—considering I hooked him at church and later told him why.

It didn't take us long to devise a simple backstory for how we ended up an item. Something believable was all we needed. A full, flowery narrative isn't necessary in a place like Apple Cart, where random details get sprinkled in every time someone spreads the story.

Apple Cart gossip is kind of like cow poop. The more it spreads, the thinner the substance.

I turn into the bank parking lot and park beside Ashley's car. It's tiny and black, with a personalized tag that reads "Ash." As I get out, I notice she has furry pink seat covers. It looks like someone shaved a poodle and dipped the fur in

Pepto Bismol. I shudder at the damage Taylor could do to seat covers like that, given her tendency to spill apple juice and goldfish crackers.

Locking my car behind me, I scan my key fob and enter the front doors. The sun shines through the glass, dancing across the tile floor as the door closes behind me. Ashley stands at her station, and looks up momentarily when I enter the swinging half-door that leads behind the counter.

I force a smile, but she's already staring down again. My nerves unbuckle when another teller walks our way. I don't like being alone with Ashley for even a second. Ever since my impromptu confrontation the day I pulled the bait money, a cloud of tension has hung between us. Not that we were ever on good terms, but still, it's grown worse.

I drop my purse in front of my stool and turn on my computer. As I'm logging in, the overwhelming scent of musky aftershave wafts my direction. Then Samuel's hands appear on my counter. I lift my eyes to his signature smug grin.

"Morning, Hannah."

"Good morning." And like clockwork, no sooner than I've spoken, Ashley is behind me.

"Hannah, I have your drawer ready. You need to recount everything to verify the amount."

"Thanks." I receive the drawer from Ashley, who's fixated on Samuel. "Good morning, Sam."

"Hey, Ashley." He turns back to me. "Hannah, I feel bad that we couldn't do lunch yesterday after church."

"That's okay."

A heavy airstream blows behind me. Either Ashley's nostrils are flaring, or literal steam is coming from her head. Not wanting to find out, I keep my gaze on Samuel.

"Maybe we can do lunch today to make up for it?" He smooths his tie and raises his brow in question.

"Uh." I'm stuck for a second, wanting a way out. Then I remember that I do have an out. I have a fake boyfriend. "That's sweet of you, but I have plans again."

"With who?" Ashley's voice is so close to my ear that the hairs on my neck stand.

I twist my head to find her a few inches behind me. "Tanner."

"Tanner Nash?" Samuel couldn't sound more surprised had I said Nick Saban.

"Yes, Tanner Nash." I glance from Samuel to Ashley, then back to Samuel. You'd think I'd pulled the bait money again by their shocked expressions.

"I didn't know you and Tanner were friends." Ashley overenunciates the word "friends" like it's a curse word.

"We're actually seeing each other." That's my clever way of calling him my someone without actually lying. We are going to see each other, after all.

A smile tugs at my lips as Ashley trots off and Samuel's face drops. Our evil plan is working.

"That's nice, Hannah." Samuel's words fall like gravel from a dump truck. He taps his hand on the counter, then turns back toward his office.

I catch myself smiling as I silently count the cash in my drawer. Once everything is in place for the day, I freeze. In order to make our story believable, I need an actual plan for lunch. One that involves Tanner.

The problem with faking something in Apple Cart is that you can't disappear into a crowded place on the other end of town. The town is so small that there is no other end.

I pull my phone from my purse and shoot Tanner a text.

Could you do lunch today?

. . .

I tap my fingernails against the back of my phone, impatiently waiting. If he can't, I'll have to make a backup plan for hiding out during lunch. After what feels like the longest minute ever, three dots appear on the thread, then my phone dings.

Not today, I'm neck deep in . . .
This is followed by a chicken emoji and the poop emoji.

I laugh a little too loud, causing Ashley to cut her eyes in my direction. I clear my throat and stare at the computer screen.

Ashley waltzes toward the front doors, full-on pageant style, and unlocks the hinges. I drop my phone in my purse and settle onto my stool. After staring at the lobby floor a few minutes while sipping my water, the sun flickers and feet come into view.

Several early morning customers file in, and one comes to my window. I go through the motions of transactions, trying not to focus on my failed plans with Tanner. I've officially lied about lunch to sidestep Samuel.

This fake relationship stuff might be harder than I thought.

The older man thanks me after I hand him a receipt and an envelope of cash. He stuffs both into his front shirt pocket as if that's the safest place in the world.

I hold back a laugh, but it's those very things that make Apple Cart the safest place in world. Much safer than even my pristine cul-de-sac in Birmingham.

The next few hours stay steady. I refill my change drawers when we get a lull in customers. Samuel walks up to my window, straightening his tie. "Where are you guys going to lunch?"

I look up from busting a roll of quarters open and halfway open my mouth. Now he's just forcing me to lie.

"It's a surprise," I say with a nervous smile.

He nods, then continues toward the drive-through window, where Ashley is standing. I suck in a deep breath and check the clock on my computer screen. It's time for my break, and I haven't a clue what I'm going to do. But I have to do something, since I'm apparently going to lunch with Tanner. Except not really.

I shut down my computer and bend down, snatching my purse. Out of the corner of my eye, I notice Ashley watching me. I hurry through the swivel door and rush out to the parking lot while she's occupied with Samuel and the teller manning the drive-through.

Outside, I exhale and hop into my hot car. *Think, Hannah.* I sit at the stop sign by the bank entrance. With no other plan, I turn back toward our house.

"No way." Samuel's Mercedes appears a few cars back, going the same direction. My palms start to sweat as I approach the traffic light that centers all of Apple Cart County. In a panic, I turn in the direction he wouldn't dare go.

Wisteria.

I don't know Samuel too well, but I get the hunch he's too good to drive through our neighboring town of Wisteria. My throat dries out as I pass the welcome sign to Wisteria, which could use a new coat of paint. And maybe some better boards to hold it in place. Or just boards, since they look like PVC pipes. Okay, so they need a new sign entirely.

A quick glance in my rearview mirror reveals nothing in the distance but a flatbed pickup hauling hay bales. I smile, relaxing for the first time since I got to work today.

Well, unless you count when I read Tanner's text with the chicken poop emojis.

Wisteria's big claim to fame is that they're usually good at sports. Kyle transferred from our school to there for that very reason. I haven't thought to ask if anyone here still holds that against him. Maybe that's why Mrs. Maudy was anxious to set me up with him.

When I drive by Dollar General and nothing more, it appears the town hasn't changed at all. In Apple Cart, we occasionally get a new boutique or food truck business, but Wisteria looks untouched since my high school days.

Of course, I've only been here a handful of times. Most were when we played against them on their field. Then Dalton had me drive him once to the county line, just outside of Wisteria. There's a sketchy liquor store by some skanky hotel past the Waffle House.

My stomach growls at the thought of Waffle House. Wow, I must *really* be hungry. I don't want to go there or the Mexican joint by the liquor store. So I pull into the Quick Stop.

The bell rings above the door, and I'm greeted with a huge paper sign displaying all the soft drink and cigarette specials. I ignore those and head for the front. I'm pleasantly surprised to see the sub station is clean and has a nice selection.

After ordering a turkey sub on wheat, I grab a Diet Pepsi from the refrigerator and pay for my lunch. Several older men with *Duck Dynasty* beards sit in a corner booth eating burgers, and a woman walks in to pay for her gas. But it's otherwise vacant, and none of them know me.

I pop open my drink and get in the car, satisfied that I might just pull this off. With my sandwich in my lap, I back out of the parking lot and find a nearby oak tree.

I park beneath the shade and roll down my windows as if I'm a cop on a stakeout. Maybe I should've bought a donut.

Two bites into my turkey sandwich, which isn't half bad

when you're desperate and hungry, my phone rings. I set my sandwich on the wrapper and retrieve my phone from the cupholder. Tanner's name flashes across the screen. I take a quick sip of my Pepsi, then answer.

"Hello?"

Before he says anything, I hear chirping. "Hey, Hannah. Sorry I couldn't do lunch. They've got me about an hour south today."

"That's fine. I know it was last minute, I just needed an excuse to dodge Samuel."

"Man, I hate that I couldn't help. I've got chicks crawling all over me. Baby chickens, that is."

I laugh at his quick correction. "Ahh, I knew I heard chirping." A picture of Tanner cuddling baby chickens pops in my head, making me all gushy.

He laughs. "They're quite a sight."

"I bet Taylor would love to see them."

"I'll take some photos and text them to you. I send baby chick pics to my niece and nephew all the time."

"Sounds adorable."

"Hey, let's plan lunch for later this week when I'm in the office. Will Thursday work?"

"Yeah. You know me, I literally work banking hours." I cringe a little at my cliché joke.

He chuckles. Tanner's a good sport.

"Maybe we can meet at Mary's around eleven thirty?" I suggest.

"Nope, I'm picking you up. Remember, we're dating."

My cheeks warm when he says "we're dating," even though it's fake. "Yes, of course."

"It's a date, then."

"Yes, a date." I swallow a huge gulp of Pepsi.

"I'll leave you to it, then. Look out for baby chick pics coming your way."

"Okay, have a good day." I hold back the phone and watch as he ends the call.

I drop my phone in favor of my sandwich. It dings a few seconds later, and I open it to a text from Tanner.

His dimpled face is all smiles, and he's cradling about a dozen chicks in his arms. Which are very tan and very muscled, by the way.

I down the rest of my Pepsi and fight the urge to make that photo my background image.

CHAPTER EIGHT

Tanner

Eleven thirty on the dot, I push open the glass door to the bank. I pull one of my favorite blue suckers from the front table and head for Hannah's window.

An older man takes up the space in front of me, so I can't see her. Judging from the brightly striped western shirt and slim build, he must be Paul. And when I watch him fist a handful of peppermints before turning to leave, I know it's Paul.

Yep, it's him. He nods my direction as we pass on my way to Hannah. She meets my eyes, and I smile—partly to sell the whole fake-dating thing and partly because something about Hannah makes me smile. She's just a good person. One of those rare women who doesn't know how beautiful she is.

Out of the corner of my eye, I notice Ashley stacking deposit slips on the center table. Maybe she'll still be around when we leave together. Short of having Ethel here to watch, she's our best bet to starting any rumors.

"Afternoon." I lean my elbow on Hannah's counter, then hold up the candy. "Sucker?"

She shakes her head. "They're not such a treat if you have to stare at them all day."

I balk. "Come on. Everyone knows banks have the best suckers."

She shrugs as I unwrap the sucker and pop it in my mouth. "Ready for some real food?" I ask around a jaw full of blue raspberry.

"Yes. I just need a second to log out."

I nod. "Take all the time you need while I enjoy my appetizer." I tap the end of the sucker stick and turn so that my back is braced against the counter. I take note of Ashley's scowl and try not to laugh while I wait on Hannah to shut down her computer.

Hannah circles around to meet me, and I instinctively reach for her hand. She takes it, but her eyebrows raise in surprise. I lace my fingers through hers and grin. She glances around the room, then lifts the corners of her lips as if she approves of my move. Which is brilliant of me, as every eye in the bank follows our hands like a pig to a trough.

Her hand is soft and tiny, fitting nicely in mine. Just the way I remember it from when we shook on our fake-dating deal. I wish mine wasn't so calloused and rough, but we are pretending after all. If this were real, I might consider using lotion.

I slowly release my hand from hers to open the door, allowing her to pass through first. My arm tingles at the sudden loss of her touch. It must be the shock of holding something tiny and warm that isn't a baby chick.

Like I would for any date, I open her truck door. She grabs hold of the handle on the side and hoists herself inside.

I try not to pay attention to her toned legs, as she's wearing another skirt. I'm pretty sure gawking wasn't part of our agreement.

Once she's settled, I shut her door and get in my side. After a hard bite on my sucker, I pull the moist stick from my mouth and flick it in the empty ash tray.

"I'm glad this is under better circumstances than the last time you rode in my truck."

Hannah laughs and shakes her head. "Isn't everything better than that day?"

I wrinkle my mouth. "I dunno. It didn't turn out so bad. You got the job, your tire was an easy fix, and Gary's gone back to logging."

"Has he really?"

I back out, then smile at her as I turn my head toward the front. "Oh yeah. Put in his two-week notice the next day."

"I'm sorry."

I laugh. "Don't be. We've wanted him gone for years, but it turns out being a lazy butthole isn't enough grounds to fire a union worker. Especially when he's actually a reliable driver."

She nods. "Thanks for picking me up. I think it really helped sell ourselves as being together."

"Well, I find it necessary for people to believe you're with me." I wink, causing her to laugh. I watch her for a few seconds before pulling out into the road.

Her laugh is pretty, but also fun. She tosses her head back and opens her mouth wide, showing off perfect teeth. Her eyes crinkle at the corners, and her petite nose scrunches.

I keep her laughing face in the back of my mind on the way to the diner, which is all of five minutes. Mary's parking lot is already filled with vehicles. Several county work trucks are parked up front, meaning we'd better hurry inside before they eat up today's special.

Like a gentleman, or someone who's desperate to appear infatuated with my fake girlfriend, I open Hannah's door and wait patiently as she climbs out rather than rushing inside to fight the other hungry wolves for the best cuts of meat.

This time, it's Hannah who grabs my hand. The nerves in my fingers fire up in shock from her unexpected touch. But in a good way. I hold open the door with my free hand, and we stroll in side by side.

Every eye turns toward the creaky door to see who's entering, and every eye gravitates toward our interlinked hands. You'd think we were a celebrity couple walking the red carpet rather than two country bumpkins walking the linoleum floor of a diner.

But in Apple Cart, anyone can be a celebrity on any given day. All you have to do is something really good, really bad, or really out of character.

The way I see it, we're covering all the bases right now. It's good for us to squash any matchmakers and to keep Samuel away from Hannah. It's maybe a little bad that we're pretending. And it's totally out of character for me to prance around town with a beautiful woman.

Not that I've never been seen with a beautiful woman. Quite the contrary. I have the reputation of dating a lot of beautiful women before they find someone more settled, mature. The few who show long-term interest in me tend to be shallow or too young to know what they want. So I stay single.

One day, maybe I'll find a real Hannah. Someone beautiful and funny, with her ducks in a row. For now, I'm content to pretend.

Several county workers hog the coveted place where

Mary puts out the lunch special. "I'm gonna check out what's on the hot bar," I say.

"Okay, want me to grab us a booth?"

I scan the room, noting the tables filling up quickly. "Good idea." I smile down at Hannah.

She releases my hand and brushes my lower back as she passes. A tingle shoots across my skin as her fingertips slide across my shirt. I wiggle my shoulders once she's gone and take in the honey scent she left behind. Maybe I should tell my senses this is pretend.

I step in line behind a few men in their water board uniforms. One turns his head toward Hannah, then smirks my way. I grin.

A few minutes later, I'm sliding into a booth across from her with my meat and three selections.

"I ordered you sweet tea. I hope that's okay," she says.

"Yeah, perfect." We've only shared two meals so far, and both were last minute, but both times I'd drank tea. I make a note to notice some of the things she likes as well. That should help make us believable.

The waitress returns with our drinks and takes Hannah's order. She gets a chicken salad sandwich and curly fries. For a moment, my mind drifts back to the french fries she shared with Samuel. I look down and rub my forehead as if I can squash the memory.

"Have you noticed that all our interactions revolve around food?"

I lift my eyes. "Not if you count the times I've come in the bank."

"You always eat a sucker."

I laugh. "True."

Hannah plucks the straw in her cup and sips slowly. I catch myself staring at her lips. They're lush and pink. I look around the room, ashamed that I'm now jealous of a plastic straw.

"Now that I think of it, everywhere in Apple Cart revolves around food."

I tilt my head, allowing myself to look her way again. "Isn't it like that everywhere?"

"Not so much in Birmingham. I mean, there are dinner parties and tailgates and such, but plenty of other things that don't involve food. But a lot that involve shopping."

"Yeah. I'd say Paul has the monopoly on that around here."

She laughs. "I'm a little surprised he's still open."

"Really?"

"Yeah. He's like what? In his seventies?"

"Gotta be. But could you imagine Apple Cart without the General Store, or the General Store without Paul?"

Her forehead wrinkles. "I guess not."

The waitress appears again with Hannah's food. Hannah thanks her as she leaves, then bows her head. I bow mine as well.

"Want me to pray?" I ask.

"Yes."

I say a quick prayer. My words stay on thanking God for the food, but my mind drifts to how much this feels like a real date. That's the idea, of course, but I'm shocked at how easy it is to fake date Hannah.

She takes a bite of her sandwich, and I start cutting my pork chop. "You know what we need?"

"What?" she asks after swallowing.

"A real fake date."

She laughs. "That's an oxymoron if I've ever heard one."

"No, I mean a date-date, not just lunch."

"Like in Tuscaloosa?"

"Could be, or somewhere more local if you want to turn heads."

"Are you saying I can't turn heads in Tuscaloosa?" She lifts a brow and bites off a fry.

I chuckle. "You're cute." And I mean that in every sense. In a town full of Ashleys, it's refreshing to come across someone so quick witted.

She laughs. "What do you have in mind?"

I swallow a mouthful of potatoes before answering. "There's a new mini-golf and go-kart place on the edge of Wisteria."

"I saw a sign for that."

"Might be fun, and there's sure to be enough eyeballing locals."

She grins. "I can see if Mama will watch Taylor if you want to go this weekend."

"Take her with us. Kids like go-karts and golf."

Hannah's grin widens into a full-blown smile. "I think she'd really enjoy that."

"Good."

We eat for a minute or so in silence, and my mind drifts to hanging curves in a go-kart with Hannah shoved beside me, laughing her contagious laugh. Maybe I hit a curve too fast, causing her to clutch my arm. For at least a few minutes, I smile to myself around a mouthful of food and daydream about our fake date.

"Another benefit to having Taylor with us is we won't have to worry about looking like a couple."

I swallow my daydream along with my pork chop. "What do you mean?"

She shrugs. "You know. We don't have to act all lovey-dovey to oversell our 'relationship.'" She makes air quotes with her fingers around the word "relationship."

Nothing like the reminder this relationship is fake to wreck my go-kart fantasy.

Hannah

I flip aimlessly through the local paper while Taylor sits across from me eating goldfish crackers and coloring. Mama sits at the end of the kitchen table, clipping coupons from the Piggly Wiggly and Dollar General flyers that came with the paper.

Yesterday, I'd told her that Taylor and I planned on checking out the new go-kart place with Tanner. By the face she made in response, I could tell she assumed it was a date. While she wasn't on our laundry list of people to fool, I'm glad she took it well.

Of course, I've been single for almost a year now, and she's sang her praises for Tanner. But it is a little strange sitting at my parents' house, waiting for a guy to pick me up. Especially when the only guy I've ever waited to pick me up was Dalton.

The doorbell echoes from the front of the house. I push aside the paper and stand. There will be plenty of time to check out who got married and arrested this week when we get back.

"I'll get it," I announce as I walk toward the front door. I pause in front of the mirror in the hallway and check my appearance.

My hair is in place and my makeup intact. I smack my lips and huff. Not that it matters, since I'm going on a fake date with a five-year-old chaperone, but I may as well look the part.

I open the door to Tanner smiling, with a bouquet of flowers. My heart beats a little harder in my chest, and I silently scold it for doing so. It's just been so long since anyone's given me flowers. Unless I count Taylor bringing me weeds from the hayfield.

I reach out and take the flowers. When I do, Tanner holds back a single daisy that isn't attached to the bouquet.

"This is for Taylor." He shrugs. "You know, since I'm taking her, too, I only thought it fair."

My face smiles but my heart melts. I swallow the heat rising in my neck at his adorable gesture. "Let me get her. We're ready."

I turn to get Taylor, not realizing that Tanner is following me until Mama speaks up. "Hello again, Tanner."

"Hi, Mrs. Richards. Enjoying your weekend?"

"As a matter of fact, I am." Mama grins at him, then eyes the flowers in my hand. "How pretty and thoughtful. Let me put these in some water for you."

I hand over my bouquet, fresh and blooming with every color in the rainbow. Mama sniffs them before crossing into the dining area for a vase. I nod to Tanner. "She's impressed."

"Good. But do you like them?"

"I love them." My face warms again at the wonderful coincidence, since I do love flowers. Well, I suppose most southern women do, and Tanner is polite.

"And this, my lady, is for you." Tanner bends toward Taylor, disrupting her concentration on a new coloring page.

She glances up and grins. "Thank you." She spins the single stem between her tiny fingers and giggles. Then she rushes toward the dining room, meeting Mama midway.

"Whoops. Watch it, baby." Mama holds her hands higher to avoid Taylor running into the vase and flowers.

"Can you put mine in a vase too?"

"Oh, how beautiful." Mama puts my bouquet in the vase and takes the daisy from Taylor. "I sure can."

Mama smiles at us on her way to the sink. Taylor runs up to Tanner and me.

"Are you girls ready to go?" he asks Taylor more than me.

"Yes, sir." She hops with excitement and grabs both of us by the hand.

"Have fun," Mama calls from behind us as we head out front.

"I can drive so that we don't have to move Taylor's seat."

"Good plan."

I buckle Taylor in her seat, then get in. Tanner gets in the passenger seat, then turns to Taylor after he buckles. "Taylor, are you good at golf?"

She raises her hands and shrugs. "I only did it once in the mountains. It's kinda hard."

"Yeah, it is. Maybe we can help each other."

She nods and smiles. A pleasant peace bubbles inside of me. Regardless of why we're doing this or who we're trying to fool, this will be a fun night.

We drive through Apple Cart toward Wisteria. Tanner gives me directions to Double Drive, which is at the edge of our county by the infamous strip mall that houses Enchilada, a liquor store, and the only hotel within an hour of Tuscaloosa.

A large wooden archway appears right before the county line. "Double Drive" is scribbled in neon pink and orange paint. Of course, the liquor store is on the other side of the line, since Apple Cart County remains dry.

"Neon paint, interesting," I say.

"Yeah, according to Earl Ed, that was a marketing ploy to tease some upcoming paintball tournaments."

I twist my lips. "Mail jail Earl Ed?"

"Yep. His parents helped him purchase this land to start the business. It's only been around since the first of the year, but done quite well."

"Huh." Earl Ed comes from a good family, so it's nice to hear he's turned to better path.

We park in front of a cross-tie signifying a space in the gravel lot. Taylor practically bounces out of her seat as soon as I undo the buckle. "I wanna do that!" She points to the go-karts racing beside us.

"We can do it all," Tanner assures her. "But first we need to pay."

The three of us go to the small wooden building with a blinking Open sign hanging from the roof. Taylor pushes past us as soon as Tanner opens the door. Her eyes widen at several claw machines filled with stuffed animals.

There's also one in the corner filled with other items. I walk over for a closer look. It's filled with pocket knives, cell phone covers, mini flashlights, and other items you might see for sale at a gas station counter.

Tanner laughs as I frown at the contents inside. "I'll have to win you a prize later."

"I'm totally good with my beautiful bouquet at home." I admire his dimples as he continues to laugh.

"Come on." He heads toward the counter near the back of the room. Taylor skips ahead, and I follow behind them, taking note of the options on the wall. "Golf and go-karts for three. One kid, two adults," Tanner says.

I glance around as Tanner pays for our package deal. Mostly teenagers mingle around, as well as a couple my parents' age from church with who I assume are their grandkids. I smile at them, noting their grins and whispers. That should get the fake-dating word out soon enough.

"Hannah?"

I turn to see Adrianne Reynolds and Daisy Duncan from

high school. Or at least that's their maiden names. I have no clue if either have married.

"Hi, how are you two?" Adrianne and I hung out some, but I never knew Daisy too well. She was a little different. Adrianne is still her usual beautiful self. She was a majorette in high school and always had the coolest clothes. Daisy's hair is now fiery red, but a natural color. Not the pink or purple or blue she alternated in school.

"Good," they answer in unison.

"I thought I saw you in church the other week," Adrianne comments.

"Yeah, I moved back with my daughter, Taylor." I wrap my hand around Taylor's shoulder and give it a gentle pat. Better to go ahead and rip the Band-Aid than wait on more questions.

Adrianne nods, taking the hint that Dalton is no longer in the equation. They both look at Tanner, then me again, and grin. If the older couple from church doesn't do the job at telling the town, Adrianne will seal the deal at her salon.

Tanner loops his arm around my waist, sending a tingle across my back. "You ladies ready to pick out your clubs?"

"Sure." I smile up at him, and he gives my side a squeeze. Swallowing nerves, I turn to Adrianne and Daisy watching us. "It was nice seeing both of you."

"Same to you. See you around." Adrianne halfway winks at me—either that or her eyelash extensions catch together. Probably both.

We turn and exit the building, Tanner's arm still around me. Taylor skips ahead when she notices the deck leading to the golf course. I help her find a small club, and she picks out a pink ball. Tanner and I pick out our clubs and balls, too, then he picks up a tiny pencil and scorecard from above the clubs.

"I can keep score," he says.

"I thought this was just for fun?" I raise an eyebrow, challenging him.

"It is, but winning is fun."

"We'll see." I lower my brow and lead the way to the first hole. Before Taylor, I played a lot of golf at country clubs with Dalton. It was part of his plan to schmooze up to big-city lawyers.

"Youngest to oldest!" Taylor hops in front of the first hole before either of us can get to it. We both laugh and back up.

Taylor takes her time hitting the ball multiple times before it clears the first hump. Tanner laughs as she chases it down a short hill and bumps it around the hole about a dozen times before getting it in.

I lean to get a look at the scorecard in his hand. He smells manly and clean. I allow myself to take in his scent, in the name of selling our fake relationship. Then I silently chastise my hormones for tempting me to sniff him out like a bloodhound. "What score did that get?"

"I'm just gonna give her ten for effort." Tanner lifts the corner of his lips into a crooked smile, activating one of the dimples. That activates a giddiness inside me. "Your turn, dear."

I step forward, away from his trance and back into the humidity. In an effort to clear my head, I start swinging my golf club. Tanner laughs behind me. But he quits laughing when I tap the ball, sending it precisely a few inches from the hole. I smile to myself as I follow the path it made and tap it in. Turning back toward him, I say, "That's two."

He shakes his head and sighs. "Two indeed." He jots down my score, then sticks the card and tiny pencil in his front shirt pocket. I stand to the side with Taylor as Tanner stretches his club in front of him like he's preparing to bat. He swings the club way too hard, sending the ball straight across the course and outside the gate. I crane my neck to watch it bounce down the hillside into the woods.

"Whoa," Taylor mumbles beside me.

"And how many's that?" I ask, trying not to laugh as Tanner joins us.

"Maybe I'll just keep score." He palms the back of his neck and grins.

I laugh. "Good call."

We continue throughout the course, talking and joking as we wait patiently for Taylor to hit her ball in every hole. I hit mine in within three or less strokes each time, baffling Tanner. In the time it takes us to go through the course, I learn that he likes motocross races and the beach. He loves action movies, especially the *Avengers* franchise, and his favorite color is orange. Nothing earth shattering, but plenty of mundane information I should know about my boyfriend.

Boyfriend. That word sounds so awkward, even in my head. I've only had one boyfriend, who morphed into my husband, then ex-husband. So I haven't called anyone "boyfriend" in some time.

As we finish playing the last hole, our balls spin down a drain pipe, amazing Taylor. Tanner jots down my hole-in-one, the fourth one of the night. Then he leads us back toward the deck to turn in our clubs.

"Who won?" Taylor asks enthusiastically, pulling at the card in Tanner's hand. He holds the paper out for her to see.

Her eyes bug. "Wow, I got a really huge number, so I must win!"

"Yes, Taylor, you got the highest number," I agree, then smirk at Tanner. He laughs.

We drop off our clubs, Taylor still high on her "win," and cross the parking lot to the go-karts.

Taylor jumps in front of a measuring stick posted to the gate.

"Stand still." I steady her in front of it. "Looks like you'll need to ride with me."

"Okay." She pouts momentarily, but quickly lightens up when she spots the go-karts coming in from the last round.

Daisy and Adrianne come up behind us. "Hey, again." Adrianne smiles.

"You two riding?" Tanner asks.

"Yeah, and we're pretty dang good," Daisy asserts.

"Oh, well, I bet you can't beat Hannah in golf."

"I bet we can't either," Adrianne says. "That's why we stick to the arcade and cars."

"Y'all come here often?" I ask.

"Not really, about every other month, I'd say. When we want something to do that doesn't involve eating or driving to town."

"Or when I can't talk Adrianne into goat yoga."

"Goat yoga?" I've heard of this but never witnessed it.

Adrianne rolls her eyes. "It's not safe to exercise with farm animals."

Daisy shrugs. "Suit yourself. I love it and so do my goats."

"I've heard of people doing that."

"You should come check it out sometime."

I half smile, actually considering it. "What could it hurt?"

"Your arms, legs, back, spine, head . . . Y'all feel free to stop me anytime." Adrianne cringes.

Tanner and I laugh.

"Seriously, it's not that bad. She's weak." Daisy narrows her eyes up at Adrianne, who has a good half foot on her, then turns back to me. "Hand me your phone and I'll give you my number in case you want to give it a go."

"Okay." I hand over my phone, happy to have any option for exercise in Apple Cart County aside from jogging dirt roads or digging out Daddy's P90X DVDs from a decade ago.

Daisy fumbles with my phone, then hands it back. "Here. I put my number and Adrianne's in there in case you want to try goat yoga or just hang out sometime. I texted us from your phone too."

"Thanks." I smile as I receive my phone.

"Hanging out will be fun. Us single gals gotta stick together." Adrianne winks. This time, I'm sure.

Tanner hugs up behind me, wrapping both arms around my shoulders. "Single?"

Both women giggle and smile at us. I catch myself smiling too as he snuggles behind me before letting go. I'd say Tanner sealed the deal on selling our relationship.

CHAPTER NINE

Tanner

I swipe a hand over my windblown hair and wait for Hannah and Taylor to join me at the gate. Hannah had to ride with Taylor, leaving me to a single go-kart. While I didn't have the pleasure of pressing up against her as we swung around curves, I did have the pleasure of beating their car.

All gentleman sportsmanship went out the window when she showed me up in mini golf.

I nod to Adrianne and Daisy as they pass while I wait for Hannah to unbuckle Taylor. Adrianne stops after a few feet and turns back. "You two make a beautiful match."

"Thanks." I grin at the compliment. It's nice to know that if this were real, we'd look good together. The girls join me a minute later, and Taylor announces she's hungry.

"We can see what food they have inside," I say.

"I want ice cream," Taylor informs us.

I raise my eyes to Hannah to check if that's acceptable. When it comes to my niece and nephew, I don't care what their parents think. When it comes to my fake girlfriend's daughter, I totally care.

"Not just ice cream." Hannah cuts her eyes to Taylor before looking back at me.

"Okay." Taylor sighs, then slowly smiles in surrender.

We walk back toward the building, passing Adrianne and Daisy in the parking lot.

"Hannah, I'm going to call you soon about goat yoga," Daisy calls out from over her car door.

"Sounds good." Hannah smiles, and we both wave to them before climbing the few wooden steps to the entrance.

Across the room from the claw machines where we paid to play sits a row of booths and a few tables. All but two tables are taken up by a gang of teenagers. When we get closer, I spot a menu on the wall.

"Huh, not your usual corn dogs and popcorn like I expected," I say.

The menu has burgers, chicken fingers, and catfish plates. Nothing fancy, but actual food from a grill. For a place called Double Drive that's next to a liquor joint and owned by an ex-criminal, I'm mildly impressed.

"They even have salads," Hannah points out. I noticed, too, but didn't even consider that option.

She bends down to discuss the options with Taylor, who chooses chicken fingers once her mom confirms they don't have macaroni. Hannah straightens and orders Taylor's food and a salad with chicken tenders for herself. I add on my burger and fries, along with three fountain drinks.

Hannah reaches into her jeans pocket and pulls out a folded bill. I put my hand on hers to stop her. "I got this."

Her lips curve slightly as she drops her hand and tucks

the money back in her pocket. I have the sudden urge to take hold of her hand again, missing the way it feels in mine. After paying for our food, I do just that.

She gives me an approving glance, sending a small flutter across my chest. Sure, it's all for show, but my head hasn't yet sent my heart the memo. I take our paper cups from the girl behind the counter with my free hand. Once we're in front of the drink dispenser, I let go of her hand in favor of fixing my tea.

It's not like me to want to hold hands with a girl. Sure, I'm a flirt and I never turn down a kiss from a good-looking woman. But I've never been much for PDA, even on a G-rated level.

I sit across from Hannah and Taylor in the corner booth, farthest from the annoying teenage group. 'Kay . . . so that makes me old. I justify it in my mind by convincing myself that Hannah and I need a quiet place to talk.

Not long after Hannah convinces Taylor she needs to try and use the restroom and wash her hands, our food arrives. Earl Ed struts out wearing a ball cap with a Double Drive logo and a chef's apron that's seen better days. He calls out each item and sets the food in front of us as we claim the plates, then drops an array of sauces, salad dressings, and ketchup on the table. I'm now slightly more impressed.

"Napkins are on the table." He nods at the roll of paper towels in the corner. "Y'all need anything else?"

I glance at Hannah, who shakes her head. "I think we're good."

Earl Ed nods. "Good seeing y'all. I appreciate the business."

"Thanks, you've done well with the place. The mini-golf course was as good as those at Gulf Shores," I say.

The tops of Earl Ed's cheeks blush above his facial hair.

"Thanks, man." He scratches his head. "I had an in with that AstroTurf place in Tuscaloosa who covered G-Maw's carport."

I lift my chin. "The one that did the church soccer field."

"That's the one. G-Maw was their first residential client, and she's sent other old folks their way. When they heard I'm her grandson, they gave me a discount on the installation."

"Sweet. You've got a pretty good menu too."

"Yeah, it's all coming together. Back when I was flipping burgers in prison, I never thought it'd come in handy."

Hannah snickers, and I choke back a laugh. "That's good, Earl Ed."

"Thanks. Y'all need to come check out the paintball field once I get it finished."

Hannah takes a sip of her drink to mellow her expression, then adds, "Thanks, we'll do that."

"All right. I'll leave y'all to it." He knocks a chubby fist on the edge of the table, then disappears toward the kitchen.

"Taylor, would you like to say the blessing?" Hannah asks.

"If I do, can I get ice cream?" Taylor wrinkles her tiny nose at her mom.

Hannah sighs. "If you say the blessing *and* eat well, then you can get ice cream."

Taylor's shoulders sag, but she recovers quickly and folds her hands in front of her face. "God, thank you for fun, food, and that I now get ice cream. Amen."

I try my best not to laugh, but I'm not entirely successful. Kids are funny to me. I envy how they can say whatever and get away with it.

I bite into my burger and swallow with an "mmmm." Earl Ed can cook. Not that I'm surprised. He probably had plenty of time to practice in prison, and he isn't exactly slim and trim.

"Mine's good too," Hannah comments. "What about your chicken, Tay?"

Taylor gives a thumbs-up while chewing.

"I know you said ice cream, but I think I saw milkshakes on the menu. That is, if your mom approves."

Taylor's face lights up. Hannah nods and smiles. "If you eat enough real food."

Taylor puts down a half-eaten piece of chicken and shakes her head. "Why do grownups always say real food? Ice cream and milkshakes are real food too. We can actually eat them, unlike the food in *my* kitchen."

Hannah giggles. "Fine, growing food. But you can pretend to eat pretend dessert anytime."

Taylor slants her eyes at me. "It's not the same." She picks up her chicken finger and nibbles off another bite.

I laugh and polish off the rest of my burger. "What did you like doing best tonight?"

"Probably—"

"Nope." I lift my hand to stop Hannah. "I know what you liked best, Miss Golf USA. This question is for Taylor."

Taylor grins. "Uh . . ." She stares at the ceiling as if in deep thought before focusing on me again. "Racing with Mommy."

"That was fun." Hannah smiles at Taylor.

"Yeah, but next time, I need to drive so we can beat Tanner."

I chuckle. "What makes you think you'll beat me?"

She shrugs and bites off another piece of chicken. Hannah and I share a laugh, and I catch myself admiring her happy face once more. Her eyes dance when she laughs, and her cheeks raise. I should turn her laugh into a GIF and replay it anytime I'm having a bad day. Then, boom, instant mood lift.

We talk a little longer and wait on Taylor to eat almost all her chicken. By the time Hannah is satisfied with the amount she's eaten, Taylor and I have decided on a milkshake.

I order a cookies-and-cream milkshake, and Taylor gets a chocolate. Hannah makes sure Taylor's comes with a flat lid. Since we're in her car, I ask for mine to come with a flat lid as well.

"You want one?"

"Nah, I don't eat desserts that often." Hannah half frowns. The girl rings up our order and turns to make the shakes. Hannah's eyes follow her every move. I can tell she wants a shake.

"Here you go." The cashier hands us our shakes.

"Thanks." As we turn to leave, I elbow Hannah. "Do you like cookies and cream?"

"Who doesn't?"

"Here, take a sip." I lean my cup in front of her face after we descend the steps to the parking lot.

She stares at the straw like it's a poisonous snake. "You sure you don't mind my germs?"

"Of course not." I drape my free hand across her shoulder and whisper so Taylor can't hear. "You're my girlfriend, so why wouldn't we swap germs?"

She giggles, then puts her mouth to the straw. My neck heats up with her lips inches away from my face. I stare ahead toward the car, not wanting to make her uncomfortable. There's a fine line between selling this relationship and keeping it real with Hannah. Even more than I want to convince Apple Cart County our relationship is real, I want to put her at ease.

Hannah lifts her lips from the straw and sighs. I'm again jealous of a piece of plastic. Under different circumstances, I'd love to replace that stupid straw with my own lips and give her a kiss cookies and cream couldn't dare compare to.

Instead, I settle for helping her get Taylor buckled without spilling any of the milkshakes.

Taylor dominates most of the conversation on the way home. She fills us in on everything that goes on while her mom is at work. Mainly a lot of junk food eating and pony playing with Nana. Sounds about like my mama with my brother's kids.

By the time we make it into Apple Cart, everything is quiet. I peek in the rearview mirror to see Taylor's head thrown back and her mouth hung open like a large-mouth bass. A tiny snore escapes her nostrils.

Hannah laughs. "It amazes me how she can go from full speed to sleep in seconds."

I turn to her. "Yeah, well, kids don't have any worries on their minds."

Hannah's smile fades, so I face forward again. I hope I didn't touch a sore subject. Maybe Taylor does worry. I've witnessed a few friends deal with their parents divorcing over the years, but never as young as Taylor. That has to be tough.

I decide to do what I do best and lighten the mood. "You know, this is the best fake date I've ever been on."

Hannah's lips turn up once more, pulling mine up with them. "And exactly how many fake dates have you been on?"

"This would make two."

"Really?" She raises a brow at me.

"Yeah. A friend in college wanted me to make another guy jealous, so we showed up all linked together at a frat party."

"Did it work?"

I shake my head. "Not for any of us. He was too drunk to even notice, and she didn't like me in that way. After about an hour, he passed out, she went home, and I joined a game of poker in the kitchen."

Hannah laughs so loud she snorts, making me laugh too.

"It wasn't *that* funny," I manage to say. "I lost forty bucks in that game."

Hannah laughs even harder. "For someone who's only dated one person and never fake, it's pretty funny."

I flare my nostrils at the memory of Dalton hovering over her in high school. Even then, I could tell he was a controlling prick. I exhale, forcing his image from my mind. In an effort to keep the mood light, I again go for the funny. "You can't say that. You went on a date tonight with me, and it was fake." Those last few words leave a bitter taste in my mouth. *It was fake.*

Hannah turns into her parents' driveway and glances at me. "True. So this is the best fake date I've been on, then, too."

I try not to focus on the fact that it's her *only* fake date. "Well, maybe I can take you on an even better one next weekend."

She parks the car and stares at her lap. Her cheeks are flushed, and her lips toy with a grin.

Maybe I'm being too flirty. But for now, I don't care. I like Hannah. As a friend, and maybe even more if she weren't figuring out her new life and I weren't . . . me.

Without giving it another thought, I unbuckle and lean toward her. My face is inches from hers when she raises her head. She closes her eyes, and my heart races as I lean in another inch. I tilt my head and close my own eyes.

Then my lips land . . . on her hand. I know I'm a little out of practice, but did I miss that bad?

My eyes pop open to her palm blocking her face. "I'm sorry," she mumbles from the other side of her hand before dropping it.

"No, I'm sorry. You're right, I shouldn't have." I jerk my head back against the seat and try to hide my embarrassment.

"It's fine, really. It felt like a real date to me too."

Yeah, until I face-planted your palm. "It's my bad. It won't happen again."

The same soft hand that all but slapped my lips is now on my forearm. "Tanner, it's fine, really." She grips my arm and shakes it. "Tanner?"

I turn my head halfway so she'll stop shaking me like a new jug of tea.

"If I didn't have Taylor or a bunch of ex-husband baggage, things would be different."

I nod and force a slight smile. It's nice of her to say that, really. But all I hear is that I'm not boyfriend material. I'm an idiot to think that someone like her would take a goofball like me seriously. Refusing to show weakness, I lift my hand. "Friends?"

She gives it a firm shake. "Friends." She holds my hand a moment longer and adds, "And fake lovers for now."

"Fake lovers." I give her hand another shake, wanting to prolong holding it. "For now." I beam at those last two words, as they can be interpreted in more ways than one.

Hannah

"Thanks." I smile at Tanner as he holds open the front door for me.

"I'll call or text you tomorrow."

I nod. "You'll be at church, right?"

"Yeah. I'll see y'all in the morning."

"Okay, good night."

"Good night." Tanner starts down the front steps.

I step inside the house, but turn my head before he gets too far away. "Tanner?" I whisper-yell to not wake Taylor. As if there were any danger in that.

"Yeah?" he calls back from the yard.

"I had a lot of fun tonight, and Taylor did too."

Even in the setting sun, I can make out his dimples. "So did I." He smiles wider before ducking his head and continuing to his truck.

I turn around and ease the door shut with my foot. Noises from the TV echo from the living room. Mama sticks her head in the hallway, but I ward her off by putting a finger to my pursed lips, then pointing to Taylor and mouthing the word "asleep." Another thing I didn't anticipate about "dating" again was the questions that would come from her.

Once I told her Tanner and I had planned this outing, she had several questions, including how and when Tanner asked me. I'm not the best at thinking on the fly, so I threw together something about him stopping by the bank, which led to lunch, which led to going golfing. All truths about our fake date.

I'll fill her in on everything after I settle Taylor in bed. Everything except for the almost kiss. I'd come way too close to convincing even myself that this date was for real. Reliving Tanner's handsome jawline and slightly opened lips tilted toward my face might lower any defenses I have left.

I huff loudly. Taylor may be tiny, but her dead weight starts to wear on me as I climb the stairs. I reach the top floor, regretting wearing wedges. I start toward her room, then stop at the bathroom after seeing her face.

"Taylor, baby?" I pat her sticky face. She whines and drops her head on my shoulder. "We've got to wash your face and brush your teeth. Then you can sleep more."

I sit her on the toilet, and she somehow manages to stay

upright with her eyes still closed. As gently and quickly as possible, I brush her teeth and wash her cheeks and chin with a warm bath cloth. Then I scoop her up once more and take her to bed.

Taylor is staying in my old room, since it has my old twin bed and brightly colored walls. I opted for the guest bedroom down the hall without all the youthfulness.

Immediately after I lay her in bed, she rolls on her side and snatches the covers. I give up trying to change her into pajamas and settle for slipping off her Crocs. Her shorts suit is comfy enough, and I did accomplish cleaning her face and teeth.

I kiss her forehead, then straighten. A wave of nostalgia hits me when I stand. Mama has left most everything the same since my high school days. The same bedspread and curtains, the same mint-green walls. There's even a photo of my senior cheerleading squad still framed on the vanity. And . . .

I cross the room and pick up the photo beside that one. It's a small picture of Dalton and me at prom. I tuck it under my arm, hoping Taylor hasn't paid it any attention. Even though there's a slew of these creeping around in photo albums downstairs, I don't want one out on display to give her false hope of us together.

Or me.

It's taken a year, but I'm finally to the point of moving on alone. Past begging him to change. Over him not wanting me, or our daughter.

Sighing, I stop by the bookshelf on my way out and grab my yearbooks. I doubt Taylor would recognize any of us in the black-and-white photos from a decade ago, or even think to flip through them. But I don't want to chance it. These can stay in my closet.

I leave her door open halfway as always, in case she needs

me. Then I round the hall to my new bedroom. It has a four-poster bed, a comfy armchair, one dresser, and nothing else. Like a bed and breakfast in a southern cottage.

I drop the yearbooks on the bed and pull out my pajamas. After brushing my own teeth and washing my own face, I come back intending to put the books away and go downstairs for a bit. But the worn leather covers stare back at me as I change out of my clothes.

Instead, I wind up propped on the edge of the bed, thumbing through the top book—my junior year. It's been a while, but not *that* long. Only a decade. But so much life has happened in that time, it feels longer.

I fight back a tear when I turn the page to prom. Dalton and I are front and center, armed up, slow dancing. Our faces are fixed on one another with nothing but love and admiration. What I wouldn't give to have that love again.

He wasn't the best person, by far. But neither am I. And up until his affair, I really believed he loved me. He sometimes got a little too controlling, but he cared about me.

I sigh and am starting to shut the book when I notice something in the background of the picture that makes me cackle out loud. Tanner. Wearing a bowtie and tux pants, swinging a shirt over his head.

A distant memory of a teacher scolding him comes to mind, along with talk of his "prank" at prom. I was too focused on Dalton to notice that night. Just like I'd been too focused on Dalton to notice a lot of things. Even when our marriage started slipping.

I close the book and toss it back on top of the others. Then I stack them neatly in the closet before climbing onto the bed. I'm not sleepy, or even tired. However, sitting in the quiet appeals to me more than answering Mama's questions right now.

She's sure to have a ton. She likes Tanner, and it's only my second first date ever. Fake or not. Besides, she doesn't know it's fake.

I roll onto my side and stare out the window into the dark sky. For a brief moment, I'd also forgotten it was fake. Tanner had mentioned going on another "date," making me blush. The sincerity in his voice had me caught in the moment. I'd wanted it to be real. Then as he'd leaned in and closed his eyes, I panicked.

I'm twenty-six years old, but I've only kissed one man. And that man was also my husband and the father of my child. I don't even know how to be intimate with another guy—on any level.

Whenever Tanner holds my hand or wraps his arm around me, it sends shivers over my skin. In a good way, an exciting way. Like I want him to hold me. Most likely, it's my loneliness and the newness of someone besides Dalton showing me affection. Not my attraction to Tanner.

Of course, I find him attractive. Who doesn't? And the more I get to know him, the more I like him. But I'm a mess. I'm supporting myself for the first time ever, plus a young child. I live with my parents. Nobody wants to deal with that. Or at least, not a guy like Tanner. He's never been married or had kids. Why would he want to settle for my complicated "bless her heart" baggage?

I close my eyes and take a deep breath. A kiss would've been nice. Even if it were nothing more than a single kiss. But I made the right choice. For me. For Tanner. Most of all, for Taylor.

My throat catches as I exhale. I can make all the excuses I want, but if I'm being honest with myself, I would've let him kiss me had it not been for Taylor. That poor child has been through enough this past year without any more confusion.

From now on, I'll make sure to keep my mind focused on platonic dating—plating. Even if it is fake. Fake platonic dating. Flating.

CHAPTER TEN

Tanner

I open Jack's front door to Jack and Jonah staring me down like they're deer caught in headlights. "What?"

"Care to share about your new romance?" Jonah fumbles a toothpick between his lips and narrows his eyes.

I hesitate. I have to play into this. I promised Hannah we'd keep the secret from everyone, parents and best friends included. That's the only way it will work around this gossip-crazy town. Nobody can be trusted. They all have lips so loose, it's like they grease them in cooking oil before every meal. Just in time to spill the tea over meat and threes at Mary's Diner.

"What's there to say?" I shrug, playing it cool as I shut the door and head toward the kitchen table.

"Lots of talk around town about you eating lunch with Hannah all the time. Then taking her to Double Drive. That's all." Jack widens his eyes.

I roll mine. I expect this kind of crap from Jonah, but not Jack. I liked him better before he got his own relationship. He's becoming too much of a busybody.

"Am I not allowed to have a friend other than you two weirdos?" I pull out a chair and sit. Jack's labs, Chocolate and Brownie, waddle my way. I pet them on the head, happy to turn my attention from the two humans.

"We just thought you'd tell us if you were dating someone is all," Jack comments.

"Who said we're dating?"

Jonah lets out a gruff laugh. "Come on, Tanner. We know you like her."

"So?" I rub the dogs behind their ears before standing to fix myself a drink. Jack and Jonah's eyes follow me to the refrigerator, and I bite back a laugh. My superpower is obnoxious immaturity.

I pour a plastic cup full of sweet tea, frowning at the Alabama logo on the front. Why Jack chose to go there instead of Auburn still baffles me. I sit down to both of them staring my way. Aside from Jonah shuffling cards, they remain motionless.

"'Kay, fine. I like Hannah. What's wrong with that?"

"Nothing." Jack purses his lips and shakes his head. "I'd have preferred you told me yourself instead of me hearing it from Paul."

"How does Paul know?" I'm now intrigued as to how far the rumors have spread in such a short amount of time.

"He saw y'all talking at the bank. Then he heard someone else talking about you two when he was at Adrianne's."

"What's Paul doing at Adrianne's? I thought he cut his own hair with that gadget he found at a yard sale."

"She had some kind of special back-to-school day for hair color. He heard they were having food and stopped by to fix a plate."

I throw my head back and laugh. "Such a mooch."

"Yeah, well. Apparently, you and Hannah were all the talk at the salon."

"Look, guys." I drop my head and give them a serious stare. "If anything were serious yet, I'd tell you two first. We've only been hanging out a week or two."

"Sure." Jack grins.

"What?"

"I could tell something was going on that day when you sat with her in church."

I cross my arms. "Fine, Jack. You are so smart. Good for you." I pat his head like I did the dogs a minute earlier, making him frown.

Jonah laughs and starts flicking cards in front of us. I gather the pile and examine my hand. Pretty good.

Jonah continues laughing until I glare at him. "Why aren't you back at Auburn yet?"

"Classes don't start for another few weeks."

I shrug. "Carol went back yesterday."

"She's starting that part-time job Monday."

I nod. Jonah always knows more about my sister than me. That's come in handy a few times when I've had him check up on some sketchy dudes for me. For all his faults, I can at least count on him to help look out for her when I'm not around.

"Is she coming back for our engagement party?"

I fight the urge to laugh at Jack. He sounds so feminine asking this.

"I'm sure she will," Jonah answers between bites of Doritos.

"Bianca will be glad. She wants her to look at this place and help redecorate."

"What, 1970s shag carpet isn't her style?" I joke about the flooring all the time with Jack.

"I don't even think it was my grandparents' style before they died." Jack removes his cap and tousles his dark hair. "Anyway, I'm glad I didn't redo it yet. She probably wouldn't like whatever I picked out."

"She gonna Atlanta it up?" I've never seen Bianca's condo, but I can imagine it's pretty prissy judging from her clothing.

Jack shook his head. "She loves the lodge. Wants something similar in here for us."

I halfway grin. It's refreshing to know she doesn't plan on totally neutering Jack. Lucky for me, I only have myself to please.

"Besides, she's the one moving to me. Least I can do is let her spruce up the old place."

We toss out our cards, Jonah raking in the hand. He mocks an evil laugh before dealing out more cards.

"So why Hannah?" Jack asks.

I flinch at the sudden question and look up from my hand. *Think fast.* I can't say because she's an attractive female our age who also wants nosy neighbors off her back.

"What's not to love about Hannah?" I bite my tongue, realizing I just used the "L" word. I should've went with "like," but it's too late now.

Jonah sneers, obviously catching that slip of the tongue. Jack's face stays solemn. "I guess I never pictured you with someone who had a kid."

"I love kids. You see how I spoil Carrie and Jacob."

Jack runs a hand through his hair. "I didn't mean it like that. I mean I didn't picture you dating a single mom."

"Well, none of us pictured you dating someone from Atlanta who wears hooker boots on hunting trips."

"Hey, I bought her some normal boots."

I lift my brows and take a sip of my tea. The hairs on my neck raise, as I'm all of a sudden protective of my fake relationship. "For your information, Taylor went with us on a date. And I really like that kid. She's freakin' hilarious."

"That's great," Jonah mumbles around another mouthful of chips. I want to slap him and tell him to stay out of it, but I refrain.

"I just don't want anyone getting hurt," Jack says.

I drum my fingers on the table and lean toward him. "What makes you say that?"

"Hannah's been through a lot of stuff you can't relate to. Heck, stuff I can't relate to. You can't nonchalantly act like you do dating random girls."

My temperature rises as I pop my knuckles one by one. Jack's Adam's apple bobs as he watches my movement. I'm sure my face is full of fury. Maybe he thinks I'm prepping for a fight. I manage to swallow some of my rage before answering.

"Hannah is the sweetest woman I know. The last thing I'd want is to see her hurt even more, especially on account of me. I love that she's a mom. Seeing how she is with Taylor makes me like her even more. She can't help it that her ex turned into a total tool and left them, and neither can I."

Jack nods. "You're right. I'm sorry, man. She is a good person."

"Thanks." I somewhat smile to satisfy Jack's apology, but my mind is elsewhere.

Everything I said about Hannah is true. It's how I feel about her. She really is the sweetest woman I know, and I admire her for so many reasons. I think she's brave for moving back to this town to give Taylor a better life, even though doing so will open her up to tons of gossip. She's hardworking and determined to not let her past define her. She has plenty of reasons to be mad, upset, or revengeful. Instead, she keeps smiling and finding the good in everything.

Even in me.

Hannah

I yawn as I pull into the bank parking lot. This weekend was filled with random outings, from taking Taylor and Skip on walks around the pasture to making s'mores in our backyard way past her bedtime. And mine.

Tanner spent most of our waking hours with us, playing with Taylor and keeping us all entertained with his stories about Auburn. My brief college days were much different in Birmingham. Of course, I'm sure a lot of the adventures had more to do with it being Tanner than Auburn.

I grab my water bottle as I climb out of the car, wishing I'd known Tanner better in high school. I'm sure he'd have kept me entertained.

The cool air hits me like a brick wall when I step inside the bank. I immediately wrap my cardigan around my shoulders. I've never understood why people overcompensate for the weather outside by blasting extreme air or heat.

Either Ashley isn't cold natured like me or she values style above comfort. I've barely made it to my station when she sashays behind me, wearing a mini skirt with a skimpy blouse that shows too much cleavage. Yes, she's a young, attractive person. But this is the bank, not Hooters.

She pushes me aside and drops my bank drawer on the counter with a thud. "Here." She holds up the thick roll of bills in the special rubber band and thumbs through the ends with her long nail. "Don't forget. We don't touch this unless it's an emergency."

I frown as she reaches beside me and shoves the bait money on top of the metal trigger that signals the cops. "Ashley, it's been almost a month since that happened. You don't have to tell me every day."

She arches an eyebrow and pouts her full lips. I swallow, a bit intimidated by her glare. Luckily, Samuel enters the lobby and rests his elbows on the counter in front of us.

"Morning, ladies." He nods at me, then scans Ashley head to toe. "Ashley, you're looking exceptional this morning."

"Why, thank you." She bats her eyelashes and jiggles her shoulders just enough to make other parts of her jiggle as well.

I turn my head to roll my eyes without anyone noticing. They chat as if I'm not there while I count the money in my drawer. All the while, I wait for Ashley to assure me that she knows it's the right amount, even though protocol dictates I double check.

When she continues flirting with Samuel instead of chastising me for doing my job, I realize something profound. Our little fake-dating plan is working. Not just on the gossiping grandmas and bored housewives, but on Samuel too.

Even better, Samuel averting his attention to Ashley takes her attention off me. I shut the drawer and hum to myself as I check off my money ledger and turn on the computer.

Ashley knocks her hips against my back while making her way around to the front. I keep my head down, ignoring the gesture. She and Samuel walk across the lobby together, leaving me in momentary peace.

That moment lasts about as long as it takes Paul to stuff his pockets full of suckers and step up to my window. He empties a leather pouch full of cash and coins on the counter. "Miss Hannah. I need to make a deposit."

"Yes, sir." I widen my eyes at the loose change rolling around. It takes moving my keyboard and a cup of pens to rein it all in.

Paul leans against the counter and pulls a sucker from his front shirt pocket. He cracks down on the sugar ball as I meticulously count each coin—twice. I admit, next to removing the bait money that day, counting hundreds of coins is the most stressful part of this job.

At least Ashley's not breathing down my neck right now. I'd prefer counting these coins another ten times to having her in my face.

I count the cash as Paul starts on his third sucker. I know because he's leaving the wrappers and sticks beside my keyboard.

"Okay, Mr. Paul. That totals out to four hundred eighty-three dollars and sixty-one cents."

Paul grins around the sucker stick. "Not bad for a hard day's work."

I clear my throat and conjure up a smile. Unless Paul's had a fire lit under his butt since I've moved away, I doubt he's put in a hard day's work.

He takes the deposit receipt I hand him and tucks it neatly into the leather pouch. Then with a click of his tongue, he finishes his sucker and starts on another before leaving the bank.

I frown at the trash beside my keyboard, then head for the supply closet for some Clorox wipes. Simply walking through Paul's store of odds and ends makes me itch for a tetanus shot.

After pulling the wipes from the bottom shelf in the closet, I stand to find myself face to face with Ashley. She raises a brow. "Did you spill something?"

I shake my head. "No, a customer left some soiled sucker sticks on my counter."

"Sticks?"

"Yes."

"Please limit it to one sucker per customer."

A laugh escapes my throat. Telling Paul to take only one of any food item is about as convincing as keeping a ravenous wolf from eating a plate of steaks.

"You think that's funny? Wasting company resources?"

"No. I think it's funny that you think Paul's gonna just eat one sucker." I shrug. "But if it really bothers you, maybe you should put a sign on the front table."

Ashley scowls and brushes past me. Again, knocking into me with her sharp elbow. What's with this woman and her sharp edges? And for someone so thin, she somehow manages to knock into everyone around. Or maybe it's just me.

I shut the closet door and retreat to my personal square of the teller station. For once, I pray Samuel will breeze back through the lobby. He's about the only one who can get Ashley off my back.

CHAPTER ELEVEN

Tanner

I check my appearance in the glass door of the bank before going inside. Not that it matters much since I'm dressed in my usual Carhartts and Top Chick Foods cap. But I want to hold up my end of the deal in making Apple Cartians believe Hannah is dating me.

The sucker bucket stares at me, each bulb begging to be plucked. I reach for a blue raspberry, but stop when I notice a sign next to the tin can. "Limit: ONE sucker per customer."

I snort at the pink, swirly handwriting better suited for a love letter from a sorority girl than a business note. Trust me, I've read plenty of both.

Despite my prankster nature, I'm a rule follower at heart. So I take the one sucker and resist my urge to grab a few others to stash in my glove box. Besides, Hannah may have written that note. I picture her to have matured past scripting in cheerleader font, but you never know.

I contemplate all the random details I've yet to learn about Hannah as I unwrap my sucker. Handwriting, subtle likes and dislikes, preferences on politics and sports teams. Things that wouldn't matter much if we weren't supposed to be dating.

Her face lights up when I cross the lobby toward her window. My insides get all twisty, and I hope her reaction isn't totally for show. I glance toward the hallway and spot Samuel behind his desk, his door half open. I nod, and he returns the gesture with the slightest smile possible.

Ashley bounds down the hall and into his office, closing the door behind her. I grin at the idea of the two of them. They'd make a great couple if they weren't both so insufferable.

My gaze returns to Hannah, who's wearing a black sweater like it's late November. Well, more like early March where we live.

"Are you cold?"

She shrugs, her grin going sideways. "They keep the air turned up in here. I'm not sure if it's Samuel, since he's always in a three-piece suit, or Mrs. Bromwell trying to make Ashley put on more clothes."

I follow Hannah's eyes in the direction of Bethany Bromwell sitting stick straight at the loan desk. She's wearing a shirt buttoned so high, it could double as a scarf. And I've never seen the woman without her hair in a tight bun. As a kid, I used to think her hair was why her eyebrows stood so high on her forehead. Now I think they got stuck that way from her looking down on everyone.

"Yeah, I'm gonna go with Bromwell." I snicker and Hannah laughs. "You ready for lunch?"

"Yes. One second." She clicks some keys on her computer mouse and reaches under her counter, pulling out her purse.

I bite into the blue sugar now stuck to the inside of my cheek as I wait for her to circle around the little saloon door by her window.

Half for show and half out of impulse, I grab her hand. She laces her fingers with mine, and my face warms at how natural it feels. I open the front door for us and nod at the sucker bucket.

"Say, what's with the sucker limit?"

Hannah pauses to read the note, then rolls her eyes. "Seriously?"

"It was up when I came in."

She shakes her head as we step onto the pavement. "Ashley must've done that."

I release her hand and open the truck door. "Ah, that explains the flirty penmanship."

"Yep. She snapped at me earlier because Paul took a handful of suckers and left the remains at my station."

"Good luck trying to limit Paul on anything edible."

"That's what I said." Hannah climbs in the truck, and I do the same.

I pull the stick from my mouth, one end now flat from where I chewed it too long. "This was my only sucker today." I toss it in the ashtray with a couple of other sticks I need to dump soon.

She laughs. "Thank you for abiding by the law."

"Of course. I'd hate for Bradley to have to come out here and arrest me."

"Yeah." Hannah sighs as she slips off her sweater, revealing a sleeveless top. "Somehow, I'm sure that would be my fault too."

I involuntarily lick my lips as I study her collarbone and the curve of her slender neck. When my eyes reach hers, I blink and face the windshield. Maybe my face didn't give away my thoughts of kissing her neck.

I clear my throat for no reason other than to break the awkward silence. "Barbecue all right?"

"Yeah." She buckles her seat belt, and so do I. Then I loosen mine a bit, suddenly feeling constricted, as if it's trying to hold me back from her. I let the strap go, and it pops against my chest as a wakeup call that I *do* need to restrict myself from her. Especially when it's only the two of us.

"I think our plan is working," she says.

"Oh yeah?" I turn on the road and head for Big Butts BBQ.

"Samuel has switched his attention to Ashley."

"I'm sure she likes that."

Hannah grins. "I sure do. Aside from rationing suckers, she hasn't really bothered me today."

"You know, my mom's been on my case a lot less since we've been hanging out too."

"That's good."

"Yeah." I laugh. "She says it's refreshing to hear of me with someone my own age."

"Really?" Hannah raises one side of her mouth in question.

I squirm, a little embarrassed to admit to dating younger girls lately. "Let's just say my last date—before you, of course—was at a Morgan Wallen concert with an Auburn cheerleader."

Hannah laughs her contagious laugh, causing me to join in, even at my own expense. "Quite different from taking a single mom to play mini golf."

"I liked our date better." I reach across the console for her hand, but decide better. I give her wrist a quick pat, then return my hand to the wheel. Lame, but better than making a move.

She must sense my awkwardness, because she changes the subject to my job. I fill her in on Gary's epic departure, which included flipping off everyone in the office and mooning my office window on his way out. Hannah's face morphs between terror and amusement a few times as I recount my boss threatening to call Bradley and Ms. Ethel calling Brother Johnny to add Gary to the prayer list.

"I remember reading his name with 'unspoken' beside it on the bulletin insert last week."

"Yep, and now you know the unspoken."

"Huh." Hannah chuckles as I park in front of the Big Butts food truck. The sun glistens against the tin of the building, highlighting the red canopy with a pig's rear end for the logo.

Several people huddle near the window, ordering, while a group of men in city uniforms take up the one picnic table beside the trailer. Big Butts is the only food truck I know that never seems to move. Even when we have a downtown event, it stays parked, thanks to its convenient location.

I open Hannah's door, noting how the city workers admire her. I make a point to place my hand on her back as she climbs out of my truck and leave it there until we reach the front of the trailer.

She orders smoked chicken and a baked potato. I've noticed she eats a lot of chicken. That's one detail I can remember, and an easy one since I work for a poultry supplier.

I get a barbecue sandwich and fries, then pay and step to the side. Hannah slides beside me and whispers near my ear, "You don't have to pay for my food every time we eat together."

"I always pay for my dates." I turn, our faces now within

inches of one another. She blushes as I drop my gaze. "Besides, I've eaten with your family on several occasions, and you can't put a price on home cooking."

My gaze lifts from her spiky heels to her eyes that are still fixed on me. I like it when she wears heels. It makes our faces that much closer. Her lips that much more accessible.

"Order up." Billy Bob's gruff voice carries from inside the trailer. I stop studying Hannah's pink lips long enough to retrieve our food.

"Here you go. I put in some extra napkins for your lady friend."

"Well, thank you." I nod to Billy Bob and carry the Styrofoam cups and boxes back toward Hannah.

She scans the grassy area that's bare except for the one large table filled with water board workers. "I guess we need to eat in the truck."

"Come on. I got an idea." I motion toward the truck with my head. We get in, and I drive past downtown to the park.

Aside from riding with my niece and nephew to see the Christmas lights, I haven't been to the park in years. But I'm certain they still have pavilions where we can eat.

Sure enough, there's a large, empty picnic table overlooking the lake. We park and get out with our food.

Hannah smiles at the lake. "I should bring Taylor here to feed the ducks sometime."

"We should bring her and Skip for a walk here."

"Yeah." Hannah moves her grin toward me as she opens her box of food. "You're really good with her. You'll be a great dad someday."

"Thanks." My heart speeds up momentarily as I spread out my own lunch. Hannah's a great parent, and her saying I'd be a great one, too, means the world to me.

A small pin of insecurity pokes at my ego, highlighting

the word "someday." Does that mean she thinks I'm not dad material now? Not that I'm wanting to be a dad now, but it'd be nice to know she thinks I could hack it.

I stare into space as Hannah bows her head, obviously praying in silence before pulling apart her chicken. We eat in silence a few minutes before she scrunches her brows. "Are you okay?"

"Yeah," I mumble around a bite of barbecue. After swallowing some tea, I shrug. "I was just thinking about how well everything's going. You know." I motion between us.

"Yeah. It's been easier than I expected."

"To faking it." I hold up my cup, and Hannah clinks hers against it and laughs. Except it's more of a squeak since Styrofoam doesn't clink.

Hannah pulls her drink to her mouth and takes a sip. "It has gone smoothly. Even my mama seems convinced we're an item."

"So do Jack and Jonah."

"Wow."

I prop my elbows on the wooden picnic table. "Jack even gave me a speech about not hurting you."

"Why would he think you'd do that?"

I pop my knuckles, hesitating to answer. "Let's just say I've never had an actual relationship. For some reason, I tend to date women I know it won't work out with."

Even though she's chewing her chicken, I spot a frown forming on Hannah's face. She swallows, then opens her mouth to speak.

"It's not as bad as it sounds. I'm not a player. It's just . . ." I pause and palm the back of my neck. Why in tarnation did I just use the word player? "Most women who want something serious aren't interested in me. They find me too goofy or say I'm not husband material."

My skin itches at admitting my biggest insecurity. I've

always been the one to make people laugh or have a good time, but not the one someone came to with a serious matter. I'm the cliché middle child.

Hannah reaches across the table and rests her hand on mine. "I don't think you give yourself enough credit."

Despite the warmth of her touch, my hand freezes. I want to flip it over and grip her palm, but I don't. Instead, I simply smile. "Thanks."

"I mean it. I don't think you're capable of hurting someone."

I laugh. "I'm not sure that's a compliment, but I'll take it."

She pats my hand gently, then moves hers back to her plate. "It is."

Almost immediately, I miss her touch. The primal part of me wants to kick the Styrofoam boxes out of the way, dip her across the picnic table, and kiss her like I'm about to ship off to war. But, I remain a southern gentleman and honor our friendly agreement—at least for now—settling on words rather than actions. "For the record, Dalton's an idiot for hurting you. And I don't just mean currently. I've always thought you were outta his league, even in school."

Hannah blushes and peers around the park. Something makes me think Dalton didn't compliment her much. Her face continues to redden, whether from the heat or the compliment, I'm not sure.

"Jack and Bianca have this engagement thing at the lodge Friday night. If you're available, would you wanna go with me?"

She glances back at me, the sun highlighting her pink cheeks. "Of course, I would."

"Good, it's a date." I grin as her face lights up at those words. Turning in a "plus one" to Bianca is sure to stir up some talk. However, the reason I'm excited has nothing to do with our deal and everything to do with Hannah.

Hannah

"Ouch." Adrianne rolls to her side, causing the goat to jump onto my back. I grunt slightly and shift my weight.

Adrianne sits up and scowls at Daisy. "You said this would be relaxing. That thing hoofed me in the boob." She rubs the heel of her hand against her chest and shudders.

"None of them weigh more than twelve pounds. It couldn't have hurt that bad." Daisy holds her perfect downward dog position with two goats on her shoulders.

"Remind me next time you're in the salon to whack your boob with a three-pound metal curling wand and see if that hurts."

Daisy rolls her eyes before dropping her gaze to the grass. I slowly arch my back, shifting weight again as one of the baby goats topples to the ground. It bleats and races toward Daisy. She scoops it in her arms and kisses its head.

"Good job, Mullet." Daisy's voice sweetens like that of a Disney princess.

This particular goat has a long strand of hair near the back of its head. Resembling, well, a mullet. In the hour I've been here, I've realized Daisy favors it over the others.

Another goat trots toward Adrianne. She stands and shoos it away. "I'll already have bruises to cover up for the party tomorrow night."

"Jack and Bianca's party?" I ask.

"Yeah, are you going with Tanner?" Daisy drawls out his name in a sing-song fashion.

"Yeah."

She stops scratching Mullet's belly and smirks at Adrianne, who returns the gesture with an arched brow. My cheeks heat up. Not so much at their reaction but at the idea of more people reacting in this manner.

Everyone in town has either seen or heard of us together by now, but tomorrow night will mark the first big event we've attended. And since it's for Tanner's best friend, a lot of people our age will be there. I'll have to bring my A-game.

"What were you planning on wearing?" Adrianne scans me carefully.

I shrug. "I guess whatever I wear to work in the morning."

Adrianne and Daisy exchange a look. One that says I've lost my mind.

With no goats currently on me, I tuck my legs beneath me and sit. "I'll refresh my makeup, of course. Probably redo my hair."

"Uh-huh." Daisy offers me a pitying grin.

Adrianne steps toward me and reaches out a hand. "Come on."

I take her hand and stand. "Where are we going?"

"My house. We're about the same size."

"You want to look in my closet first, since we're already here?"

Adrianne turns to Daisy. "No offense, hon, but aside from sweats, your regular clothes are a bit crunchy."

Daisy stands and groans. "What's that supposed to mean?"

"Let's just say our girl Hannah here is more of a Rachel than a Phoebe."

Daisy purses her lips. "Fine. Let's at least finish our yoga first."

Adrianne glances around at the goats wandering through the yard. "Oh, honey, I've been finished."

"Come on, kids." Daisy rounds up the goats. I'm amazed at how they go from aimlessly trotting around to falling in line behind her.

"Let's go." Adrianne is already at her car when Daisy locks the goats in their pen. I start toward my car, but Adrianne motions me over. "I'm just down the road. Y'all can ride with me."

I open the back door, and Daisy stops beside me. "Best buckle up and hold on," she whispers.

I get in and buckle, not thinking much about her warning until Adrianne jerks the car into reverse and gasses it out of Daisy's drive. I grab the "oh crap" handle, as my daddy calls it. Well, he calls it something a little more colorful at times.

Daisy makes eye contact with me in the rearview mirror as we bolt out of her drive and onto the county road. Sure enough, about two miles down the road, we turn down a dirt driveway. Gravel flies as Adrianne's car spins down the narrow path.

We pull up to an adorable midcentury home, and she jerks the car into park. Both Daisy and I do a head bob at the sudden stop. Adrianne cuts the engine and hops out as if it's nothing. Maybe since she was the one driving, she could better anticipate the upcoming impact.

I unbuckle and give myself a few seconds for my heartbeat to steady before opening the door. When I do get out, Daisy is staring at me. "Told you."

"Wow. She's an even worse driver than in high school."

Daisy nods. "So I hear. I didn't ride with her up until a

few years ago. But the first time nearly sent me into cardiac arrest."

I laugh.

"Come on, ladies." Adrianne is on the front porch, hands on hips.

"Yes, ma'am," Daisy calls in a sarcastic tone.

We walk together toward the house and follow Adrianne inside. Her home is sleek, with neutral tones. Very minimal but inviting.

"Okay." She twists her head toward me as we continue following her into a bedroom. "You're a little shorter, but you wear heels a lot, right?"

"Yeah."

I stop in the doorway. "This is your bedroom?" Instead of a bed, there's a large makeup table. One wall is a full mirror, while the other three are lined with racks of clothes.

"No silly, my spare bedroom."

I nod. I've never known anyone who used an entire room for a closet. Especially someone who lived in a small house.

Daisy plops on the cow-print chair in front of the makeup table. She props her elbows on the table and drops her chin in her hands. I think if she had her way, we'd still be rolling around in the grass with goats.

Adrianne thumbs through a rack filled with dresses. She pulls a lavender satin dress and holds it in front of me. "Perfect. I'm loving this with your eyes and skin tone. Daisy?"

"Hmm?" Daisy raises her eyes from a compact she's studying. "Try it on."

"Yes, here you go. There's the dressing room." Adrianne points a hot-pink nail toward the closet door.

I take the dress, trying not to laugh at the irony of this room. The main room is a closet, and the closet is reserved for changing. Nevertheless, I flip the switch in the closet and slide the door shut behind me. A normal-sized full-length mirror is mounted on the wall.

I step into the dress and channel my yoga moves to zip the back by myself. That's generally Taylor's job when I wear something with a full back zipper. After smoothing out the skirt, I turn slowly in front of the mirror, taking in all angles of the dress. Wow. It really does look good on me.

"Need help?" Adrianne calls from outside the closet.

"No," I answer as I slide the door open.

Both women's eyes widen as I step into the room.

"You look beautiful," Daisy mutters, sitting straight for the first time since we've entered this giant wardrobe room.

"Thanks." I feel my cheeks blush.

"You really do, Hannah." Adrianne steps toward me and sticks her hands in my hair before I can answer. She untwists my bun and tousles it loose, then tugs the ends of my hair over both my shoulders. "I'm doing your hair and makeup tomorrow."

I catch a glimpse of myself in the mirror wall behind us. From neck to knees, I look good. But my hair is crimped from the damp post-shower bun I put it in after work, and I'm wearing tennis shoes.

"Tomorrow?" Adrianne moves her face in front of mine and raises her eyebrows in question.

"Yeah, sure. Anytime after work. I get off tomorrow around five."

"Perfect. I have one foil to do tomorrow morning, and then a few men's cuts. After that, I'm free." Her pearly teeth appear between her bright red lips, making her mouth resemble a candy cane. I smile back.

Adrianne moves behind me and plays around with my hair. "You can take this home with you."

I nod as she pats my shoulder and moves back to the rack of clothing. I take one long look in the mirror, trying to imagine my hair fixed and my feet in something shiny. Then I return to the closet for my gym shorts and tank top.

As I change, I hear Daisy argue with Adrianne that she doesn't need to borrow anything. I open the door to Adrianne's rebuttal. "Why not dress up? All you wear is cotton."

"Technically, it's hemp."

Adrianne rolls her eyes. "Whatever. It won't hurt anything for you to gussy up now and again."

I hang the lavender dress on the end of a rack by the door, facing forward. They continue bickering while I pick through the dresses. When I come to a hunter-green lace dress, I hold it out. "What about this?"

Both of them turn and stare. Daisy comes and touches the material. "Now, that's not too fancy."

Adrianne rolls her eyes again. "For real. It's fancy like Applebee's, which is where I wore it last, by the way."

"I think it would look nice with Daisy's red hair, and it's semiformal. I'd wear it to a day wedding," I add, studying Adrianne's expression.

Her face softens. "I do like it better than anything of Daisy's."

Daisy huffs.

"What? I'm just being honest."

Daisy lifts then lowers one shoulder. "Fine. I massage people, pour candles, and mess with goats all day. That doesn't exactly require a *Gossip Girl* wardrobe."

"I'm sorry. All I really mean is that you're welcome to borrow anything of mine."

Daisy smiles. "Apology accepted." She takes the green dress from the rack. Adrianne curves her lips into a slight smile as well, but the corners of her mouth twitch as if it's forced. I assume she doesn't care for our choice in the green dress.

"What are you wearing?" Maybe getting Adrianne to talk about her own outfit will lighten the mood.

She scratches the back of her ponytail and stares at the racks. "I'll throw something together tomorrow." Despite her lack of enthusiasm over her own clothes, she looks back at us with a more pleasant expression this time. "You girls want some lemonade?"

"Sure." I pick up the lavender dress and follow her into the living area. Daisy is on my heels with the green dress.

I sit on the couch and drape the dress over the back beside me. Adrianne appears from the kitchen opening with three glasses of lemonade. "Thanks." I take my glass, as does Daisy.

"Daisy, you need to at least wear wedges with that dress."

Daisy nods. "I know."

"No flip-flops."

"I know," Daisy snaps back.

I take a huge gulp of my lemonade, contemplating what I can say to break up this war of wardrobes.

"Hannah, those wedges you had on at the go-kart place were cute," Daisy comments.

"Thanks." I almost offer them to Daisy for the party, but decide that might trigger another debate.

"You two look good together." Adrianne beams.

"Thanks." It takes me a moment to realize she's referring to Tanner rather than my shoes.

"When did you two get together?" Daisy asks.

I shift on the velvet couch, a little nervous about giving a backstory without first consulting Tanner. We've thrown out details here and there about how we started dating, but no particular dates.

"A month ago." That would be around the time we agreed on this arrangement.

CHICKEN ABOUT LOVE

Adrianne's smile widens. "Well, I've never seen him like this with anyone. You're good for him."

At the risk of sounding like a broken record, I answer with another, "Thanks."

We continue chatting about anything and everything for a few minutes until our lemonade is gone. Then we head back to Daisy's house. Adrianne's driving doesn't bother me as bad this time. Not so much because I'm getting used to it as because I'm less focused on the ride and more focused on tomorrow night.

Something about dressing up, getting my hair and makeup done for the first time in forever, excites me. Most of all, I know I'll have a great time with Tanner.

CHAPTER TWELVE

Hannah

Adrianne fluffs the back of my hair with a skinny comb. My hair hasn't been this big since the pep rally when us cheerleaders switched places with the majorettes. Come to think of it, Adrianne helped me tease my hair then too.

Funny how we've come full circle.

"There." She smiles at the mirror in front of us. "Now I just need to finish your makeup."

She layered several moisturizers I'd never heard of on my face before starting my hair. I can't imagine taking this much time to get ready on a daily basis. I pretty much wear a full face of neutral makeup and run a straight iron over my hair, then call it a day.

I sit in silence as Adrianne gabs about anything and everything going on around town. Apparently, more stories come through her doors than the county paper's. However, I imagine not all her sources are trustworthy.

"Look up."

I do as I'm told while she flecks my bottom lashes with mascara. She continues talking about all the people who dye their hair. I make a note that whatever I say to her is equivalent to putting it on Facebook and then using my paycheck to boost the post statewide.

Adrianne gets quiet for the first time since arriving at my house. She stares down at me and drops her mouth open into a small O shape. "Perfection."

She steps to the side so that I can see myself and smiles. I tilt my head, taking in my profile. "Wow, you made me look—"

"Like your best self," she gloats.

"Yeah," I mutter, for lack of better words. The last time I had my makeup professionally done was my wedding day.

"Tanner is going to faint when he sees you."

My face morphs into a smile as I imagine Tanner's reaction to my makeover. He's used to seeing me in slacks or pencil skirts, with my hair pulled back. Not A-line dresses, with curls draped across my shoulders.

Adrianne smiles at me in the mirror like a proud mom about to send her daughter to prom for the first time.

"Hey, Mommy." Taylor bounces into the bathroom, disrupting our appreciation for Adrianne's art.

"Hey, pumpkin." I wrap an arm around her, pulling her to my side to discourage her from jumping in my lap and wrinkling the dress.

"Nana and PawPaw are taking me to a movie!"

"That sounds fun."

Taylor nods enthusiastically before running a hand on my skirt. "You look like Cinderella." She taps her tiny pointer finger against her chin. "Or maybe Rapunzel. She wears light purple."

"Thanks. Adrianne's my fairy godmother."

Taylor smiles at Adrianne and wrinkles her nose. "You did good."

"Thanks." Adrianne laughs.

"Taylor." Mama's voice echoes up the stairs.

"Oh, gotta go. Huggy?"

"Huggy." I squeeze Taylor and kiss her lightly on the cheek so as to not smear my makeup.

She bolts out of the room and down the stairs as soon as I release her. Adrianne packs up her makeup and closes the black leather bag. "I'm going home to change. I'll see you in a bit."

"Thanks again, Adrianne. You made me look so good, I hardly recognize myself." I smooth a hair as I examine myself in the mirror.

"Oh, hogwash, Hannah. You're gorgeous. I just brought to the surface what was already there."

"Well, thank you." I smile.

"Anytime." She turns and winks on her way toward the stairs.

I puff out my bronzed cheeks before going to my room. My feet tingle as I cross the carpet to my closet. I hold my stomach in an attempt to calm my nerves. Something about dressing up always makes me anxious. Maybe because I only do so for big events.

Proms, formals, my wedding. All of which involved a guy. All of which involved Dalton.

Until now.

Dressing up for a night with Tanner stirs a mixture of anticipation and uneasiness inside of me. I'm both looking forward to tonight and worried I might slip up and make a wrong move. Either by not convincing everyone around us we are an item, or by convincing myself that we should be.

I bend down and grab my strappy summer heels. After buckling them at the ankle, I head downstairs. Almost immediately, I get the urge to pee. For some reason, my bladder shrinks three sizes when I'm nervous. And it shrank about five sizes after I had Taylor. So my bladder is currently eight sizes too small.

I rush to the downstairs bathroom, not bothering to shut the door since I'm alone. With one hand, I bunch the back of my dress and clutch the purple satin like a debutant would her most precious pearls. I do my business, then stand before flushing. Only when I drop the skirt do I feel something wet hit the back of my knees.

Swallowing, I turn so I can view my backside in the mirror. Sure enough, the tail end of my dress somehow made it in the toilet. Correction: the tail end of *Adrianne's* dress.

Slight panic wells up in my chest, and I wring my hands before snatching the towel beside the sink. Then I remember that I still need to wash my hands, so I do that first. Once my hands are dry, I wet the end of the hand towel and blot the dress. Except I can't see it that well, so I climb onto the vanity to try and get a better look.

Now I'm halfway in the sink, with the end of the dress pulled up beside my head, wiping the urine-soiled fabric. And that's when the doorbell rings.

I crane my neck to yell toward the front door, "Just a minute." When I try and straighten, I topple forward toward the floor. I manage to catch myself, but my heel hangs in the netting under the skirt.

Jerking at the heel of my caught shoe, I abandon the towel and grunt. I don't want to force the shoe and cause a rip, so I work on unbuckling it from my ankle.

About the time I undo my shoe, I hear a door shut. I scramble to stand just in time for Tanner to walk in front of the bathroom. Glancing down, I notice my skirt is half up, so I slap it down against my legs. The hanging shoe hits the tile floor, taking the netting down with it.

Tanner's eyes are the size of quarters. Embarrassed beyond repair, I turn my head to hide. That's when I notice my hair is messed up as well. I sigh and slap my hand on my head.

"I was gonna ask are you ready . . . but . . ."

"Give me five?"

"Yep." Tanner stares at the floor as I collect the loose shoe and stagger upstairs to change into something less torn and, uh, less urine-y.

I unzip Adrianne's dress, already dreading how I might explain its condition. Then I find a plain navy dress in my closet. Not at all the stunning factor Adrianne's dress conveyed, but it'll work. I smooth my hair back out of my face, combing my fingers through it. To top off my new look, I put on my second shoe.

"Ready," I call out as I tiptoe downstairs, cautious as possible.

Tanner comes to the bottom of the stairs and grins. "A little wardrobe malfunction?"

My mouth tugs at a smile in spite of my embarrassment. "Something like that."

"Well, you look great, again."

"Thanks." My cheeks heat up at the word "again." There's no telling what all he saw of me earlier.

I take my purse from the table by the front door and lock up behind us. We walk to his truck in silence, and Tanner opens the passenger door. I stare at him for an extra beat, impressed that he'd open my door when there's not a soul here to witness it, aside from Daddy's dog. He smiles at me before circling the front of the truck to his side.

Except for a few random comments, we ride in mutual silence to Gamer's Paradise. Not awkward silence, though, which draws me to Tanner even more. In a situation like this, I tend to make small talk for no reason.

Tanner turns by the sign for the lodge, which is flanked with gold and silver balloons, dancing in the breeze. At the end of the dirt drive, Jonah stands in khakis and a dress shirt, directing people where to park. We're right on time, but dozens of cars already sit in front of the tree line bordering the lodge.

We park where Jonah points. Tanner nods at him, and he smiles back after noticing I'm in the truck as well.

Tanner laughs. "You ready for this?"

"Isn't this like the best way ever to solidify our relationship?" I say the word "relationship" in a mocking tone.

"Absolutely." Tanner grins at me with those adoring dimples, making it easy to play my role in this charade.

He shuts off the truck and meets me at my door before I pull the handle. As I climb out, he takes my hand and continues holding it even after I'm safely on the ground.

We walk hand in hand toward the lodge, nodding and greeting people along the way. I catch Jonah smiling at us from the corner of my eye. Having his and Jack's approval will make things run so much smoother.

Balloons matching those on the sign arch over the double doors. I take a deep breath as Tanner pushes the door open to a room filled with people, chatter, laughter, and food.

Everyone knows and loves Jack, which is evident by the crowd. I've only seen Bianca a few times at church, but everyone seems to like her too. I don't realize I'm squeezing Tanner's hand tighter until he rubs the back of my hand with his thumb. A warm calm rushes over me, and I grin at him.

"What are you wearing?" I turn to Adrianne making a beeline our way. That warm calm gives way to a nervous chill. She's wearing a short black dress, with her hair pulled into a high ponytail. But what I notice most is her eyes glaring at my outfit.

She reaches us and picks at the shoulder of my dress

before leaning closer to whisper. "Why are you not in the lavender dress?"

"I had a bit of a wardrobe malfunction."

Her face scrunches like one of Paul's discarded sucker wrappers. "What?"

"I'll explain later." I fight off a frown.

"Who did you come with, Adrianne?" Tanner leans toward me so that Adrianne has to take a step back.

She shrugs, dropping her hand from my shoulder. "I just drove myself."

"Well, it's good to see you. We're gonna find Jack." Tanner presses his lips together and walks away, tugging me. I follow, happy to put off the dress confrontation.

"Thanks."

"No problem. I like Adrianne, but she can be a bit bossy."

I give his hand another squeeze, this time intentionally. Then I open my mouth to respond, but before I can, Jack finds us.

"Hey, glad y'all made it."

"Hi, Hannah. That dress looks great on you." Bianca scans me head to toe before meeting my eyes.

"Thanks." I grin, secretly hoping Adrianne is in earshot. Of course, her dress was better. That is, until it had the toilet-water stain and ripped netting hanging down. But hey, if an Atlanta gal who always has the best shoes approves of my look, then it must be good.

I glance down at Bianca's shoes and notice that the gold sparkles across the toes of her heels perfectly match the gold sparkles on the neckline of her dress. If she ever gets bored with finance, she could have a great career in fashion. "You look great, as always."

Bianca smiles. "Oh, thanks. I just threw this together to go with the silver-and-gold theme."

I nod. Why is it people like Adrianne and Bianca always say they just threw something together, yet look like royalty? Kind of like how my mom says that about a meal that ends up tasting like the special at Paula Deen's restaurant. Here I am trying to throw together my life.

"Hey, everyone." A loud female voice disrupts our chitchat.

"Oh boy," Tanner mumbles in my ear. His sister steps to the center of the living room and speaks again. "If I can have everyone's attention. I'd like to welcome y'all all to Jack and Bianca's engagement party. We have appetizers circling around, but there's also a self-serve meal set up on the patio off the kitchen. Drinks are outside in the barrels. Let me know if y'all need anything, and enjoy."

Carolina smiles and shrugs before disappearing into the crowd. People continue talking, and some meander toward the back for food. Jack and Bianca start a conversation with someone else, leaving Tanner and me in a sea of people we've known most our lives.

"I haven't seen all these people together in one place since high school," I say.

"Then you clearly haven't gone to any Apple Cart football games since then."

I laugh. "Nope. The last time I went to that field was when I cheered my last home game."

"Wow." Tanner's eyebrows shoot up. "You seriously haven't gone to one game since?"

"Nope. I mean, I lived in Birmingham since graduating, and we haven't had my reunion yet."

"How can you say you're from Apple Cart and not cheer on the Armadillos once since high school?"

I laugh at the memory of our mascot. "Does the armadillo still wear that homemade shell?"

Tanner drops my hand and crosses his arms. "I'm not

telling you. You'll have to come to a game with me and find out."

"Okay, maybe I will."

I imagine sitting on the bleachers with him, snuggled under a blanket. He reaches one hand around my waist and brushes my side with his fingertips. I sigh lightly, allowing myself to enjoy his present company, regardless of what the future holds.

"Speaking of armadillos, are you hungry?"

The fairytale in my mind gives way to laughter. "Gross."

"Hey, they could have one of those *Steel Magnolias* cakes. You never know with Jack."

"True." I lean into him as we walk toward the kitchen, his arm still draped around me. My mind again drifts to Tanner, Taylor, and me in the stands at an Apple Cart Armadillos football game. However, football is more than a month away.

We haven't discussed how long we plan to fake date. Truth be told, I didn't want to think of it ending. I'm having too much fun. And the idea that this might carry into the fall excites me . . . maybe a little too much.

Tanner

I pile a plate with deer poppers and set it on top of my main plate that's filled with steak, potatoes, and a roll. Hannah laughs as I try and balance the deer poppers on top.

"Need help?"

"Always."

She takes the deer-popper plate and holds it in the crook of her arm, between her plate and her elbow.

"You're good at that."

"Remember, I waitressed some when we were younger."

"Oh yeah." I follow her off the patio, which is congested by people either fixing plates or sitting at the closest tables.

We find a table closer to the edge of the property, underneath a tree with Christmas lights hanging from the branches. I guess they're Christmas lights. They're the kind with the big, round bulbs. I'm no romantic, but even I can appreciate a decorated outdoor setting with Hannah beside me.

I set my plate and drink in front of me, then take her hand. "I'll have to tell Mama that Carolina forgot to bless the food during her little speech."

Hannah snickers, then bows her head as I say a quick prayer. I keep my head bowed for a beat after saying "amen," not yet ready to drop her hand. When she slides her hand away from mine in favor of her sweet tea, I use mine to grab my fork.

Holding Hannah's hand has become a natural comfort to me over the past few weeks. Familiar and satisfying. My eyes trail her hand as it lifts the cup of tea to her mouth. A large diamond ring catches the lowering sun and sparkles on her ring finger.

"Wow, that's a nice rock. I've never seen you wear it."

She lowers her cup and blushes, then spins the ring around her finger. "Thanks."

I drop my gaze to the table and grab a deer popper. She obviously didn't like me mentioning the ring.

"It was my grandmother's engagement ring."

"Oh, nice," I answer around a mouthful of deer and bacon.

"And mine."

I cough on my food and reach for my own tea. No wonder she didn't want me to notice it. I swallow a gulp and wipe my mouth with the back of my hand. "I didn't mean—"

"No." She shakes her head. "It's fine, really. I haven't worn it since . . ." Her voice trails off, leaving me to fill in the blank.

I avoid all D words: divorce, diamond . . . Dalton. Instead, I focus on her grandmother. "I love family heirlooms. That's cool that you have your grandmother's ring."

"Yeah." She twists her lips and glances at her hand as she peels a piece of shrimp. "That's why I kept it."

"Hannah, there's nothing wrong with you wearing it, especially on your right hand." Her lips straighten and flirt with a smile, so I continue. "Heck, if it makes you feel better, tell everyone I bought it for you."

She giggles, and I laugh along with her. My shoulders relax as we both let go of the momentary tension.

Once the laughter settles, she clears her throat. "It's not that the ring makes me think of him." She stares at the tree branches overhead and sighs before looking back at me. "It's more of how it reminds me that I wasn't able to keep my vow like my grandparents did. I mean, they were married over fifty years."

I drop my fork and cup my hand over hers. I mean it as a comfort for her, but my own mood lifts as soon as we touch. "Hannah, from what I know, you tried everything in your power to make it work. You can't help what Da—he does." I cringe at almost saying the worst "D" word. "You can't beat yourself up for your marriage ending."

She squeezes my hand as she's done several times tonight, ticking my heartbeat up a notch. It's like she's sending a secret signal just between us. I smile at her, wishing she could see herself as I do.

"I worry about Taylor, is all. Not growing up with a mom and dad like I did."

I stroke the back of her hand with my thumb and sigh. "You're such a good mom, it won't matter. Besides, you have your dad to father her. And I'm always happy to keep hanging out with her. Even after."

I leave it at that, not wanting to add the phrase "we quit dating." Or faking, or pretending, or whatever else you might call it. Although I constantly remind myself that this is all one big, fat jinx on everyone in town, every time we're together, my mind plays tricks on me. Either we're *that* good at faking it, or some of this really is real for me.

"I don't want you to be a stranger, and I don't think Taylor does either."

"That's good to know." I stare at her pretty face, mesmerized by the fact that she's just as pretty on the inside. What I admire most about Hannah is how I can be myself with no judgement. My entire life, I've lived in my older brother's shadow. Never able to live up to my parents' expectations. And even Jack thinks I'm somewhat of a joke when it comes to serious matters.

For the first time in my life, someone gets me.

Music starts playing low and slow from the back patio. I turn my head to see several couples dancing nearby the house. "Come on." I stand, pulling Hannah up with me.

A napkin falls from her lap as I pull her in close. "Oh." She stumbles a tiny bit, then smiles when she realizes I want to dance.

I wrap my arm around her waist, resting my hand on the small of her back. We sway in the grass beneath the pine tree. After a minute or so, she lets go of my hand and wraps her arm around my neck, resting her head on my shoulder. I rest my free hand on her back and hold her tightly, relaxing at the honey scent streaming from her hair.

The last time I held a woman in my arms like this, a drunk Auburn chick had braced herself against me to try and not fall off a retaining wall. I'd saved her from her ill-timed fate, then released her ASAP. This time, with this girl, I want to stay this way forever.

For one solid slow song, I allow myself to live in the moment. No worrying about who might be watching us, how we're acting, or even what Hannah thinks. She's okay with this or she never would've snuggled closer. So I close my eyes and inhale her honey aroma, memorizing every sensory detail of holding her in my arms in case this never happens again.

For one song, I'm not pretending. She's mine.

Then, like most playlists in rural Alabama, the Tim McGraw and Faith Hill ballad ends and "Bubba Shot the Jukebox" blares across the speakers. I sigh into Hannah's hair at the realization that the moment is over. But I don't want it to be.

She lifts her head off my shoulders, our faces dangerously close. Before I can talk myself out of it, while we're still armed up, I tilt my head toward her lips.

CHAPTER THIRTEEN

Hannah

Is he going to kiss me?

Tanner's face is headed toward mine, and with every centimeter closer, my heart beats faster. Last time this happened, I threw my hand in his face like Regina George to her haters. And I've regretted that ever since. Partly because I didn't want to embarrass him, and partly because I wanted the kiss as much as him. But I couldn't kiss him with Taylor there, even if she was asleep.

Tonight it's adults only, and to everyone here we're old news. Still, a kiss wasn't part of the deal. A kiss will make this real.

I need to duck my head, move away, fake a sneeze. Yeah, a sneeze. That way he won't think I'm intentionally breaking contact.

I scrunch my nose to feign a sneeze just in time for his

mouth to meet mine. My eyes shut and my nose unfurls as the warmth of his lips brush against mine.

Against my better judgment, I wrap my arms tighter around his shoulders and lean into the kiss. I haven't kissed anyone in well over a year. And not *really* kissed anyone in maybe two years, thanks to Dalton directing his passion elsewhere.

I try and convince myself that's what this is about for me —a kiss. A good kiss—rather, a great kiss. I'm a lonely woman in need of some male companionship, that's all. But deep down, I know that's not all.

Several men have asked me out since the divorce, including one friend in Birmingham whom I found promising. When it came down to it, I couldn't picture myself with him in this way. The same for anyone else who showed interest. Taylor or no Taylor, I didn't see myself with them. Then Tanner popped up out of nowhere and reignited my desire to date.

My chest rises and falls as his hand crawls up my back and ends in my hair. I kiss him deeper, not caring that we're full-on making out in the middle of Jack's party. Besides, we knew all these people in high school. It's not like they haven't ever made out in front of us.

After what isn't long enough for me but way too long for proper southern-belle etiquette at a dinner party, I pull back. I stare into Tanner's eyes, dancing with something sweet and a bit wild at the same time. Then there's those dimples, popping around his full smile.

"You're a great dancer," he says.

I laugh. "Same to you." I loosen my grip around his shoulders and slide my hands down his chest before dropping them.

He drops his hand from my back and twirls a lock of my hair around his finger before letting that hand fall too.

"Did I ever tell you that your hair makes me crave pancakes?"

I laugh again. "That's weird."

He shrugs. "I mean it as a compliment. It smells like that local syrup."

"Thank you?" I narrow my eyes at him as I start to sit in my chair.

The honky-tonk music transitions into another slow song. Tanner catches my wrist. "One more dance."

"Okay." I drape my arms around his neck once more and rest my head against his chest. For the full song, I close my eyes, not wanting to focus on anyone or anything but us.

We sway in tandem. His fingers make tiny circles on my bare upper back, sending tickles across my skin. I want him to kiss me again, but I know we shouldn't. Instead, I hold onto the memory of our one perfect kiss. Especially since there may never be another.

The song ends sooner than I want. A goofy Luke Bryan song is next, signaling us to break away this time and finish our food. We talk, laugh, and eat for the next little while. With only a few tables near ours at the end of the yard, we mostly have the area to ourselves. A few people come by while mingling to say "hi" or comment what a nice couple we make.

I can't help but think that we would make a nice couple. Then I immediately scold myself for letting my mind go there. We have a deal, and we're at different stages in our lives. Tanner doesn't need someone with a kid and a domineering ex.

After the sun is well set, we take our plates and head toward the lodge. Several people meet us on the way down, carrying cornhole boards and bean bags. The tree lights twinkle around us as the crickets start to chirp. I slap my arm at a rogue mosquito swarming nearby.

Tanner peers around. "Yep, bugs are coming out. Time for us to go in."

I nod. "Someone should make perfume that doubles as bug spray for nights like this."

He smiles. "That's actually a good idea. You should suggest that to Jack and Bianca. They might could get Ronald to put it in the store."

"Really?" I wrinkle my nose. On the back of Jack's property sits a huge hunting store by the interstate. He sold the land to the men who own the chain not long after he met Bianca.

It was that business deal that first brought them together. Tanner told me many stories of when Bianca first come to Apple Cart to meet the men for business at Jack's lodge. Although amusing, I believe her coming here was fate. How else would two people so different ever get together?

We dump our plates and cups in the trashcan by the back door and enter through the kitchen.

"Hello, lovelies." Mrs. Mary pulls a pan of pies from the oven and smiles our way.

"Hi." I step over and give her a hug after she sets the tray on the counter. She pats my back with a mitted hand before letting go.

"Is that a fish?" I focus on her hand.

She opens and closes the mitt's mouth. "Yep. It's Jack's. Dessert will be out in a second." She takes the mitt off and fans her face with it. "Whew, it's hotter than Satan's house cat tonight."

"Do you need us to help with anything?" Tanner steps toward the oven.

Mary fans the mitt our way and shakes her head. "Uh-uh. That's the last of them."

I follow her gaze to dozens of miniature pies spread

across the back counter. "Have you been baking this whole time?"

"Yep. You know I gotta serve my pies fresh. Can't ruin my reputation. You two enjoy yourselves."

Bianca and Jack file in the kitchen before we can say anything else.

"Well, if it isn't Apple Cart's second-hottest couple." Mary winks at Tanner and me.

"Haha." Jack runs his hand over his hair, then pulls a cap from above the refrigerator.

Bianca slaps his wrist. "I told you. Please, no cap until after the party."

He sighs and tosses it on the kitchen island. "Okay." He takes his fish mitt from Mary and puts it on. "Thanks again, Mary. I can put out the pies."

She steps back for him to get a tray.

"I'll help." Tanner grabs a second fish mitt and makes a goofy face at me as he slides it over his hand. Mary starts spouting off what is what, explaining how the pumpkin and apple cinnamon look really similar.

Once the boys exit onto the patio with pans of pies, Bianca takes Jack's cap and hides it in a drawer. She smirks at me and takes a seat at the island. "Hannah, I know we've only met a few times, but I've known Tanner for a year and a half now. I can honestly say I've never seen him this happy."

My cheeks heat up, and I drop my face to hide the blush. "He's a great guy."

"He really is, but he's always seemed a little unsettled, you know. Until lately. I think you've been really good for him."

"Thanks." I smile at her. "He's been good for me too."

I watch Tanner through the glass door off the kitchen. He's laughing and chatting with everyone who comes by to get a pie. He has a unique ability to make anything fun. And fun is one ingredient I need to make my life a little more sweet than sour.

The door opens and Tanner comes in carrying empty pans except for two pies. He sets down the trays and removes the hideous fish mitt. "My lady, would you care to join me for dessert?" He picks up a mini pie in each hand and tilts them toward me.

"Of course." I stand and smile at Bianca before following Tanner to the front porch. Aside from the people occasionally trickling out to their vehicles, it's just us and the porch lights. We lean against the hand-carved porch rail to eat our pies.

Tanner holds his pie up and taps the tin against mine. "To a great date."

"To a great date," I repeat before biting into the delicious pecan filling. The nutty flavor fills my mouth, and Tanner's grin fills my heart.

As we end the night sharing dessert on the porch, I think back to what I told Bianca. At the time, I was simply repaying the compliment, but every word is true.

Tanner has been good for me.

Tanner

"Stop it." The words come out breathy between laughs. Taylor and Skip roll off me, and I raise my upper body, breathing heavily from the tickle attack. From Taylor, that is. Skip gave me more of a lick attack.

Hannah laughs from her front-row view on the back porch as I brush grass from my hair and back. I smile at her and shake my head, then watch as Taylor attempts to play fetch with an overly hyper Skip.

I stand and flick off the remaining blades of grass, then join Hannah on the porch. The last two days, I've lived in a daze. Last night, Hannah and I kissed . . . like for real kissed.

When I took her home, I wanted so badly to kiss her good night. But I didn't dare press my luck. I kissed her at the party when the moment was right. For now, I've got to play my cards right and not get greedy with stealing kisses. If I'm lucky, she may initiate the next kiss. Either way, I'm not going all in until she lets me know she's done pretending.

With any luck, that will happen sooner than later. It surprised me when she texted me after she got off work today and invited me over to grill out with her family.

Everything is sure starting to feel real. If I'm honest, it's felt real to me a week now, maybe longer.

I never would've considered dating someone with a kid. Not because I don't like kids. I love kids. More because I never pictured myself as a potential stepdad to someone. The more time I spend with Hannah, the more I enjoy spending time with Taylor too.

Oddly enough, I could picture us three becoming a family sometime in the distant future. That both excites and scares me at the same time.

"They're a little rough, huh?" Hannah says.

I shake my head. "She's tough for a little girl."

"I blame it on Daddy. They wrestle all the time, and he has her helping him change oil and rotate tires."

"Good life skills. I like it."

Hannah nods. "I'm glad there's someone around to teach her. I should've paid more attention when Daddy taught me. I guess I never thought I'd be without him or Dal—anyway . . ."

I stare at the wood floor beneath my feet, thankful she

didn't finish his name. I've never cared for the guy, even in school, but finding out he was unfaithful to Hannah makes me want to hunt him down at the mention of his name.

The mood's too heavy, so I bring up something a little lighter. "As long as Taylor doesn't use up all the bubbles, you've got my trick." I lift my eyes to Hannah. Her mouth tugs at a smile.

"She spilt the rest of them on Skip last week."

We share a laugh. "Well, there's plenty more at DG."

"I don't know. Have you been down the toy aisle lately?"

"No, I have not."

"All the summer stuff is wiped out since they marked it down seventy percent."

"Better put it on your list for Walmart, then."

"I'm more of a Target girl."

I shake my index finger at Hannah. "See, I knew you were classy."

She laughs. "Not for snobbish reasons. They have good clothes for someone on a budget."

I fan my hands down the front of my Auburn T-shirt and Wrangler jeans. "Clearly, I wouldn't know. I have two looks: Carhartts and button-downs or T-shirts and jeans."

"As do most men around here."

I nod and start rocking my chair. She said that neutrally, but does she prefer my look or a Birmingham businessman? I press my lips tightly as I imagine Dalton dressed in a suit and tie, with some of those shoes they make you wear in weddings. The real shiny kind. We all hate them. Jack's already promised Jonah and me that we could wear boots in his wedding. Shiny boots, according to Bianca, but still boots.

"What are you thinking?"

"Hmm?" I turn my head to Hannah.

"You look deep in thought."

"Not really." I don't care to admit that I'm picturing her ex in Brooks Brothers and clown shoes.

Hannah's eyes search my face for an answer. Somehow, she can sense I'm not telling the truth.

"Honestly, I was thinking how much fun I've had hanging out with you and your family." I smile. I had been thinking that up until the southern-men wardrobe options entered my mind.

She smiles back and reaches over, grabbing my hand. I thread my fingers through hers and rock steadily, focusing on her pretty face. I'm not sure if she offered her hand out of friendship or even out of pity. It may be nothing more than a kind gesture to her.

But to me, it's a shred of hope that one day, this can be something really real.

Tanner

I open the door to the scent of wasabi and grilled meat. Jack, Bianca, and I enter to people chattering, spatulas clanking, and a drum beating in the distance, which means someone came for a birthday dinner.

"When you said sushi place, I expected something quieter," Bianca says.

Jack and I exchange a look and laugh. "Trust me, babe, this is the best sushi in town." He rubs her back and grins.

I nod. "And steak, and rice, and chicken, and scallops, and shrimp. Need I go on?"

Bianca snorts. "I'll take you guys' word for it."

"*Y'all!* You gotta quit saying 'you guys' if you plan on moving to Apple Cart." I smirk.

Jack draws her close to him and kisses the top of her blonde head. "Ignore him, you talk just fine."

"Eh, at least you don't have a northern accent."

She balks. "I'm from the south too."

"Atlanta's the least southern place around."

"Still in the south." She raises her thin eyebrows to challenge me.

"Whatever, you'll like this food." I step to the podium, where a girl scribbles names on a white board. "Table for three."

"Grill or table?"

"Uh." I glance over my shoulder at the lovebirds. "Let's do the grill. We wanna give our gal the authentic T-town experience." That'll teach Bianca. I can't wait for her to witness mine and Jack's game of who can catch the shrimp first.

"All right. Name and number?"

I spout off my digits, then stop before saying my name. A playful grin creeps across my face. "You Guys."

"Did you say 'You Guys'?"

"Yeah, you never heard someone with the last name 'Guys'?"

She shrugs. "Okay. We'll text you when a grill is ready."

"Thanks." I nod at the accomplishment of potentially ticking off Bianca. All in the name of fun, of course. If she's gonna join our tribe soon, she needs some initiating.

I join the canoodlers in the waiting area. "How long's the wait?" Jack asks.

"There were only a few people ahead of us on the list."

"I'm gonna run to the restroom, then."

"'Kay." After he stands, I slide beside Bianca to make more room for the people coming in.

CHICKEN ABOUT LOVE

"Tanner Nash?" A perky voice calls my name from the door. I twist my upper body toward a group of college-aged girls bounding inside. All of their clothing put together might make one normal-sized shirt.

It takes me a moment, but I recognize the redhead from somewhere. She must be the one who called my name, because she dives toward me with open arms. I give her shoulder a quick pat, then shrink back so she'll get the hint.

Bianca chuckles under her breath and cuts her eyes my way. I frown.

"You don't remember me, do you?"

I clinch my jaw, trying to conjure up a memory. "No, ma'am, I can't say I do."

"I'm Deanna's cousin. We met at a party in Auburn a few months back."

I snap my fingers. "That's right." My eyes bug as I realize how I know her. She's the drunk chick I saved from falling. I don't mention that out of respect for her—and myself.

She runs her hand through her hair in a flirty way. "I just wanted to say 'hey' before we eat."

"All right. Hey."

She giggles, then practically skips over to her group.

Bianca leans close to my ear and whispers, "Have I mentioned how good Hannah is for you?"

I turn to her and smile. "Only a zillion times."

She pats my knee. "Good."

I laugh and rest my head against the wall behind us. My phone buzzes, and I check it. "Looks like our table is ready."

"You Guys, party of three. You Guys." A different young girl calls us out, hesitantly saying the name.

Jack returns as Bianca jabs me in the ribs. "Real cute, Tanner."

I laugh, and Jack puts his hands on his hips. "What did you do?"

"I'll tell you in a minute. We gotta go before they give You Guys' table away."

Bianca rolls her eyes as we lead her to the grill. Time to culture this woman in an authentic Alabama Japanese experience.

CHAPTER FOURTEEN

Hannah

"So, word on the street is you and Tanner made out to 'Bubba Shot the Jukebox' at the engagement party."

My mouth opens to answer, but I can't find the words. No "hi, how's your day been," or anything. Adrianne leads with this as soon as my butt hits her chair.

"I, uh, we kissed, and I believe that was the song playing at the time."

Adrianne steps behind the salon chair and squeezes my shoulders. "I'm just messing with you. I think it's romantic."

"You do?"

"Yeah. Would've been more romantic if you had on my lavender dress, but yeah."

I wince. "Sorry about that, again. It's at the dry cleaners, but I've still got to fix the netting."

She lets go of my shoulders and starts fumbling through a drawer of combs. "Nah, just keep it."

"I can pay you back, then."

"No, seriously. I was probably gonna donate it soon anyway. I've worn it like three times already."

"Oh . . . thanks." That's when I realize I've never seen Adrianne wear the same clothes twice. No wonder she loaned me a dress. I wear the same black pencil skirt at least once a week to work.

Adrianne drapes a leopard-print cape over me and buttons it behind my neck. Then she fans out my hair and examines it like a million-dollar bank statement. "You need a trim."

"Whatever you think."

She combs my hair and starts snipping the very ends while filling me in on all the local gossip. Who's seeing who, what scents Daisy's added to her candle shop, Mrs. Maudy getting her to make a house call each week until her hip fully recovers.

I mainly listen, not having anything to add to the conversation. Even if I did, I'm not much for gossip. That's the one thing I miss about Birmingham. You could actually have a private life. Here, it's like living out the personification of Facebook.

Once my hair is straight across the bottom, Adrianne picks at my head with the pointy end of her comb. Piece by piece, she folds tinfoil beneath and paints a purple goop on top before folding it up like a piece of leftover pizza.

Half an hour and tons of rumors later, my hair could easily boost a cell phone signal on any dirt road if I tilted my head just right.

"Come on." I follow Adrianne's lead to a row of dryers. She flips the switch on one and points to the chair. I sit and reach for the back of my head.

"Uh-uh." She swats my hand. "No scratching. You'll get color all over you."

I sigh and lean back in the chair. Adrianne closes the hot helmet over my head. I reach for the stack of magazines on a side table and find a copy of *Magnolia Journal*, then thumb through to see what Chip and Joanna are up to these days. Or more like a few months back, when the magazine came out.

My ears itch where the tinfoil heats up around the edges, but I don't dare scratch. I've forgotten how much this stings, as I haven't had highlights in more than a year due to saving money and the fact that my hair wasn't the biggest priority at the time. Adrianne told me she'd do it for the cost of the color if I let her experiment on me. I'm not sure what made me agree to that.

Adrianne cuts the hair of an older woman who just came in, then hurries to the back to mix more color once the woman leaves. The bell jingles above her shop door, and two pretty girls walk in. Wiping her hands down the front of her leather apron, Adrianne heads up front. Their voices are muffled beneath my space helmet, but I can make out some of what they say.

Adrianne seats the blonde in her chair before going back and bringing out color. The redhead sits near me in one of the dryer chairs. They all chat as I read about Joanna's new line of dinner plates. Well, new last season. She may have something else out by now. I swear, that woman never sleeps.

The redhead is close enough where I can understand every word she says. I gather that they're talking about someone dating. The redhead says she saw him in Tuscaloosa Sunday with a pretty woman in fancy clothes.

I continue scanning the magazine, not paying them much attention. That's until the redhead says the words, "Yes, Tanner Nash."

I bite my bottom lip and suck in a breath before

slumping slightly in the chair so that my ears are more exposed. That helps me hear the other two more clearly.

"What woman?" Adrianne asks as she foils the blonde girl's hair.

"I dunno. She had really light hair and really expensive shoes. I guess she's from Tuscaloosa." The redhead announces this casually between smacks of gum.

My face flames like I've stayed out all day without sunscreen. A swirling sensation hits my stomach. The redhead continues talking about how cute Tanner is and how she met him at Auburn. I don't want to sit here, a prisoner to this dryer, hearing any more of it.

In a panic, I throw back the hood to the dryer and rush toward the door with my cape flailing around me. I step outside and hurry to the side of the building. Pacing the parking lot, I fan my face. I'm burning up from the dryer, the outside humidity, and hearing about Tanner with another woman.

It shouldn't bother me. He owes me nothing—loyalty, explanations, nothing. We had an agreement to be a couple to all of Apple Cart. What he does in Tuscaloosa when I'm not with him and all the county isn't watching is his business. Besides, we never discussed exclusivity or not real dating someone elsewhere.

There's no breech in our verbal contract. But if that were all it was, I could easily let this one slide. That's not why my stomach is in knots and I'm standing in the middle of downtown dressed like a sack of leftovers.

I care about Tanner.

In more ways than I want to admit. I've liked him from the time he offered me a ride, saved my interview, and fixed my flat. Since then, I've liked him on such a deeper level. A level that dangerously resembles love.

I swallow and half smile to Paul, who's making a strange

face at me from across the street. I didn't want to acknowledge him staring at me, but otherwise he may think I'm some quirky statue and try to come buy me for his store. Realizing that I'm a moving person, he scratches the side of his head, then goes inside his store.

I bury my head in my hands and try to hash out my feelings for Tanner. What a mess I've gotten myself into. As I'm debating whether to go back inside or rip the tinfoil out and make a run for it, Adrianne calls my name.

"Hannah, what in the world? You're gonna ruin your hair."

I lift my head and sigh. She marches toward me and points the painful end of the comb in my face. "Get your little butt back under that dryer. Now I gotta calculate how long you've been out here, along with the heat index, to figure out how much time to tack off the dryer."

My shoulders droop. "Sorry. I just heard that girl saying she saw Tanner with a fancy woman."

Adrianne rolls her eyes. "That's Deanna's cousin from south Alabama. She ain't got a lick of sense. Almost flunked out of Auburn. I wouldn't give what she says any merit. Tanner likes you. Trust me, I can tell."

"You sure?"

Adrianne lowers her weapon of choice. "Uh, yeah. He took me out to eat one time, and he didn't act near as interested as he ever has in you. The whole night he treated me like a friend. I'm not even sure why he asked me out."

I half smile, wanting to believe she knows Tanner better than the redhead. Sadly, I'm not sure if I know Tanner as well as either of them. I thought I did, but how can I really know someone in half a summer? I thought I knew Dalton, too, after dating and being married long enough to total a decade. And I was wrong about him.

If my ex-husband can hide an affair from me for months, then surely a friend can hide his dating life in another town.

"Come on." Adrianne puts her hand on my back and pushes me toward the front door. I sigh up at the Cut and Dry marquee as we enter. She leads me to the dryer and resets it for me.

I scoot up enough to not hear anything too clearly, relieved that the redhead is now across the room studying a shelf of products. Regardless of the deal I have with Tanner and how it's none of my concern what he does in real life, I need some time to think before I see him again.

Tanner

I hum to myself as I leave the local gift shop with a bouquet of summer flowers. It's actually a pharmacy inside the local hospital, but also the only place to buy flowers. Unless you want the fake ones in the garden aisle at Dollar General.

They have some pretty nice things in there for women. Maybe that's why so many girls register for their wedding stuff at the pharmacy. One table out front is dedicated entirely to Jack and Bianca, and a quick glance as I walk by lets me know all this stuff is for her.

Heck, Jack would register at the General Store for fish mitts and boots. I laugh at the image of Jack and Paul setting up a table of gifts. The old woman behind the front desk at the hospital shoots me a scolding face. I frown and nod, remembering I'm now back in the main hospital.

I sniff the flowers to get the sterile scent of Clorox and

sick people out of my nose on the way to my truck. Hannah will love these.

As carefully as possible, I secure them on the dash of my truck before backing out of the parking lot. Then I pull on my sunglasses and start toward the bank. We haven't spoken since Sunday after church, so I wanted to surprise her with lunch.

I drum my thumbs on the steering wheel to the song on the radio. Sunday night, I agreed to go eat with Jack and Bianca last minute, and I spent most the week checking chicken houses in a neighboring county. Although we've texted, I've missed talking to Hannah in person and seeing her even more. And I haven't heard anything back from her since my text late last night.

A few minutes later, I park in front of the bank and hop out with the bouquet. When I stop at the sucker table, which still has the "take one" sign—now taped to the bucket—I decide to hide the flowers. I take my one allowed blue raspberry treat and tuck the hand holding the flowers behind my back.

The sunlight streams across the tile floor, lighting a thin path to Hannah's station. I follow the line as if it's directing me toward a long-awaited heavenly prize. She's counting cash with her head lowered and typing something on her keyboard. Not wanting to interrupt her train of thought, I step up quietly and hold the bouquet in front of her.

After shuffling through the stack of bills once more, she looks up. I expected her to be surprised, but not shocked. Her face doesn't suggest any pleasantness in the flowers . . . or me.

"Wanna go to lunch?"

She sucks in a breath and stacks the bills. "I can in a minute."

"'Kay. These are for you." I push the flowers forward. She

takes them and offers me a slight smile with about a tenth of the enthusiasm she usually has when I bring flowers.

"Thanks." She turns and sets them on the counter behind her, not bothering to smell them first.

My shoulders sink, taking my heart down with them. Does this have something to do with me not seeing her all week? Surely not. Hannah isn't needy or clingy. However, if it *is* that, then maybe what I have planned will go better than expected.

I open my sucker as I wait for her to put the money in the drawer and shut down her computer. "I'm ready." She joins me on the other side of the swinging door, purse on her shoulder.

I want to reach for her hand, but she's gripping her purse strap with one hand and the top of her purse with the other. Also strange, but maybe she's got a gun in there or something.

We walk outside in silence, and I open the bank door and her truck door, like always. She climbs in quietly and continues holding onto her purse once she's settled.

"Did you like your flowers?"

She presses her lips in a tight smile before answering, "Yes, thanks. I'll put them in water once I get back to work."

I lift my chin and study her expression. It's so neutral, I can't decide if she's mad or tired, or if an alien robot has kidnapped Hannah and is standing in her place. "Any suggestions on where to eat?"

She lifts then lowers one shoulder, still clutching her purse for dear life. "Could we maybe get something to go and eat at the park? That will give us more privacy."

A grin creeps up my lips. She wants to be alone with me, so she can't be too mad. I back out of the parking lot and head for Big Butts. It's the quickest to-go option around. Not that there are any other options aside from Mary's Diner and the gas station. I've heard it rumored we're getting a Jack's, but no signs of that yet.

Wanting to test Hannah's death grip on her purse, I allow her to open her own door at Big Butts. We step out of the truck, and I nod to all the water board workers hogging the one table by the food truck. Hannah has her purse with her, raising my suspicions again. Did she rob the bank or something?

We order, and she pulls out her wallet. "This one's on me. Please."

I drop my hand from my back pocket where I'd started retrieving my own wallet. Her expression communicates that I best not protest this one. Hannah pays for our food, and we step to the side so the person behind us can order.

"Have you had a good week so far?" I kick the dirt in front of me, frustrated that I'm resorting to small talk.

"Yeah, you?"

"Pretty good. I had to go out of town a lot."

She nods, saying nothing.

"Order up." Billy Bob cranes his neck outside the trailer window. I take that opportunity to break away from whatever weirdness is between Hannah and me.

I take the food and Hannah meets me at the truck. Out of habit, I open her door. Our hands brush as she's reaching for the handle to open it herself. My chest swells for a moment until she lets her hand fall. I miss having her close.

Instead of grabbing her and kissing her right then and there for Billy Bob and all the water board to see, I settle for a quick smile before getting in the truck. We'll be alone in a minute, and I can tell her everything I want. And if she feels the same way, I'll get my kiss . . . along with many more.

I'm content to sit in silence with my thoughts the next few miles. By the time I turn into the park entrance, I've rehearsed my speech for proposing a real relationship to

Hannah. One where everything we've conjured up to please others becomes a reality. One where I'm officially in her life, and Taylor's.

As I climb out of my truck, I'm smiling so big my cheeks hurt. I open Hannah's door, and her eyes meet mine. Those chocolate diamonds focus on my face for a split second before she blinks and steps down.

We head to the pavilion where we've shared several meals. It's vacant, and I take that as a good omen. After opening our food, I offer up a quick prayer. I'm more than ready to ask Hannah out on a real date.

My eyes pop open when I say, "amen," and I reach for her hand. Instead of embracing my touch, she slides her hand across the table and into her lap. My face falls. "Is everything all, right?"

Hannah sighs deeply and stares at her plate. After a long pause, she lifts her eyes to mine. "Tanner, we don't have to pretend anymore."

"I agree."

"Good." She perks up almost immediately, confusing me further. "Because I was thinking since we've convinced everyone we're together, the job is done."

I open my mouth but nothing comes out. I'm not sure what she means by "the job."

"All that's left to do is plan our breakup." Hannah pops a fry in her mouth, as if she just suggested we plan a party rather than a breakup. She swallows, then continues. "It doesn't have to be dramatic. I'd prefer it not be. We just need word to spread that we're no longer together."

The words "we're no longer together" stab my heart. I sit there stunned at how she can talk about this as if it's no big deal. Even more so at how she has an appetite right now.

"I just think with summer ending, it's a good time for us

to move on so that we're free to really date without worrying about rumors, you know?"

No, I don't know. What the heck does it matter whether it's summer, fall, or Armageddon? I'd still want Hannah in my life. And the only person I want to date is her—real, fake, however I can get her.

I grip the edge of the picnic table to steady myself. This must be some sick nightmare.

"Tanner, do you agree?"

I inhale a huge puff of humid air and release it through my nostrils. Then I somehow manage to stand without passing out and pace the length of our picnic table.

"Tanner?"

My nostrils flare again, as I can't seem to breathe through my mouth. How could I have misread her this much? All this time we were together, our kiss at the party. Did that mean nothing to her other than a big, fake bomb? She'd confided so much in me, spent so much extra time with me that wasn't needed to convince our nosy neighbors, and allowed me to befriend her family.

I stop and face her, contemplating what to say. Should I tell her my true intentions of this lunch? Should I blow up on her for leading me on, even though I agreed all this was fake in the first place? No, I'm too prideful to admit defeat. Instead, I do what Tanner Nash does best. I go into persuasive mode.

I prop my hands on the edge of the table and lean toward her. "How about we wait just a little longer." I hold up my index finger and thumb about an inch apart. "Maybe, say, after football season is well underway. Or at least until after school is started."

"Why?" Hannah's face is full of shock, as if us continuing to hang out is my dumbest suggestion ever.

I lift my hands and shrug. "Why not?" Dropping my

hands, I plop back down on the bench. "I think this is going well. Don't you?"

"Well, yeah. That was the whole point. But eventually we're both going to want real relationships, and doesn't us fake dating get in the way of that?"

Not if us is the us I want. It's on the tip of my tongue, and I should say it. She may even find it romantic. But I'm too cocky and stubborn for my own good. Instead, I get defensive.

"Hannah, I am one part of this fake relationship and I get fifty percent of the vote."

"That's exactly why we're having this discussion."

"I didn't want to have this discussion. Not today. That's not why I brought you to lunch."

She drops her head in her hands for a moment before looking back at me. "Tanner, we can't keep pretending forever."

"I agree. But I see no reason why we have to stop what we're doing."

Hannah stands so fast that she knocks her Styrofoam cup on the ground. "Tanner, I can't do this anymore."

"You at least owe me an explanation as to why." I stand, meeting her gaze. Her chocolate eyes have a burgundy flare inside them.

"No, I don't. You're my fake boyfriend. We did each other a favor. We've both played our parts, and what's done is done. I'm ready to stop the charade." She starts toward my truck way faster than someone in spiky heels and a tight skirt should be able to travel.

I jog and catch up to her. She opens the truck door and grabs her purse.

"What are you doing?"

"Leaving. You won't respect that I want this to end."

"I've shown you nothing but respect, but I demand an answer as to your sudden change of heart."

Hannah slams the truck door and starts walking toward the park entrance.

"Where are you going?"

"Back to work," she calls without looking back, still speed walking in shoes unsteady enough to break an ankle on anyone else.

I glance at the picnic table with my uneaten ribs, then back at her. I sigh and hop in my truck. My stomach will have to wait in line behind my heart. A minute later, I'm driving beside her. "Hannah, get in."

"No."

"Yes."

"No." She stops, as do I. "I tried to tell you nicely, but you won't accept 'no,' so I'm leaving."

She speeds up again, and I continue to drive beside her. "Give me a reason, please."

"No." We're now outside the park, and she's running toward downtown.

I drive beside her, yelling out my window. "Hannah, come on. Talk to me."

She shoots me a death glare and rushes down Main Street. I get caught by the one stoplight in town, which almost never turns red. "Are you kidding me?" I beat my fist on the dash and watch as she scurries down the road and into Piggly Wiggly.

CHAPTER FIFTEEN

Hannah

I practically fall into the sliding doors of Piggly Wiggly, embracing the air conditioning. When I ran away from the park, I neglected the fact that it's over ninety degrees outside and I'm wearing stilettos and a black pencil skirt.

Blowing a sweaty strand of hair out of my eye, I lean against the wall filled with "Help Wanted" and "Hay Bales for Sale" flyers. I'll stay here a few minutes until Tanner has time to pass. Shouldn't take long, since that light hardly ever goes red. Thank God, it did today.

A loud engine roars outside and I lean forward. Tanner's Tacoma pulls into the parking lot, sending a sliver of fear down my spine. I hate confrontation, and the last thing I want is to admit that I'm hurt by him being in Tuscaloosa with another woman.

He's done everything I've asked of him, and more. He's free to really date whomever. But why did he have to kiss me a few days before going on a date? And why did he allow me to get so close to him? Not to mention Taylor.

His truck door opens, and I panic. With no other options, I rush toward the registers and duck behind a lane. Boots come into my view, and I swallow. *Please don't be Tanner.* I force my eyes upward to find Jonah holding a bag of Doritos and a jug of sweet tea.

"Hannah, are you all right?"

"Shhhhh." I jerk my index finger in front of my lips and shush him. Then I put on my best puppy dog stare, pleading with him to keep quiet.

His face lifts, and I hear Tanner's voice. "Jonah, have you seen Hannah?"

My heart beats so fast, I fear I may have a heart attack. Oh dear, I can't die on the floor of Piggly Wiggly. Who will take care of my daughter? My parents, of course. But still, what a way to go.

I scrunch my eyes shut and send prayers for patience, strength, and any other fruit of the spirt I can remember. Then I tug Jonah's pant leg in desperation.

He pulls at his pants as if he's heard my plea. "No, not today. Why?"

I sigh and look up at him. He's still facing the door. *Good boy, don't give me away.*

"I thought she might've stopped by here on her lunch break. That's all."

A long beat passes. I shift my weight before my legs fall asleep. All I need is to crash and cause a commotion.

"Thanks, man. I'll call her later."

"No problem." Jonah puts his food on the conveyor belt, then glares down at me.

I mouth a "thank you," and he frowns. Then he pays for his food and extends a hand to me. I take it and allow him to pull me up.

He rushes me toward the back of the store where they stock supplies. We stand behind a cardboard case, hidden between the stockroom door and a large display of Little Debbie snack cakes. "Do you mind explaining to me why I just lied to one of my best friends?" He scans me head to toe. "And why you look like you've been rode hard and put up wet?"

I roll my eyes at him comparing me to a sweaty horse. But if the stickiness of my blouse is any indication, I'm sure the comparison isn't far off. The door flies open in my face and a stock boy comes out with a rolling cart full of bananas.

I grab Jonah by the collar and jerk him inside the stockroom before the door shuts.

He grins. "I've had similar fantasies in high school, but they usually involved the girl taking me to the back of Daddy's hardware store."

"Oh please." I huff and pinch the bridge of my nose. "I can tell you what's going on with Tanner, but you have to swear you won't tell a soul. Especially not Jack."

His goofy expression softens. "Something serious?"

"Yes." I press my lips together and glance around to make sure nobody is nearby. "We had a fake relationship."

"Do what?"

"The whole time we were dating, it was fake."

He rests his bag of groceries on a nearby stack of boxes. "Seriously?"

I nod.

"But y'all were so good together."

"I know." My heart sinks a little when I admit it. We were good together, and still could be, if not for him wanting to actually date other people. I toy with the wrapping on a box to loosen some nervous energy, then gaze up at Jonah. "But it was all an act to get everyone off our backs about our love lives."

CHICKEN ABOUT LOVE

"Oh." Jonah's face saddens. "For what it's worth, he was really happy around you. I could tell."

My heart pricks, wanting so much to believe that. But Tanner has a way with words. I'm sure he convinced Jonah and Jack better than anyone that he was really into me.

"So why did you hide from him?"

I stare at the wrapping, the memory of my desperate escape tinting my cheeks with embarrassment. "I decided it was time to end things, and he didn't agree. We argued, and I stormed off."

"Why end it? I mean, I know y'all were faking, but still."

I twist my lips. If I can't manage to admit my insecurity to Tanner, I can't dare tell Jonah. I lift my eyes before answering. "Personal reasons."

He nods. "You know he's gonna call you, or see you in town. You can't hide long in Apple Cart."

I inhale and exhale as if I'm doing downward dog with a goat on my back. "Yeah, I know. I just needed some time first." I raise the corner of my mouth in a lazy grin. "Thanks for saving me in there."

"Sure thing. I tipped the cashier an extra ten to keep hush as well."

I laugh. "You didn't have to do that."

He shrugs. "We've all been in weird situations now and again. Your secret's safe with me."

"Thanks."

"You bet. Just promise me one thing, Hannah."

"Yeah?"

"Don't shut out the possibility of Tanner. I know you guys had this little pretend thing going on, but the reason we all believed it wasn't because y'all are such good actors."

"Really?"

He chuckles. "Trust me. I remember Tanner's rendition of Huck Finn in the school play."

I laugh with him for a moment. Then Jonah's face goes serious. "It's none of my business and all, but I think you two would make a great couple for real. And I think everyone else agrees. That's the only reason y'all were able to trick so many of us who know y'all so well."

He pats my shoulder, then frowns at his hand. He wipes my sweat down the front of his shirt before picking up his grocery bag. "Catch ya later."

Jonah disappears out the back door of the Pig. I stand between fabric softener and strawberries for a brief moment, but what feels like eternity, with the weight of Jonah's words holding me down. At last, I manage to shake what he said about Tanner and me long enough to exit through the front as if nothing strange just happened.

Then I cross the street to the bank and try to ignore Ashley's snarl as I fix two glasses of water in the kitchen. One for my flowers and one for me.

Tanner

Three voicemails and half a dozen texts later, I toss my phone on the floor and give up. My pathetic groveling ends here. The only successful call I've made tonight is ordering a large meat lover's pizza from the Quick Stop.

Hannah has more than made it clear she doesn't care to speak to me. I'm still confused by why she ran from the park, but for whatever reason, she doesn't want anything else to do with me.

Message received.

I'm sure she's received my messages by now too. Sighing,

CHICKEN ABOUT LOVE

I fall back onto the couch and fumble for the remote. I find it right where I left it, in the crack between cushions.

The TV glares, filling the otherwise dark room. It's not quite dark outside, but I plan on going to bed as soon as I eat supper. Thankfully, the gas station started delivering in town. I have zero desire to put on a shirt and shoes.

I scroll through channels, debating between an Adam Sandler movie and the Outdoor Channel. Even though they're goofy as all get out, all Sandler movies still have a love interest, so I opt for watching old men track squirrels.

My eyes glaze over as the main dude spiels off a monologue about the proper bait to use for squirrels. I've all but fallen asleep when the doorbell rings.

I grunt and open my eyes, regretting ordering a pizza. There's at least enough cereal and chips in the pantry to tide me over tonight. The doorbell rings a second time, and I stand. After a quick stretch, I grab my wallet from the coffee table and stagger toward the door, then open it.

My eyes widen when Jonah stands on the other side. Out of impulse, I slam the door shut. In his face. He opens it, and I slam it harder.

After our run-in at the Pig, I'm sure he'll have questions. I have no reason to be a butt to him, except that I don't want to bring up Hannah. Not now and not with him.

He opens the door a second time and shoves his body in front of it before I can shut it. "I have your pizza."

I cross my arms and glance at two pizza boxes in his arms. "Are you moonlighting at the Quick Stop now?"

"No." He snarls. "I was picking up my own food and saw your name on a box. Told the delivery kid I'd take it to you."

"I'm not tipping you."

"I didn't expect you to. Can't two friends share a meal on a Friday night like usual?"

I say nothing and flare my nostrils.

"Come on. You know we'd be at Jack's playing poker if he were home."

I swallow so hard, my Adam's apple jerks like a bobber with a fish on the line. Jack going to Atlanta this weekend had given me the perfect excuse to lie low. Eat my pizza in peace. Then this buffoon shows up on my doorstep more determined than a church leader peddling religious pamphlets.

Since Jonah shows no sign of leaving, I begrudgingly step aside and allow him to enter with our food. He sets the pizzas on my small kitchen counter and goes for the fridge.

I shut the front door and sloth inside. Leaning against the opening between the kitchen and living room, I cross my bare arms. Jonah grabs a jug of sweet tea, which is easy to find among the milk jug, bottle of ranch dressing, and nothing more. Then he fumbles around my cabinet for some cups.

"You need a drink too?"

Assuming the Mountain Dew melting on my coffee table is urine hot by now, I nod. He gives me a nervous grin, as if he's afraid I might lash out at him at any moment. And I might, depending on what he says.

Jonah pours two cups of tea and sets them on the counter by the pizzas. I uncross my arms and slide away from the threshold to retrieve my food.

We walk to the living room, each holding a cup in one hand and a pizza box in the other. Jonah glances around the seating area before sitting in the extra chair. It's not comfortable at all. Something stupid Carolina picked up at an antique auction. But I get the sense he's a little afraid to sit in my recliner right now, and the nest of covers and chip crumbs pretty much solidifies that I've claimed the couch for myself.

I try not to laugh as Jonah settles into the ancient chair

with a back straighter than a Southern Baptist deacon. He squirms a bit before flipping the lid on his pizza and grabbing a slice.

No sooner than I reach for a slice of my own pizza, Jonah starts. "So what's the deal with you and Hannah?"

I drop the slice in the box and sigh. "We got in an argument, she left, and I wanted to make things right."

He shifts his shoulders and takes another bite of his pizza. Jonah's eyes get that faraway glaze while he chews. That means he's thinking. I bite into my own pizza and watch him reposition himself toward the edge of the chair.

After I've eaten an entire slice and reach for another, he hops up, holding his box. He circles the coffee table and plops down on the opposite end of the couch.

"Feel better?" I smirk, finding it hard to stay mad at him.

"Much." He reclines against the couch, relaxing his features. "The whole time I was hauling it back from Auburn, I tried to tell your sister that chair sucked."

I laugh. "Thanks for trying."

He shakes his head. "You know how stubborn she is. Said it would give your place some character."

I roll my eyes and bite off another hunk of crust. "She's definitely a fixer," I say around a mouthful of bread. "I feel for whatever poor sap marries her one day."

Jonah shakes his head. "I'll try and warn him too."

I burst out laughing. Aside from me, Jonah probably knows Carolina best. Including her obsession with HGTV and trying to spruce up anything and everything—including me.

The tension lifts as Jonah joins me in laughing. We talk a little more about how we've both bought hideous decor before just to tick her off. It's almost become a game: Who can find the ugliest decoration that looks normal enough to convince Carolina we seriously like it, then bring it home.

Once the laughter subsides, Jonah takes a sip of his tea and clears his throat. "Look, man. It's none of my business, but you seemed pretty shook up when you ran in the Pig today."

I gulp down most of my own tea in an effort to prolong the Hannah talk just a few seconds longer. Jonah's staring at me as I put down my cup. "Yeah." I set the half-eaten pizza beside me and slump down. There's no way of explaining what's going on between us without actually explaining what's going on between us.

My palms grow clammy and I swipe them over my knees. "It's complicated." So I've gone with the most cliché excuse in history. And Jonah doesn't buy it for a second.

He rips off a piece of crust with his teeth and rolls his eyes. "Come on, bro. You owe me more than that." He talks around a mouthful of pizza, but the sarcasm somehow seeps through.

I shrug and fall back into the cushion behind me. The one that's practically indented to fit my head thanks to the last few hours of wallowing in pity.

"All I know is you two were thick as local honey a few days ago. I assume nothing bad happened to her or I'd have heard about it by now. So what's really going on?"

My nerves tingle as I try out words in my mind. I'd promised Hannah I wouldn't tell anyone about our little charade. But I guess it doesn't much matter now. And I've got to talk to somebody. Better Jonah than my meddling sister or lovestruck Jack or my parents, who'd probably confess they were skeptical of Hannah falling for me in the first place.

"We were faking it."

Jonah's eyebrows raise and his jaw hinges open. I expected him to show shock, but his face is so contorted, it's as if he's putting on more emotion than he should or he's simultaneously trying to hide a smile and not smell a fart.

Whatever the reason, I stare at the TV instead. "I'm sick of my parents blowing through here every month between RV trips and criticizing me for still being single. Sick of Ms. Ethel and her casserole brigade trying to set me up. Sick of people questioning my seriousness because I randomly date now and again but never have a relationship."

I turn to Jonah, whose face is now somber. "And it turns out, Hannah's sick of everyone trying to find her the perfect man too. Ever since she's come back to town, the before-mentioned older ladies of Apple Cart have tried their darndest to find her a new husband. She can't go to church, work, or even the Pig without someone suggesting someone for her. She'd rather focus on Taylor and restarting her life, not play small-town bachelorette."

Jonah rubs his jaw and nods. I sigh, then continue. "After the chicken-truck wreck, we kinda became friends. Then I stepped in at church one day when Samuel was trying to schmooze her and the casserole queens had been after me. Turns out, us sitting together at church solved a lot of problems that morning. So we decided why not do that more often? Be seen together around town. Go on a few local, friendly dates. Start some talk and get people off our backs."

One side of Jonah's mouth tugs into a slight smile. "You two sure fooled me. And Jack too."

I take a sip of my tea before melting my head into the indented cushion once more. "What can I say, I'm a good actor."

"No, you're not."

"I tricked you."

Jonah snorts out a chuckle. "Man, you suck at acting. I remember from school. Yeah, you started out as a salesman and can talk, but I don't think that's why you and Hannah convinced everyone what you had going on was real."

"Is that so?" I cross my arms in a challenge.

"Yep. The only way you two managed to pull this off is because deep down, y'all really care about each other."

A nervous laugh trickles from my throat. I don't like being called out like that . . . especially when it's true.

"Seriously, Tanner. If you didn't 'like' like her, do you really think you'd be this upset over a fake relationship?"

I blink, the vulnerability slicing me like a knife. Memories of our kiss flash through my mind like all the best parts of my favorite movies playing at once. My heart speeds up at the memory of her touch, and I swallow back the sadness of never having it again.

There's nothing I can say to refute Jonah's argument. After a long moment down memory lane, I turn to him with a nod. "I do 'like' like her. Maybe even 'love' like her."

Jonah's eyes grow three sizes. "Are you going to tell her that?"

I pop my knuckles and let out a huge breath of air I didn't realize I'd been holding. I've never said "love" about any woman aside from my mom, sister, and grandmas. Which means I've never used it in the context of romantic love.

"I don't know, dude. What if she doesn't want to talk to me?"

Jonah leans closer to me and stares. "Don't you owe it to yourself to at least try?"

Behind the goofy grin crawling across his face is a ray of hope, a glimmer of encouragement. Maybe he's right? I've never felt this way about anyone else in my life. It's got me scared stupid, but if I could potentially end up with Hannah, wouldn't it be worth putting myself out there and risking rejection?

CHAPTER SIXTEEN

Hannah

As I turn down my parents' driveway, I review a mental list of what needs to get done before Taylor starts school. It's quickly approaching, which is why I promised her we'd play outside the rest of today when I got home from work.

Halfway down the drive, a newer black truck comes into view. My pulse races. It's the same kind of truck Dalton drives. Surely not . . . I park opposite the truck and get out of my car. As I'm walking toward the house, I get a glimpse of the back tag. "D Law."

My stomach bottoms out as nausea and anger war inside me. What the heck is that moron doing here? This is my safe place, my family's home.

I march up the front porch, heat surging through my body with every step I take. By the time I've made it to the living room, my skin is boiling to the point that I itch all over. My ears sting, clouding my sense. The top of his arrogant head peaks out from above the armchair where Daddy usually sits. How dare he sit in my daddy's chair.

I stomp around the sofa to meet him face to face and open my mouth to give him a non-Baptist tongue lashing. My mouth slaps shut when I notice Taylor sitting in his lap.

"Mommy, you're home." She hops up and runs to me with outstretched arms. "Huggy." I pick her up, and she wraps around me. "Daddy came to play with me."

"Oh, he did?" I plaster on the old pageant smile for my angel, then turn to the devil defacing Daddy's chair. My eyes narrow as Dalton smooths out his starched shirt and grins.

"I did, but I want to talk to you as well."

I swallow the lump in my throat and squeeze Taylor tighter. Right now, she's the only thing keeping me from snatching one of Mama's porcelain bells from the mantel and ringing the side of his head.

Speaking of Mama, she appears in the threshold between the living room and kitchen. "Taylor, you want to go with me to check the blueberry bushes while your parents talk a minute?" Mama offers me a sympathetic smile, and I manage to lift my lips a little as a slight thank you.

"Okay." Taylor runs to Mama as soon as I lower her to the ground, oblivious to what's going on here.

"Come on." I waste no time walking into the kitchen after Mama and Taylor head outside. Dalton follows me, and I exhale at no longer having to watch him squirm in Daddy's chair.

I lean back against the kitchen countertop and kick off my heels. Dalton steps toward me and puts his hand on my cheek. All the fire coursing through my body gathers at that spot. It's as if I might explode from him touching my face. Not in a good way either. In the way of "he has some deadly disease and now I'm infected."

I put my hand on his and jerk it away from my face. "Dalton, what are you doing?"

"I'm such an idiot."

I laugh, some of the tension finally escaping with it. "I know that, but what are you doing *here*?"

"Hannah, I'm serious. I never should've walked out on our marriage."

I cross my arms in a "don't come near me" stance and huff. For almost a year, I'd prayed and begged for him to say that. To admit his faults and fight for our family. It never happened, and I eventually learned to move on.

"I'm serious, baby. I want my old life back."

I exhale through my nose like a bull seeing red. As much as I love hearing him admit his wrongs, having him grovel for me to take him back sickens me. I want to spout off about all the times I cried myself to sleep on the bathroom floor or how I waited to feed Taylor right before her bedtime in hopes her daddy would make it home in time to eat with us. All the while, he was "working late" with the new lawyer. But he doesn't deserve that. I can't allow him to know how he hurt me then or how he's scarred me for life.

"No."

There. That one little powerful word says it all. And, as I suspected, Dalton still isn't used to hearing that word. His eyebrows shoot up and he takes a step toward me. I squeeze my arms tighter around my middle as if that will ward him off. It does keep him from coming closer, but it doesn't make him shut up.

"Please, just hear me out. I didn't realize how much I would miss you and Taylor in my life. I hate going home to an empty apartment and eating takeout in front of the TV."

"Oh, so you want us there to entertain you and cook you dinner?" I raise an eyebrow in protest.

Dalton rakes his hands through his perfect hair, a gesture

he only does out of frustration. He never messes with the gelled perfection otherwise. "That came out wrong. Yes, I realize all you did, but that's not why I want you back."

I frown. I should be changed into shorts and pushing my daughter on a swing right now. Instead, I'm cornered in the kitchen by this imbecile, still wearing my work clothes.

"Dalton, I don't care if you want me for your maid, your arm candy, or your love slave. I don't care if you want me at all, because, frankly, I don't want you."

He blinks like I just dashed a gallon of ice water on his face. Metaphorically, I guess I did. And if I could pull it off without uncrossing my arms, I might do it tangibly as well.

"You don't want to give me another chance? Give *us* another chance as a family?"

I sigh. Of course, he'd play the family card. And six months ago, it would've totally worked. Even two months ago, maybe. But after all I've been through this summer, I just can't.

Tanner and I never were together, but the time we spent together proved I'm capable of having a life with someone other than Dalton. There's more to me than Dalton's plus one. I have a job, friends I didn't meet because of him, and a newfound confidence in myself as an adult.

"No."

Wow, my vocabulary is stellar today. However, the shock on his face lets me know I'm communicating solidly.

"No?"

I shrug as nonchalantly as possible. "Yep, no. I want you to be a dad to Taylor and spend time with her. She needs that. She needs you, and you need her. But I don't need you anymore. And I certainly don't want you anymore."

Dalton grows eerily still, as if Elsa herself froze him in place. I blink my eyes in an effort to make him blink. Then I feign a yawn. Everyone yawns when the person in front of them yawns, right? Still, nothing. As I contemplate actually stepping toward him to check his pulse, his shoulders sag, taking his face with them.

"I hate to be so blunt, Dalton." Good Lord, I'm actually feeling sorry for him now. But not so sorry that I reach out to console him. My arms are now so tightly crossed that they've begun to tingle.

"I get it," he answers at last. "Like I said, I'm an idiot, and I have been for a long time."

Well, I can't argue with that.

"I do feel badly about all I've put you and Taylor through, and I would like to see her more often."

"Of course, you're still her father." I can't bring myself to say daddy yet, or even dad. He has to earn that title.

"Seeing how much she's grown lately makes me realize all the time I've missed."

I frown and stare out the kitchen window at Taylor and my mom in the backyard. "It's only going to get worse. She starts school in a few weeks. All my neighborhood friends back in Birmingham said once they start school, it flies by." I glance back at his solemn face.

"Yeah." He sniffles, and I swear he chokes back a tear or two.

I sigh, as his sincerity about Taylor softens me a bit. "Look, Dalton, you're welcome to see Taylor anytime. But I'd like to know first. I didn't expect to come home from work and find your truck in Mama's driveway."

"Yeah." He rolls up his sleeves and follows my gaze to the window. "It was an impulse move, I guess. I'm working a lot more now that I'm alone, and I really missed her today."

I allow myself to smile and ease up on my arm tension before I pass out. "I get it. I'd miss her too."

Dalton continues staring out the window and smiles.

"You know, for all I've done wrong in my life, when I look at Taylor, it's proof I did at least one thing right."

The tension lifts, and I drop my arms. I'm now confident Dalton won't continue to make the case for the three of us to get back together. My smile widens as I watch Taylor laughing outside as she plays with Skip. "I know exactly what you mean."

Tanner

I run my fingertips over my freshly shaven jawline. My little one-man intervention with Jonah renewed my hope in having a real relationship with Hannah. After Jonah left, I immediately started planning what I'd say to plead my case for us to be together.

Jonah just thinks I'm a bad actor. I'm actually the best actor I know, because I act confident every day of my life. My entire life, I've lived in my big brother's shadow. I'd assumed after he got married, it would stop. Nope. My parents even left my college graduation because my sister-in-law went into labor early with their first grandchild.

Then, there's Carolina. We've always been close, but Daddy and Mama baby her like no other. I somehow got stuck in the middle trying to keep up with Matthew or stay little like Carolina. Along the way, I developed thick skin and an overly confident act to overcompensate for being the mediocre middle child.

Then Hannah happened. She understood me in a way nobody had before. I shared more with her in six weeks' time than I had with anyone else in my life, including Jack and Jonah.

That had to be love, right? Why else would I tell some random woman I haven't seen since high school my life's troubles? My insecurities and hang-ups. My life's desires and dreams.

I run a comb through my hair and smile at the mirror. At least I look good. If I can't find confidence in what I can offer her as a boyfriend, maybe I can at least charm her with my straight teeth and dimples.

Sighing, I turn down the hallway toward my bedroom. I pop my knuckles as I stand in front of my open closet. Green. Everyone says I look handsome in green. I pull a green polo shirt from the top rack and a newer pair of Wranglers to go with it. Then I grab a pair of boots I reserve for church and special occasions. I can't profess my love with my feet covered in chicken crap.

There. I'm ready. At least on the outside. A quick stop by the gift shop for some flowers, and then off to Hannah's. I play out the scene of Hannah and me in my mind all the way to the hospital. As I imagine her crying and leaping into my arms, I smile.

Thud. That smile is quickly smacked off by the revolving door to the hospital. I blink a few times and rub my temple. Maybe I shouldn't get lost in the passionate parts just yet and focus on what I'm gonna say.

I nod to the older lady behind the reception counter, who smirks my way. No doubt, she caught a front-row seat to my misfortunate slap in the face. I stroll toward the gift shop as if the side of my head isn't throbbing and scan the selection of flowers. Not much to pick from.

I pick up the two options sticking out among all the empty holes in the flower cart. One is already wilting. The other has some sort of plastic wrapper around it that reads, "I

Love MOM," with red hearts and swirls. Must be some sort of Mother's Day wrap, although the other bouquet looks as if it's been left out since Mother's Day.

"Uh, got any more flowers?"

A slouchy woman with a nose ring hooked through both nostrils raises her eyes. She shakes her head so hard, her hot-pink bangs dance across her forehead.

"All right." I glance back at the two bouquets in my hands. I can't suggest we start fresh with a bunch of dying flowers. "'Love Mom' it is, then." I drop the sad bouquet back in its slot and slide Mom across the counter.

After a few awkward moments of trying to get a pleasant face from the girl running the cash register—and failing—I'm cautiously maneuvering the revolving doors on my way to the truck.

I drop the flowers on the dash and shake my head. I can't give Hannah a Mom bouquet. She is a mom, but still. That's not how I see her. Too bad they don't have a bouquet wrapped in "the most beautiful, caring, fun, and adorable woman ever who I'd gladly spend the rest of my life loving." Loving. There I admit it. I love her. I stare down at the flowers, and before I can think better, I rip off the Mom wrap.

Bad idea.

They start to fall apart. Luckily, I fist them before the whole group spreads too far to recover. There's no way I can rearrange the flowers to look decent. And while I might can drive down the road holding them together, I can't hand them to Hannah like that.

I need something temporary until she puts them in a vase. Squinting my eyes, I fumble through the contents of my toolbox in my brain. A metaphorical light bulb goes off when I remember the colored zip ties. If they can cling to a chicken leg for identification, then they can hold a couple of flower stems steady.

I hop out of the truck and have the flowers secured in under a minute. The flowers stay in place, and the green tie is barely noticeable . . . when I cover it with my hand.

Satisfied with my Hail Mary, I climb back in the cab and head for Hannah's house. Despite a few hiccups along the way, I'm confident Hannah will hear me out and like what I have to say. Or worst case scenario, Taylor and her mama will spot me before she can toss me out. I smile to myself. Those two would never toss me out.

My smile starts to fade as I picture Taylor's joyful little laugh. I've grown close to her as well, and to Hannah's parents. Cheesy as it sounds, I fell in love with the whole family. Even Skip. I've always wanted a dog, but my mom didn't care for them when I was growing up, and I haven't bothered getting a big dog like I want since I live in town.

When I turn onto Hannah's drive, my nerves are so on end that I sense every piece of gravel rolling beneath my truck. I tug at the collar of my shirt, suddenly hot from anticipation. What if she doesn't like what I have to say? What if despite all we've been through and the way she looked at me and the way she kissed me back, it really was all an act for her?

I swallow and grip the steering wheel tighter. Now that I'm here, there's no turning back. I park beside her car and let out a huge breath. Then I lift the flowers from the dash and start toward the front door. Every step I take gets heavier, until I plant myself on the doormat.

My palm sweats around the flowers, and I'm grateful the slick Mom wrap is gone. Otherwise, they might slide right through my fingers. With my free hand, I ring the doorbell. The subtle ding echoes through the house, raising the hairs on my neck. I've done it now. No turning back.

I stare at my boots, waiting for Hannah to open the door.

Better yet, Taylor. I can pull a flower from the zip tie for her and get ushered in to her mother.

Instead, the door swings open and I lift my eyes to meet . . .

"Dalton?"

"Tanner Nash?" He's as shocked as I am to see him, if not more.

"Yeah." I shrug and hide the flowers behind my thigh.

"What are you doing here?" Dalton tilts his head in the same way he did whenever someone eyed Hannah for a second too long.

"I can't say I expected to see you here either."

Dalton's jaw twitches. There's no need to tell him why I'm here. For one, it's none of his business. And for two, I have as much right here as him.

We stare at one another the same way two guys in a western do right before they draw weapons. But we're civilized, modern-day citizens, and my only weapon is a zip tie filled with flowers, so I settle for clinching my jaw until he speaks again.

"You haven't heard?"

"Heard what?" I rock back on my heels, my body involuntarily repelling his smug grin.

"I'm back in Hannah's life."

I swallow, gulping down mounds of frustration. The last person I expected to see behind this door was Dalton. And in my naivety, I expected him to say he was here to pick up Taylor. But he never even mentioned Taylor, just Hannah. *My* Hannah.

Or at least, I thought she was mine. If her ex is back, then she never will be mine. Dalton is a first-class tool, but I can't stand in the way of a family trying to make it work.

"Did you need something?"

I jerk my eyes from the doorframe, where I've been

staring for some time. How long have I stood here lost in my thoughts like an idiot? "Uh, no."

I need to leave. I need to get on with my life. Accept that this Hannah and Tanner thing ain't gonna happen in the real world.

I nod my head and take a step back. Then I turn and jog down the porch steps, hurrying toward my truck before anybody else realizes I'm here.

As soon as I crank my truck, I back out and focus on the gravel road ahead. No looking back. I can't stomach Dalton standing in that doorway where I've gone to pick up Hannah and Taylor or taken them home so many times. Where I've walked through the door to join them all for a family meal.

Dalton's living the life I'm meant to live . . . or I'd hoped to live. But it was his life all along. He's the one who married her and fathered Taylor. Not me.

And as I leave their driveway and turn onto the county road, it hits me. All that talk about really dating and other people, then Hannah acting so vague about details. She was trying to spare my feelings. She didn't want to admit that she's back with Dalton.

CHAPTER SEVENTEEN

Hannah

I haven't slept decent since running away from Tanner. Running down the road and squatting behind a Piggly Wiggly register is by far the most immature act of my life. Well, at least in my adulthood.

I'm not sure what possessed me to do all that. Was Tanner with another woman in Tuscaloosa? Maybe, maybe not. But he owed me nothing. He kept up his end of the bargain. So why did I go all desperate housewife over a potential sighting of him with someone else in an adjoining county?

Because I care for him. Like, a lot. I don't like admitting that to myself, and I'm way too cowardly to admit it to him. Especially since there's a small part of me that believes it might be the beginning of love.

I groan. That's a word I reserve for my immediate family only. No more men. I've already accepted the fact that I might stay a single mom forever, and I'm totally good with that.

Or I was, until Tanner Nash happened.

Whoa. I blink at the mirror, realizing I've been swiping the same eyelashes with mascara this entire time. I pinch my lashes between my index finger and thumb nails and scrape away some of the caterpillar crust so that I don't walk into church with a makeup-induced black eye.

I add some mascara to the other eye to even it out too. There, that's better. My stomach churns as I anticipate seeing Tanner at church. Will he try and sit with me? Doubtful. Should I invite him to anyway? How should I play this? Should I pull him aside and apologize first thing, or act chill during church and then apologize?

"Ugh." I drop my head and groan even louder this time. I've tortured my brain enough for an early morning. It's time to wake up Taylor and face whatever demons are waiting for me at Apple Cart Baptist. Nosy old ladies, Samuel, Jonah giving me a knowing look. Who knows what?

I cross the hallway to Taylor's room, where she's halfway awake. I sit on the edge of her bed and give her a gentle shake. "Taylor, sweetie. It's time to get ready for church."

She blinks a few times then wrinkles her nose. "What's wrong with your eye?"

I sigh. Maybe I didn't do such a good job evening them out. "Nothing."

She sits up and yawns. "Can I take a toy to church?" Several stuffed animals hang over her arms.

"Just one."

"But they need someone to talk to."

A smile tugs at my lips, but I manage to keep a straight face. "Not in church."

"How about two in the car, and I only take one in church?"

"Fine." I smile. She definitely got the negotiating skills from her daddy. As long as she doesn't take entirely after him, we'll be fine.

I pat her on the head and go to her closet. She has way more clothes than Mama and me put together. I pull out a cute sundress and her pink sandals, along with a coordinating hair bow.

"I have your clothes out. When you're changed, brush your teeth, and then I'll help you with your shoes and fix your hair."

"Okay." She yawns widely, but gets up.

I walk downstairs to cook us some breakfast, but Mama has beat me to it. She's standing over a waffle iron, still in her pajamas.

"Well, you're ready early."

"Yeah, I couldn't sleep." I sit at the island and stare out the window. A vase of colorful flowers glisten in the sunlight. "Where did those come from?"

"Oh, Taylor said her daddy gave them to her."

"Huh. I didn't notice them until now."

"She brought them to me right before he left, so he must've had them in his truck until then."

I roll my eyes. "It's amazing they didn't wilt. He's never been the smartest at giving gifts."

Mama grins back at me. "I'm proud of you for handling him coming by so well."

I shrug. "I guess I did. As much as I want nothing to do with him, I know he and Taylor need one another."

Mama nods. "As it should be." She steps back and turns off the waffle iron. "I need to go get ready. There's plenty waffles here for everyone. If Taylor wants to go a little early with us to Sunday school, she can."

"Thanks." I watch a random bird out the window fly into Daddy's gourds. I should start Sunday school myself, but as a twenty-something divorcée in a small town, I don't really know where I'd fit.

That's what I liked best about hanging out with Tanner. It was never awkward around him. Like he was spending time with us out of pity or trying to fill Dalton's spot. He was just himself, and he fit in perfectly with me . . . and Taylor.

Mama disappears toward her bedroom, and I start pulling out plates, syrup, and whatever else we might need to eat waffles. Busy work always keeps me going when my mind wants to throw a pity party. I have no clue how Tanner will react to seeing me again. I'm sure Jonah's probably caved by now and filled him in on the Pig incident, which will make me more pathetic in his eyes.

Thankfully, Taylor rushes in, jolting me from a spiraling sense of humiliation.

"Pancakes!"

"Waffles."

She raises her hands and shrugs. "Same thing. One just has square holes."

"True." I fix her a plate and pour myself some coffee. We sit at the table and chat about yesterday. She hasn't seen her dad in at least half a year. I pray he sticks to his word of seeing her more regularly. She can't take any more heartache right now.

And neither can I.

Mama and Daddy come in dressed for church and eat, then announce they're headed to Sunday school. Taylor goes with them, leaving me alone. I put away the plates and leftover food in silence, then wipe down all the countertops. After that, I decide to sweep and mop. Anything to keep me busy before it's time to leave.

Once the kitchen is sparkling, I retrieve my shoes from my room and head to church myself. I'm glad Taylor agreed to go with Mama and Daddy. A small part of me hopes riding alone will ensure I can stay after and talk to Tanner. Maybe even go someplace alone with him to hash out what happened.

I haven't decided if I should bring up the woman in Tuscaloosa. Would it make me sound possessive and desperate to do so? Plus, it could be nothing. Maybe it's someone he works with, or a cousin or something. Wishful thinking on my part, but maybe.

I park near the back and scan the parking lot for Tanner's truck. I don't see it, but that doesn't mean anything. There's still a few minutes before service starts. I get out and sneak in the lobby before Sunday school lets out. As soon as the sanctuary doors open, I slide into a back pew.

My parents and Taylor roll in a few minutes later with a crowd of others and join me. More and more people file in, talking and shuffling in the pews. I see Jack come in, followed by Jonah. Later, Carolina comes in and sits with them. But no sign of Tanner.

Brother Johnny steps up into the pulpit and welcomes everyone, and the choir takes their seats behind him. Still no sign of Tanner. I stand and open a hymnal like everyone else and go through the motions of singing "Amazing Grace." All the while, I keep an eye out for Tanner.

By the time the worship leader announces we can all have a seat and Brother Johnny comes up front again, I give up. Tanner isn't coming, and there's a good chance I'm the reason.

I've really done it this time. I've kept someone from going to church, and I've possibly ruined what could be the best thing for Taylor and me in a long time.

Tanner

A loud buzz sounds beside my head. I reach for my phone and turn off the alarm after hitting snooze more times than I can count. About the fifth snooze, I made the executive decision to skip church.

I'm not one to mope around and lay out of church or anything, really. But the whole Dalton thing really got to me. The last thing I wanted was to run into him with Hannah at church of all places. Not that I don't think Dalton could use a good sermon.

It's just that church is our place. Where all this rescuing each other from matchmaking began. Even more than that, I've enjoyed sitting with her family and joining them for lunch afterwards. With my parents RVing half the time and my sister hit or miss thanks to living her best life in Auburn, I've missed sitting with a family in church. And I didn't want to transition to the new church my brother goes to where the music guy wears skinny jeans and they have a smoke machine. That's a little too much for a true Apple Cartian, in my opinion.

Hannah's family welcomed me in from day one, and I've enjoyed it. I'll miss her parents and Taylor almost as much as her. Almost.

I check the time on my phone. Crap. I haven't slept this late in years. I throw back the covers and force myself to stand. After twisting around to pop my back, I go to the bathroom.

It's almost lunchtime and I have nowhere to be, so I decide its perfectly acceptable to not put on pants. I brush my teeth and floss, then head for the front of the house in my boxer briefs.

Is this my life now? Transitioning from the bed to the couch? Maybe so. Well, not totally. I have a job.

The idea of watching mindless TV annoys me, so I reach for the local paper sitting on my coffee table. Might as well get my mindless fix by reading.

As expected, the main story is the ongoing saga of a zoning war between two citizens. One wants to move in a modular home, while the head of the HOA in that neighborhood opposes. For the last half year, there's been back and forth between the two at the county commissioners' meetings over whether the pro-built modular home is a trailer or a house.

I couldn't give two bird turds either way, but apparently this is a heated topic in Apple Cart that warrants the front page almost monthly.

The next few pages are filled with all the people Bradley arrested this week when he busted the latest meth lab. I went to school with a few of them. Seeing their rotting teeth and wrinkled faces shines some light on my current situation of messy hair and underwear. See, I'm not a total bum. It could be worse.

Across the fold from the villains of Apple Cart County is an engagement announcement. Two good-looking recent college grads are armed up in a hay field, all smiles. Good for them. I read the article of how they met at UA and plan to marry in the fall at Jack's lodge.

I stare at their faces and think of how nice it must be to find your person. I've got half a decade and many more miles of living on them, and I'm still sitting here alone in my underwear. Funny thing is, my situation never bothered me until recently.

Until Hannah.

I like kids, and I like women even more. But I was in no hurry for either. If I got married one day and had a family, great. If not, I had my friends and my niece and nephew to spoil. No need to try to make it happen. I had a great life already.

I guess I didn't know anything was missing until Hannah came along. Now, she's what's missing.

Sighing, I rub my face and fall back against the couch. That indentation swallows me up like it's been waiting for me all morning. Why, of all people, did I have to fall for someone who went back to her ex?

It doesn't even matter that she's been married before. What matters is she had a long history with someone who wasn't me. Yet, at my age, most women do. At least, most women worth having a relationship with. Huh, now that I think about it, that explains why I tend to date younger women. Less life experience, less likely to have romantic history with someone else. Less likely to leave me for their past.

I fold the paper together and toss it on the coffee table. The Apple Cart football team, complete with cheerleaders and the armadillo mascot, stare at me from the back page. My mind drifts to high school, when Dalton and Hannah were the hot item. The Ken and Barbie of student athletes. Both good-looking, straight-A students. Quarterback and head cheerleader. Such a small-town cliché.

I was the wise-cracking wide receiver. Good athlete, decent grades. Good looking, but too goofy to pull off that suave demeanor. If they were the king and queen of Apple Cart High, I was the court jester.

Despite having a little time in the limelight with the queen, I know my place. I've always known it. And the goofy guy never gets a fairytale ending.

CHAPTER EIGHTEEN

Hannah

I lock my car door and push open the glass door to the bank. The sun dances in front of me, so I keep my sunglasses on halfway to my station. With as little sleep as I've had the past few days, I may as well be hung over.

My eyes adjust to the mediocre florescent lights above as I slip my sunglasses into the side pocket of my purse. I greet Mrs. Bethany, who always beats me to the bank no matter how early I arrive. She half smiles my way, then glares at my pencil skirt. My guess is she thinks it's too tight.

I ignore the gesture and circle behind the counter to my station. I turn on my computer, then straighten the few things around my desk, before a strong, musky scent fills the air and heels click across the tile floor. I don't have to lift my head to know it's Ashley. In fact, I choose not to and continue staring at the static screen of the bank's web landing page.

A few minutes later, a sharp elbow jolts me to attention. Ashley's shoving me over to put my money in the drawer. "Now, remember."

With no cares left to give, I throw a hand in her face. "If you mention the bait money one more time, I swear, I'll tackle you right here."

Her big eyes widen even more. She steps back and clears her throat. "Alrighty, then. Just remember, I'm watching you." Her eyes narrow and she points two fingers at them and then me before strutting off to the next teller station.

I sigh and smile to myself for finally standing up to that thin, blonde bully. A quick sip of my water, and I dive into counting the money in the drawer. As soon as I total everything and mark that it's correct, I lift my gaze to Samuel standing in front of my computer. I'm surprised I didn't smell him coming too. Either he's laid off the aftershave, or Ashley's scent is still taking over the place.

"Morning, Hannah."

"Good morning," I manage to greet him after a slight yawn.

"You look tired."

"I am tired."

Samuel shakes his wrist to move back his sleeve, then checks his massive gold watch. "How about I take you to brunch in a bit? Help you wake up."

"My break isn't until eleven, and I'm really not hungry."

A loud yawn breaks out behind me, and I follow Samuel's gaze to Ashley slumped against the countertop behind my station. "Wow, I'm sleepy too."

"There's fresh coffee in the kitchen," Samuel calls out behind me.

Ashley stands, suddenly fully awake, and marches toward the kitchen. I'm still watching her when Samuel continues talking.

"How about lunch, then?"

"No thanks, I have plans." Total lie, but at this point what does it matter? I lied to the whole world about Tanner and me for over a month, including my daughter. No matter if I came out and said we were faking it or not, I still lied.

"I'm assuming the plans are with a friend, since you and Tanner are no longer together."

I open my mouth to comment on how forward he's being, not to mention nosy. However, the sheer shock of him knowing we're no longer an item silences me. Especially since we haven't officially said we're no longer an item. We simply had a fight, which was all on me, and that's it.

Unless . . . heat crawls up my neck as I imagine Jonah telling Tanner what really happened in the Pig, then Tanner telling all his friends how we faked everything. Then it somehow making the rounds to the hair salon and proving to the entire county how desperate I am to keep people out of my business. Or worse, how desperate I am to prove that I can have another meaningful relationship. Ugh.

I suck in a deep breath and dip my head. When I raise it, Ashley is standing beside Samuel with two cups of coffee in her hand. "Here, Sam. I made you one as well. Just like you like it."

"Thanks," he mumbles. He takes the cup but keeps his eyes on me. "Are you sure you're okay, Hannah?"

"Yeah," I lie again. I haven't been okay in a long time, and these two weirdos staring at me isn't helping.

Ashley enters through the little swinging door and shuffles some papers behind me. Most likely, she's finding some excuse to eavesdrop.

"But you aren't with Tanner anymore, right?" Samuel wastes no time making this more awkward for me.

"It wasn't good timing for Taylor." As soon as the words leave my mouth, I want to kick myself in the teeth. But thanks to losing most of my flexibility, that isn't possible. Plus, I'm way too young for dentures.

However, I deserve some sort of punishment for that lie. Taylor loves Tanner, and he loves her as well. They've become the best of buddies this summer. Sometimes, it's easier to play the kid card than admit I'm a pathetically jealous person. But getting cheated on can do that to a person.

"Word on the street is you're back with Dalton," Ashley speaks up from behind us. Literally proving she will talk about me behind my back.

"No." I swivel on my stool to face Ashley. "More like he's back in Taylor's life. That's it. I'm very much single."

Without saying a word, Ashley slams the filing cabinet she's rummaging through and prisses off toward the drive-through window. I'm not sure which part of that ticked her off, but it got rid of her, so I couldn't care less.

"You're single, then."

Oh great. I swivel back to face the other source of my growing migraine. This one is smiling wider than a snake-oil salesman after killing a ten-foot copperhead. "Yes," I squeak out through the lump forming in my throat.

Samuel glances around the lobby, then leans forward, putting both elbows on my counter space. He reaches across the slick surface and takes my hand. His hands are softer than mine and not the least bit comforting. I jerk my hand free from his and take a step back.

"What's wrong, Hannah?"

"Why did you just hold my hand?"

"I want to make you feel better."

"And you thought holding my hand would do it?" I arch a brow to challenge his reasoning.

"You need someone to take care of you."

I scoff. "No, I don't."

"You told me yourself you needed this job."

"Yeah, to take care of myself."

"Let me take care of you and you can quit." He makes some sort of schmoozy face that sets my stomach on fire.

I bend slightly and pick up my purse from the floor. "How about this? I'll just quit now and I'll never have to deal with you again."

His greasy grin melts into bewilderment, and I love it.

"Then what are you going to do? Live off you parents?"

I bounce through the swinging door and look him in the eye. "Get another job."

He crosses his arms and the gold watch pops out again, catching the light of the morning sun. "You said yourself nobody is hiring."

"There's always somebody hiring. And I'd rather scramble eggs at the Wisteria Waffle House than have you breathe down my neck every day."

Even with his overuse of tanning cream, his face goes pale enough to match his hay-colored hair. A smile cocks across my lips and I turn on my heels, then march out into the parking lot.

The sun blares my vision, but I don't care. I haven't slept but a few hours in days. Yet, for the first time in over a year, I feel more awake than ever. I'll enjoy the last little bit of Taylor's summer break and go to work somewhere by the time school starts. Even if it is Waffle House.

Tanner

I meander through the chicken house, checking off all necessities, from temperature to air quality. Tons of growing chicks

CHICKEN ABOUT LOVE

prance around my ankles as I shift through the sea of feathers. All day, I've worked as a robot. Laser-focused on whatever needs to get done with as little human contact as possible.

A far cry from my usual joking, outgoing self, but much needed for now. Maybe I'll get out of my funk someday, or maybe this is the new Tanner post-Hannah. Either way, I've avoided any excuse to engage in small talk with anyone. That includes buying a gas station burrito for lunch rather than hang around one of the local eating establishments. I'm sure I'll pay for that one later in more ways than one.

Right now, though, any ounce of indigestion is worth it to lie low.

I walk to the edge of the chicken house and sit against the wall, not caring that a pile of poop-covered hay is beneath me. Or that chicks are now climbing on top of my outstretched legs. Lying around like a lesion all weekend is starting to catch up with me. Either that or the burrito.

I need a break. Not just from work but from life. In all my twenty-eight years, I haven't wanted to hide from people. Even with all the embarrassing antics of my teen years and all the times I disappointed my parents in some way or another, I never flat-out felt ashamed.

Now, I do. My little fake-date scheme has hurt Hannah somehow, and that's the last thing I wanted. Of all the people in the world, she's the last one I'd want to hurt. Not only that, but I drug Taylor and her parents along for the ride.

I drop my clipboard beside me, then I rest my cap on my knee and bury my head in my hands. A chick climbs up my shirt and sits on my head. I don't even care at this point. For the longest few seconds of my life, I sit in chicken poop and imagine growing old as a bachelor. Nothing more than checking on chickens and eating gas station pizza. Maybe the occasional splurge of going to

Tuscaloosa for Japanese and a Chick-fil-A milkshake. Man, what a sad scenario.

"Mr. Nash?"

I raise my head slowly so as not to disturb the chicken nesting in my hair. My eyes scan boots, then overalls, then the concerned face of Mason Magill, the chicken-house manager. His gray eyebrows are squatted together over his nose. "Are you all right, son?"

I brush the chick from my head and another from my notes before standing. "Yes, sir. Just a little dizzy spell." I don't add that it's self-induced from living in a disoriented state all weekend.

"You might wanna get that checked out. I had a bad case of vertigo once. Woke up to a goat nibbling my beard."

"That'll do it, I'd say."

"The vertigo or the goat?"

I chuckle. "Both."

"I suppose."

I replace my cap on my head, then remove the pen from my clipboard. "Everything looks great, Mr. Magill. You just need to sign here below my signature for the inspection."

"All right." Mason removes a pair of bifocals from his front overalls pocket. Wearing them makes him resemble Santa Claus. He signs with a slightly shaky hand, then pushes the clipboard back to me.

"Seriously, son, you need to get that checked out if you're feeling bad."

"Yes, sir." I muster a slight grin, then nod and make my way to my truck.

If only finding help for my condition were that easy. Short of a heart transplant, I'm not sure I'll ever shake what happened between Hannah and me.

I climb in the truck and buckle up. A quick stop by the office, and I'll be done for the day. Then I can retreat to my

CHICKEN ABOUT LOVE

house, change into shorts, and watch the Outdoor Channel.

I keep my eyes fixated on the road ahead as I drive toward my office. I managed to avoid everyone this morning before leaving to make my rounds. Maybe I can do the same before heading home.

I park and get out, hurrying before anyone exits the building. A few shreds of hay remain on my seat, so I dust those out the door before closing it. Most likely from my pants, thanks to collapsing on the chicken-house floor.

Pulling my cap down over my eyes, I sneak in though the side door and hurry toward my office. I've almost made it there when I bump into something. Warm liquid spills down the front of my stomach. I clench my teeth in slight pain when it reaches my crotch.

"Tanner Nash, watch where you're going."

I've run into Ms. Ethel's walker, and her coffee mug splattered onto me.

"Sorry." I set the mug upright and make a mental note to buy her an actual travel mug for Christmas. She should know better than to set a mug without a lid in a cup holder on a walker. But I refrain from telling her so. I'm in enough trouble as it is.

"Hang on." I dart into the bathroom down the hall and grab a fist full of paper towels. Then I rush back and start mopping up my mess. She hasn't moved an inch, including the scowl on her face.

"What were you doing rushing around without watching where you're headed? That's dangerous."

"I know, Ms. Ethel. I'm sorry." I move the wad of towels around with the toe of my boot, then ball up the mess and toss it in the trash can inside my door. I continue into my office, and the squeak of her back wheels follows me. Clearly, I'm not shaking Ms. Ethel that easily. Not today.

"Aren't you gonna mop up the stickiness?"

I sigh and remove my cap. "The cleaning person's coming today, so . . ." I shrug.

She steps closer and narrows her eyes at me. "Is that poop in your hair?"

I pat the top of my head until I feel a stiff glob right above my temple. Just great. "It appears so."

Ms. Ethel shakes her head. "What's wrong with you?"

"What's wrong with me?" That comes out a little too harshly, especially when speaking to an elder, but I'm at my wit's end.

Ms. Ethel isn't the least bit fazed. She rolls toward me and shakes a feeble finger in my face. "You shot outta here like a bullet this morning, then ran slap into me this evening. And you're not fooling anyone skipping church yesterday. We all saw your truck in the driveway when we went to Mary's."

I shake my head and sigh. "I'm having a moment or two, 'kay? Everyone else in this town has their issues. Am I not allowed to have one minor breakdown?"

The look on her face is a mixture of sympathy and terror. "I suppose so. It's out of character for you is all."

I scratch my head. When I bring my hand down, I cringe at the stale chicken poop under my nails.

Before I can say anything, Ms. Ethel leans closer. "It's Sheila's daughter, isn't it?"

Ms. Ethel is the last person I want to discuss my love like with, or lack thereof. The fact that I'm even considering having a heart to heart with her shows my desperation. I rub my chin and glance back at the chairs behind us. "You got a minute?"

She checks her tiny wristwatch and nods. "I've got about an hour before *Matlock* comes on."

"'Kay. Well, have a seat." I motion behind us, then sit at

my desk chair. She rolls in front of one of the chairs across the desk and sits slowly.

Against my better judgement, I unpack all the details of mine and Hannah's charade. Her face transforms into a million emotions as I explain what we did and *why* we did it. I don't hold back a bit, even when it comes to naming all the people we aimed on fooling, her and Maudy included.

After a ten-minute monologue, Ms. Ethel is reaching across the desk, hugging me with tears in her eyes. Not the way I expected this day to end, but hey, I've already had a chicken poop on my head. What's a sobbing granny to add to the mix?

CHAPTER NINETEEN

Hannah

It's been five days since I told Samuel to take my job and shove it, in my own way, and the endorphins from standing up for myself have diminished to nothing.

Now I'm settling on the reality that I'm again unemployed and back to browsing LinkedIn like a middle-aged, white-collar stalker. Which is pointless since the only Apple Cart employers on LinkedIn are the community college and the mines. I've already applied to the first. The latter had no office openings, and I'm pretty sure they wouldn't want to send me underground to do their dirty work.

Was I totally stupid for quitting the bank? Possibly. But when Samuel wouldn't let up about taking me to eat and then grabbed my hand, I'd had enough. It was either quit with my dignity intact or slap that fake tan off his face and get fired. Somehow, quitting to avoid sexual harassment

CHICKEN ABOUT LOVE

made me more employable in my mind than becoming the harasser.

I sigh deeply and rock back and forth as I watch Taylor and Skip from the back porch. Her dad is supposed to come and take her out for the day. He said it would be closer to noon, but bless her heart, she got up early to not miss him.

The empty rocker beside me sends a sharp ping through my heart. I miss Tanner sitting beside me on Sunday afternoons, talking about everything and nothing all the same. Watching Taylor play and eating pie. We'd sit and rock for over an hour like an old married couple. Effortlessly talking and watching the sun lower before joining Taylor in the yard.

I'd never realized how much I longed for that. Dalton and I never sat and talked unless we were eating a meal. Even then, it was hurried so he could get back to his computer and work on cases or check the stock market. Law school changed him. Each conversation had a purpose or a mission. No more casual talks, as he didn't have time to sit around and talk. His exact words.

Maybe he didn't mean it that way, but I interpreted it as him not having time for me or Taylor.

I close my eyes and rock harder, sucking in the air from the fan circulating overhead. The beginning of August in Alabama always feels like the threshold of hell. Thank God for sweet tea and air conditioning.

A few minutes into my failed effort to get Tanner out of my mind, my phone rings. I open my eyes and reach for it on the table between the two chairs. It's Dalton's number. Maybe he's close. It's already near noon.

"Hello?"

"Hi, is this Hannah?" a sultry female voice answers.

"Uh, yes. Who is this?"

"Tabitha, from the office."

My blood boils so much, it's a wonder my skin isn't bubbling. Seriously? Anyone but that floozy. I inhale and exhale through my nose, trying my best to remain calm. My last conversation with her was the day Dalton moved out and she came to help transport some of his stuff. I got in her face, crying, accusing her of wrecking our home. She laughed, saying it was all in my head. She was just a "friend from work" helping him.

Only by the grace of God am I able to answer calmly. "Could I please speak with Dalton?"

"He's busy at the moment."

I grind my teeth so hard, I expect to see chiseled enamel fall to my lap at any moment.

"He wanted me to let you know that we decided it would be best not to get Taylor today. Dalton had a rough court case yesterday and has a terrible migraine."

I nod for a minute, then realize she can't hear my head. "Okay," I squeak between my gritted teeth. "Can I please speak to him for just a minute? I promise it won't be long." My entire body tingles at saying "please" to this vixen.

"I guess I can see if he's up."

Wow, how generous of her. I stand and pace the space in front of my rocker, waiting. Tabitha's voice is muffled as she speaks to Dalton. "Honey, Hannah wants to talk to you. She said it would only be a second."

I said a minute, but whatever. I'll take what I can get. I'm sure I can fit a few choice words in a second.

"Hello?" Dalton sounds hungover. Either he's really got a migraine or he's laying it on thick.

"Dalton, while I appreciate you calling"—I cringe at the notion of even saying that, but someone has to act maturely—"I don't really want Taylor with Tabitha."

"Why's that?" His voice is miraculously void of pain now.

"I don't want her confused. She's supposed to spend time

with her daddy. Not her daddy and whatever Tabitha is to you."

"Whatever Tabitha is? We've been together for a year."

"So you admit that now?"

"Yeah. Right *after* our divorce."

I bite the end of my thumbnail. "How convenient that you would have someone waiting in the wings as soon as the ink dried on our divorce papers."

"Look, you've been a belle through most of this, but I don't appreciate this new attitude. I didn't say anything about you and Tanner Nash."

My eyes widen as I blow fumes through my nostrils. "What about me and Tanner?"

"Come on, Hannah. Don't act like I don't know."

I sit back in the rocker, suddenly feeling sick. Word really does travel fast thought Apple Cart, and beyond.

"What's wrong with me having someone? It's been a year since us. More if you count how long since you've treated us like a couple."

"I don't give a . . ." I pull the phone back as he uses a few choice words I don't care to hear. "You can have whatever you want with whomever you want. But don't go sleeping around with people from high school and then get mad at me for having a relationship with Tabitha."

That's it. I bolt from my chair so fast that it rocks back and forth, hitting against my thighs. "I am not sleeping around with anyone. The only man I ever slept with was you, and the only regret I don't have about that is our daughter! Tanner and I barely kissed." Okay, not barely, as it was the best kiss of my life and a thousand fireworks went off in my brain while the rest of me melted into a puddle at his feet. But Dalton doesn't need to hear that.

A chuckle comes from the other end of the line. "Yeah, I didn't expect Tanner to be so romantic."

My eyes narrow and I glance around for something to throw before remembering I can't hit Dalton through a cell phone. "Tanner is plenty romantic. There's more to romance than getting someone in bed, or in the bed of a Z71."

"How dare you."

"How dare you!" My head is so hot, my scalp itches. I pace again, waiting for him to reply. I expect another string of curses. Instead, I actually get a mature response.

"Hannah, I know I haven't been a good companion. Ever. And I'll try better with this whole Tabitha thing when it comes to Taylor."

My blood pressure drops from boiling to simply sky high. "Can you please not make promises to Taylor? She was really excited about you coming today, and now I have to tell her you're not."

"Yeah. I'll do better."

"Good. I really do want you to have a relationship with her, but you have to understand what comes with that. You can't let her down like you did me and expect her to love you just because you're her father. You have to earn her trust."

"I promise to try harder."

I wince at him promising me anything, but I let that one slide since he actually sounds earnest.

"And I know the Tabitha thing is none of my business now, but I don't want Taylor seeing you two sharing a room or anything like that unless you're married."

"We still have our separate apartments."

My blood pressure finally lowers back to a semi-normal level. "Good."

"Look, Hannah, I know that kind of stuff is important to you and I respect you raising Taylor that way, I really do. That's why I know she's better off with you."

I sit back in the rocker and sigh. "Dalton, I want you to be in her life—really, I do. But we have to be on the same page when raising her, whether we're together or not. We can do this, but you'll have to talk to me about things. Not have Tabitha call last minute saying you can't make it."

"I'll try to be better, I swear."

"I'd appreciate that. Remember, we've got to put Taylor first in this to make it work."

"I agree."

I laugh.

"What's so funny?"

"I think that may just be the first time we've ever agreed on anything."

He laughs a little too. "We both liked the paint color in our old house."

I roll my eyes. He's such a nerd. "Seriously, though. It would mean the world to Taylor if you work with me and put her first. No matter what people come and go in our lives, she's always the most important."

"I know. You're right."

"Wow. I've never heard you say that."

He laughs again. "True, but I actually mean it. When it comes to Taylor, you do know best."

"Thanks."

"Please explain to her why I didn't come."

"I'll try."

"Talk to y'all later."

"Bye."

I hang up the phone and sigh. That was a way more productive conversation than I ever could've anticipated. On the downside, I've got to go break the news to my daughter that Daddy isn't coming today.

I stand and start to tuck my phone in the back pocket of my shorts before going to Taylor. Instead, I bring the phone back in front of me and click on the contacts icon. Then I scroll down to Tanner's name. A big part of me wants to shoot him a text and ask what he's doing. If Dalton can't come, Taylor would enjoy doing something fun with Tanner and me.

After selecting his name and hovering over the keys on my phone, I shove it in my pocket. Who am I kidding? He doesn't want to be anywhere near me. He literally went through the bank drive-through last week, slumped down, wearing dark sunglasses. And I don't even work the drive-through.

I've lost him for good—as a friend and potentially more. And it's all my fault.

Tanner

"Get up." My face stings as something, or someone, pops across it.

"Ouch!" I blink and raise onto my elbows, then prop my pillow behind my head. Nothing like a slap in the face to wake me.

"You're gonna be late for church."

I yawn. "What time is it?"

"Almost time to go." Carolina crosses her arms and gives me the same look my third-grade teacher did whenever I got caught horse playing in the restroom.

She stayed here last night after eating supper at Matthew's house. While I don't mind, I tease her for not staying at our parents' house while they're gone. She's such a scared baby princess. "Why don't you go ahead without me? I'll drive myself."

She flings my extra pillow at my head, causing me to

flinch. "No, you won't. You'll go back to sleep. Now get up and shower. You smell like crusty pizza."

As I should, since it's the last thing I ate. Skipping a steak dinner was worth it this time to not get the third degree from my sister-in-law on how I never should've let Hannah go. Like I had a choice in the matter. I yawn and shove the pillow she assaulted me with to the floor. Then I head for the bathroom. About halfway there, I relieve my stomach of gas from the before mentioned crusty pizza.

"Gross." Carolina coughs.

"Get over it. My house." That should get her out of my room.

She rolls her eyes as she passes me on her way toward the living room. "Don't waste time."

"Yes, ma'am." I smirk, and she gives me that same condescending teacher stare.

I disappear behind the bathroom door, undress, and hop in the shower. As much as I want to sleep, it's for the best my sister woke me. She didn't have to slap me and throw things, but if not, I'd probably still be in bed. Aside from Ms. Ethel pitying me, nothing's really changed from last week. I've continued going through the motions at work, then going straight home.

Warm water washes down my back before I turn for it to hit my face. Carol was right. I did need a shower. Maybe I do stink, but I also need to wake up. I blink through the stream of water and soap up, then rinse off and shampoo my hair. Ever since that chicken pooped on my head, I've used extra shampoo.

A few minutes later, I step out of the shower a new man. At least on the outside. I shake the water from my hair and grab a towel from the nearby rack. I dry off and wrap the towel around me before heading back to my room.

Once I'm dressed, I stop back by the bathroom to comb

my hair and shave. Carol can pitch a fit about me taking too long if she wants, but I refuse to go to church with scraggly whiskers. Especially when I expect to see Hannah there.

I rinse off my razor and stare in the mirror. Best I've looked all week. Maybe Hannah will think so, if she cares to look my way. I put away my razor and dry off my chin. As I walk toward the front of the house, a million questions funnel through my brain.

Should I try and sit by Hannah and her family? Nah, that might catch everyone's attention. Maybe I should sit near them instead. On the pew behind them? Or should I play it cool and sit with Carol? People wouldn't think much of me sitting by Hannah or not if I'm sitting with my sister. That would be kind of me since she's home this weekend.

"You ready?"

"Huh?" I jerk my head to Carolina staring at me.

"You seem a little dazed. You sure you're awake?"

"Yep. Let's go." I step toward the kitchen and grab my Bible from the edge of the counter.

I follow Carol outside to her car. "You can ride with me."

"Sure." Normally, I want to drive myself anywhere, but sitting back gives me a chance to sift out my thoughts.

I don't live far at all from the church. As soon as I make the decision to sit with Carol and avoid any controversy, we're pulling in the parking lot. I scan the space for Hannah's car, but don't find it or any of her parents' vehicles. Strange, since I know we're not early.

We enter quietly with a few more stragglers. Music plays across the foyer, signaling that we're already late. Carolina frowns at me, and I shrug. "At least I came."

She lifts one corner of her mouth and opens the wooden door to the sanctuary. We slide in the back and find a spot on the pew behind Jack and Jonah. They nod, acknowledging us, then continue singing.

The songs are on a screen today. I stare ahead but don't pay much attention to the words. I'm too busy cutting my eyes around the room in search of Hannah. Soon enough, the music fades and everyone sits. I lean back against the pew and give up trying to find her.

My mind wanders throughout the sermon, which defeats the purpose of me coming to church. Guilt washes over me as I stare at the pew where I sat with Hannah's family for so many weeks. Where are they?

People bow their heads, and I follow suit. Instead of listening to Brother Johnny, I voice a silent prayer for my current situation. I want to work through things with Hannah, and if not, get over her. Moping around in a fog isn't doing myself any favors.

A few minutes later, we all stand to leave. Jonah turns toward Carolina and me. "Mary's?"

Carol grins. "Unless brother dear has a roast in the oven back home."

I scoff. "And by brother you mean Matthew, right?"

She giggles, then turns to Jonah. "I think that means yes."

"Sure." I follow Jack, Jonah, and my sister to the parking lot. A few people greet us along the way, but I make sure to keep walking so I can avoid interrogations.

The only misstep is when Ms. Ethel scoots by us and squeezes my arm. "Praying for you, son," she whispers not so quietly. She's the only person I know who whispers louder than most people talk.

I nod at Ms. Ethel, then keep walking. My sister scrunches her nose at me when we get to the car. "What was that about?"

I climb inside before answering in case any of the busybodies have their antennas up. "I had a rough week, that's all."

"By rough week, you mean you and Hannah breaking up?"

"Who told you that?"

She smirks at me as she turns her head to back out of the parking lot. "Jonah."

"What did he say?"

She straightens the car and shrugs before pulling into the street. "Not much, just that y'all aren't seeing each other anymore. A shame, if you ask me. She's the best girl you've ever dated."

"Yeah." My voice is breathy like an eighties rock singer. I clear my throat and fake a cough to cover it. The last person who needs to hear desperation in my voice is my little sister.

"If you don't mind me asking, what happened there?"

Since Jonah didn't spill the beans about our fake relationship to Carol, I'm not going to. "We're really different."

"Yeah, but opposites attract, right?"

"Not always. That girl Jonah dated for a while didn't work out."

"Sasha doesn't count. She was weird."

I laugh. "How was she weird? She was hot and really sweet. At least the few times I met her."

Carolina snarls her nose like she's smelling a fart. "I dunno. She never would go anywhere without a full face of makeup, and she didn't like macaroni and cheese. What southerner doesn't like macaroni and cheese?"

"See, opposite of Jonah."

She rolls her eyes. "Enough about Jonah and his oddities. Look at Jack. He's nothing like Bianca, and they're all but married. Then there's Daddy and Mama. Oh, my friend Kendra and her fiancé."

"'Kay, I got it. But that doesn't mean it always works between two opposites."

"Is it her kid? I mean, you're great with Carrie and Jacob, but the whole stepdad thing seems a little overwhelming."

"Nope, I love Taylor. She's hilarious."

"Well, then what is it?"

I clinch my jaw before anything about Dalton seeps from my mouth. Carolina is a few years younger, but still old enough to know I never cared for the guy in school. And I refuse to torture myself with recounting the incident of him answering the Richardses' door.

"Let's just say it's complicated."

"Ugh, please. Don't feed me that crap. Everyone says that when things get hard. You gotta hang in there if you really like the girl." She shakes her head and swoops into a parking space my big truck could never fit in.

Carol cuts the engine, and we sit in silence for a second. I sense she's waiting on me to answer, so I do. "I wasn't the one not willing to hang in there."

Her face saddens and she reaches across the seat and pats my knee. Then she unbuckles and climbs out in silence. I grin as my sister heads toward Jonah and Jack, who wait on us by the front of Mary's.

Either she's matured to the point of being sweet or she knows I'll kick her tail if she badgers me any more about Hannah. Regardless, I appreciate her dropping it. Now if only I could somehow convince Hannah I'm worth a real shot.

CHAPTER TWENTY

Hannah

I close the back of my mom's SUV and survey our pile of . . . stuff. "Why don't I go get one of those luggage carts?"

"Good idea, honey. I'll stay with Taylor, and your daddy can check us in."

"Okay." I pull my hair back with the hair tie on my wrist and head toward the elevators to find a cart.

The sticky beach breeze hits my face as soon as I turn toward the condo entrance from the parking deck. I breathe in the mixture of salt and sun, hoping I can relax over the next few days. Mama convinced me to go with them on their vacation since I'm off work. At first I resisted, but decided a little change in scenery couldn't hurt. Plus, Taylor has never been to the beach with my parents.

They've come to this same condo as long as I can remember. Playing in the pool and hunting snow crabs with Taylor is sure to bring back fond memories from my own childhood.

I spot a cart and grab it, then head toward the parking deck. Before I can make it back to the SUV, Taylor yells, "Mama, can we go to the beach?"

When I'm closer, I answer, "As soon as we take everything up."

"Please, please." She bounces up and down on her tiny toes.

"Hannah, go ahead and let her see it. Your dad and I can unload all this now that you have the cart."

"Are you sure?"

Taylor tugs at my shirttail. "Please, Nana said so. She's your mama, so you have to listen to her."

Mama laughs. "She's right."

"Okay, in one minute." I peel Taylor from my shirt and pat her head. Then I start stacking some of the bigger bags on the cart. When I've got most of them settled, I take Taylor's hand.

"Yes!" She drags me through the parking lot the way I came, then stops.

I laugh. "You don't know where you're going, do you?"

She shakes her head.

"Come on." I lead this time, taking us around front, past the lobby to the side of the condo.

Taylor's eyes widen at the two pools flanking either side of the walkway. "Cool. I wanna swim after the beach."

"We can swim in a bit." I lead her down the wooden walkway until it transitions into pearl-white sand.

"Kick your shoes off."

She shuffles off her Crocs, and I do the same with my flip-flops. I hold a pair in each of my hands. "Go play."

She smiles up at me as if asking permission. I nod toward a row of umbrellas. "I'm right behind you. Find some sand."

Her smile widens, and she takes off running as fast as she can. Which isn't all that fast considering she weighs maybe forty pounds and the sand is as thick as sugar. I trail a few feet behind and suck in more of the salty air.

I regret not bringing her here sooner. Dalton and I took her to Disney a few years back, and we mostly went to his parents' cabin in the mountains. But the beach has always been a special place for me.

Taylor squats down on a pile of sand. Most likely, it's the remains of a sandcastle built earlier in the week. She starts sifting it through her hands as she does in the sandbox at home. I sit on my knees beside her.

"This sand is stickier than the sand I have at home."

"That's because you have play sand that PawPaw bought. This is actual beach sand."

She makes a surprised face and blinks. "And it's so shiny."

"Yep." I set our shoes down and run my hands across the white surface.

"Did we bring my sandcastle stuff?"

"We did. It's in some of the luggage. In a few minutes, we can go up and change into swimsuits and get sunscreen and bring it back with us."

"Will Nana and PawPaw come play with me too?"

"I'm sure they will. They love the beach too. We used to come every year when I was little."

Taylor rakes a pile of sand into her tiny fist. She holds it up sideways, letting a stream of white dust fall from the middle of her hand. "You know who else I wish was here with us?"

I sit silent for a second. I'm quite certain she'll say her dad, and I need to prepare myself to explain why he can't come on vacation with our family. "Who, sweetie?"

"Tanner."

My mouth drops and I fall from my knees onto my butt. "Tanner?"

Taylor nods and gives me a "duh" expression. "You know, our friend. He builds the best sandcastles."

"Oh, yeah." I'm still in shock at Taylor wanting Tanner here with us. Of course, he built a number of sandcastles with her in the big green turtle box at home. That has to be why. She's five. Too young to understand the concept of going on vacation. "I'm sure if he were here, he would build a castle with you."

"He'd swim with us too."

"Maybe so."

"And probably fish with PawPaw."

Okay . . . this is getting a little weird. "You sound like you really want Tanner here."

"Well, yes, Mommy. He's my friend. He's your friend too."

"He is my friend."

"I miss him."

I wipe my hands together to shake off the excess sand and pull my knees toward my chest. "It's only been a little over a week since you've seen him."

"Kids don't know how to tell time. You know that."

I laugh. "I suppose so."

"Can he come play when we get back?"

"We'll see." My words trail off as I stare over Taylor's head at the ocean.

I never can expect what's about to come from her mouth. But of all the crazy things she's said, there's no way I could've prepared myself for this conversation. I'd worried about her getting attached to anyone I might date in the future. That's the main reason we'd been so platonic around her with our fake relationship.

Maybe taking the focus off of us led her to get even more

attached to him. Or it could just be that Tanner's such a likable guy and great with kids.

I hate that she misses him. Even more, I hate that I miss him.

Tanner

Somehow at lunch, I agreed to playing poker at Jack's tonight. I blame it on my sister. She talks as fast as a manure salesman with a mouthful of samples. I'm certain poker came in somewhere between her talk about classes and teasing Jonah about falling over a fence at the rodeo.

Now Carolina's on her way back to Auburn and I'm left holding the bag. Of Doritos, which I also volunteered to bring, apparently.

I start to knock on the screen door of Jack's place out of habit, then remember Bianca had a new doorbell installed. One of those fancy ones that plays a little tune and lights up. Jack can see people through it on his phone. A little freaky, if you ask me.

I hit the bell and wait for the music to end. "Come on in," it answers me in Jack's voice.

After dusting off my boots on the rug—yet another addition from Bianca—I step inside.

"You brought my chips." Jonah grins.

"Yep."

Jonah jumps up and takes the bag of Doritos. I step toward the kitchen to see Jack sitting in his usual seat. My usual seat is occupied by someone. Before I can speak, the guy turns around.

"Michael?"

"Hey, Tanner."

I'm both confused and hurt. What was Jack thinking inviting Michael into our group? "Jack, what is he doing here?"

"Playing poker like the rest of us."

I prop my hands on my hips as if I'm a mad mother and Jack's my son. "He can't play with us." Not the most mature response, but the most accurate to relay my feelings.

"Why is that?" Jack crosses his arms and puffs out his chest to challenge me.

I point to Michael, who's sitting in silence while we fight about him. "His wife worked at a freakin' casino, for crying out loud. And he can shuffle cards like Rain Man. For all we know, he's here to take our lunch money."

Jack scoffs. "Michael's an honest guy, and frankly, I've enjoyed his shuffling. It's entertaining."

"Well, I'm not playing with him."

"Now, that's mature of you."

"I never said I was mature." My face heats up at admitting my childish ways. Insecurities creep through the back of my brain. *Hannah thinks you're immature too. You can't be with someone like Hannah acting like this.*

That's all it takes for me to mellow out. I shake my head. "Fine, but I want my chair. I'm still not *that* mature."

Michael stands and stretches his legs. "Take it."

Jack goes toward the back door and grabs a five-gallon bucket he reserves for extra seating. I'm surprised Bianca hasn't upgraded that. It would've been number one on my list, way above the doorbell and mat. Jack flips the bucket upside down between our chairs. "Here you go, Michael."

Michael eyes the couch and yawns. "If it's all the same to you guys, since Tanner's back, I'll go nap on the couch a few hours."

All of us give him a wondering glare. Even Jonah, who's been lost in the Doritos bag until now.

"Y'all will understand when you have a baby one day. They never sleep. So if it's all the same to you, I'd like to catch a few winks before Krystal expects me home."

"All right," we mumble, almost in unison.

Michael smiles and backs up to the couch a few feet away in the living area. He kicks off his boots and is snoring before we can shuffle the stack.

I glance back at him, a little jealous of how quickly he fell asleep. I've tossed and turned all week, trying to shake situations from my mind. Then I give up and turn on the TV. "Why did y'all invite him here?"

"Shh . . . He's right there," Jonah barks between bites of chips.

"Dude, he's snoring."

"You've been so sketchy lately, I needed a backup player."

I frown at Jack. "Sketchy?"

"Yeah, I haven't seen or heard from you in over a week. At church, you acted all out of it."

"Shouldn't you have been paying attention to the sermon?"

"Shouldn't you?"

I frown. He has a point. "Sorry, I've had a lot on my mind."

"Hannah?"

I sigh. "I'd rather not bring her up."

As if right on cue, Jack's dogs mosey over, wagging their tails. They're followed by Skip. Jack pets his dogs. "You girls want a treat, don't ya?"

"What's Skip doing here?"

He glances up at me. "Oh, he's staying here while the Richardses are at the beach."

"When did they leave for the beach?"

"This morning." Jack walks to the kitchen and opens the freezer. He grabs an ice pop. The long, skinny kind in a clear wrapper.

I watch Jack break the frozen stick into chunks within the wrapper before taking his pocket knife and cutting the end off. Then his dogs line up in front of him. He holds out the ice pop as Chocolate and Brownie take turns biting off the chunks. It's the most bizarre thing I've ever witnessed. Before long, Skip realizes what's going on and steps up to get a bite.

In a weird way, I'm thankful for dogs eating Popsicles, as it took my mind off Hannah for a brief moment.

Once all that remains of the frozen treat is the wrapper, I'm back to picturing Hannah . . . on the beach . . . in a bikini . . . with the wind in her hair. It's getting hot in here. Maybe I need a Popsicle. A metaphorical bucket of cold water hits my face when Dalton walks up in a Speedo and wraps his arm around her.

I shake my head to break apart that terrible picture. Instead of point blank asking if Dalton's in the picture, I skate around the question and ask about Hannah's location. "Is Hannah back in Birmingham? You know, since you've got Skip."

"Nope. The whole family's at the beach."

"And by whole family?" Maybe this will answer my question. I swear, he better not make me say Dalton.

"Dalton's not with them," Jonah says around a mouthful of chips as he wipes cheese dust on his shirt. He picks up the cards to deal them out.

Now that the elephant in the room is visible, I may as well ask all I want. "How do you know that?"

"Your sister."

"Carolina?"

"Unless you've been hiding another one all these years?"

"How the heck would she know? She's in Auburn ninety-five percent of the time."

Jonah takes a gulp of tea and wipes his mouth with the back of his hand. "She heard it from Adrianne at the gas station. Mrs. Maudy told Adrianne that at the salon."

Relief washes over me, and I'm suddenly ten pounds lighter. "You're sure?"

Jonah shrugs. "I'm sure that's what they said. Now if it's true or not, who knows?"

I sigh and slump down in my chair. I pick up my hand and rearrange my cards, trying to focus on something other than Hannah . . . and stupid Dalton.

Jack puts his cards upside down on the table. "Tanner, what happened with y'all?"

I shake my head and put my cards down as well. Something tells me Michael won't be the only one skipping poker tonight. Guilt runs rampant through me as I regret coming clean to Jonah, then Ms. Ethel, of all people. Word would've spread slower had I just published it in the local paper. But she swore to stay silent. We'll see.

Jonah gives me a pitying look. The cluelessness of Jack's face lets me know Jonah's kept my secret.

I turn toward the living room to make sure Michael's still out of it. The drool making its way to his facial hair lets me know I can talk freely. I face Jack and shrug.

"You're not gonna believe this, but I never was really with Hannah."

Jack narrows his eyes in question. I continue to unpack the story of how we came to form a fake relationship. Jonah stays solemn during this bit so as not to reveal he already knows all this. That is, until I get to the new part where I broke down in front of Ms. Ethel in my office and she pointed out I had chicken poop in my hair.

I should've left that last little detail out, because I had to back up and explain how the chicken pooped on my head. Of course, that made them laugh and did help relieve some of the anxiety of me reliving that last fight with Hannah.

"Worst of all, my feelings became real. As much as I tried to keep reality separate from pretending, I started to fall for her. We only kissed the one time, but I've never felt that way from any other kiss from any other woman."

Jack sighs. "I get it, man. It was like that with Bianca."

Jonah's chin is propped in his hand as if he's listening to a bedtime story. "So I can't relate to a life-changing kiss or anything, but I could tell y'all had something real. Whether you two saw it or not."

Jack fumbles with the cards in front of him before looking back at me. "Have you tried to talk to her?"

I sigh heavily. "Well, after the incident of her disappearing at the Pig, I sent a bunch of texts and tried to call. Then I went to her house once."

"You did?" Jonah perks up at another new bit of information. "What happened?"

I swallow and pop my knuckles. "Dalton answered the door."

Jack and Jonah's jaws drop simultaneously. "So that's what started the talk about whether they were together," Jonah comments.

"Yep. And my guess is Ms. Ethel had to have started it, since sadly, she's been my confidante in this. And since your fourth-handed info trail started with Mrs. Maudy, who's her BFF."

Jonah shakes his head. "I still believe they're not together. You should go see her again."

"She's a hard woman to catch. I'm beginning to think she'll hide from me forever. Besides, she said something about us being free to date other people when we had that fight in the park."

Jack takes the dripping Popsicle wrapper to the trash can and pulls off a paper towel. On his way back, the dogs follow him in case he's bringing back another treat. He sits and wipes the table, then pats their heads.

As he's petting Skip, he says, "What if she had to see you?"

"What do you mean?"

He grins at Skip, then me. "I've got a plan."

Jonah and I exchange looks. Last time Jack had a plan, it involved rolling a stuffed deer with bullet holes through the Atlanta airport.

CHAPTER TWENTY-ONE

Hannah

Yesterday threw me for a loop. No way did I anticipate Taylor bringing up Tanner. In fact, I'd hoped this trip would give me a break from him. Not that I don't miss having him in my life. I do, very much so.

But I need some time to chill and heal. Hmm, maybe I should get a shirt that says that?

I jog a little farther and try to refocus on the music streaming through my earbuds. Bad decision, as the next song in the shuffle is none other than "Bubba Shot the Jukebox."

"You've got to be kidding me," I yell loud enough for the older couple walking past me to take a few steps up the shoreline. No doubt, they think I'm crazy, and maybe I am at this point.

I jerk my earbuds out and find a nearby beach chair. With the sun barely over the ocean, nobody's had time to claim it yet, including the people who put out the cushions. I swipe some stray sand from the seat and recline back.

There's few people on the beach at this hour, so I can hear the waves clearly. Much preferred to "Bubba Shot the Jukebox." Who knew that would be the song to set me on edge? Not the least bit romantic, but somehow the unofficial background noise to my falling for Tanner.

I inhale and exhale deeply. Not from running, but from all the angst building inside of me. What if I really screwed things up this time? What if Tanner was my second chance at a happily ever after? For me and Taylor.

She's made it abundantly clear that she likes him, so I'm certain she'd have no issue with us dating. Neither would my parents, as they already thought we were dating.

That's another can of worms in itself. Mama mentioned something on the ride here about Tanner missing us while we're gone and how she hadn't seen him a while. I brushed it off as us taking a break since we're both busy. Which is pure bull. I'm less busy now than ever. I have my parents to help with Taylor, who's about to start school. Plus, my recent change in employment status.

I run a hand across my sticky hair and comb my fingers through my tangled ponytail. Was I a complete idiot for quitting the bank? I mean, it was kind of a hostile work environment, with Ashley talking down to me and Samuel breathing down my neck. But still, it can't fare well for me to quit the first adult job I've ever had after about two months. Not to mention that I stormed out like a Broadway rendition of *9 to 5*.

Needless to say, I won't count on anyone from Smart Money Credit Union for a reference.

I pull my phone from my fanny pack and pause my music. Yes, I wear a fanny pack. May as well, since I'm a mom now. However, I draw the line at driving a minivan. I have some shred of dignity left. At least for now.

The urge to text or call Tanner is strong. I run my thumb across the screen of my phone, daring myself to select the contacts app. It wouldn't hurt to talk to him. It's not like I could see him right now anyway.

But what would I say? *Hey, sorry about running away from you at the park and hiding in the Pig. Oh, then ignoring your texts and voicemail checking on me. So how've you been?*

Ugh. I cringe and pull my knees into my chest. There's really no coming back from my temper tantrum turned cold shoulder. If I were him, I wouldn't even answer me. So why add another stab to my wound?

I go back to my music and pray Bubba doesn't shuffle through again while I finish my run. Even though I told my parents last night that I planned on running early this morning, I don't want Taylor waking up and hunting for me.

After adjusting my fanny pack, replacing my earbuds, and dusting the sand from my shorts, I'm ready to run. I head toward the pier, concentrating on how fast I can run in the sand to keep my mind off other issues.

The pier gets closer and the sun gets bigger the farther I run. I've about made it to my destination when the song in my ears tunes out in favor of my ringtone. I unzip my fanny pack and notice a number I don't recognize. It's local to Apple Cart, but that doesn't mean much nowadays with stealthy telemarketers.

On impulse, I decide to answer. A small piece of me hopes its Tanner's office number. Maybe he thinks that's the only way I'll answer.

"Hello?"

"May I speak with Ms. Abner?"

"This is she."

"This is Olivia Carter, dean of Apple Cart Community College."

I hold out the phone a second and catch my breath from running. Now that I know this call is legit, I don't want to pant though the receiver like a Saint Barnard.

"We closed the job board this morning for the dean's secretary position, and I've started going through resumes."

I lean forward, resting my free hand on my knee to steady myself.

"Ms. Abner, are you still there?"

"Yes, ma'am." I straighten to steady my voice.

"If you're still interested, I'd love to have you in for an interview."

"Yes, ma'am." I try not to sound too eager, but I'm not sure I succeed.

"Great, when could you come in?"

I slap my forehead, regretting not staying home. I could meet with her today if not. "I'm actually at the beach with family this week. We come home this weekend. So next Monday?" I clinch my teeth and pray that isn't too late.

"Sure. I can see you at eight a.m. a week from now."

"Yes, ma'am. I apologize for not being in town sooner."

"No problem, you'll just be my last interview. Come to the front of the college and ask for me at the lobby desk."

"Yes, ma'am. I look forward to it."

"I as well. See you then."

I keep the phone to my ear until I hear her hang up. I try not to focus on the part where she said "last interview." Of course, she plans on interviewing more candidates.

Turning around, I speed walk toward our condo. Working at the college was the job I'd hoped to get all along. Maybe this will work out.

I tuck my phone and earbuds in the fanny pack, then speed up even more. This gives me something to look forward to back home. Now, if only I could work things out with Tanner.

Tanner

My phone buzzes in my pocket. It's Jack.

"Hey."

"Hey, man. I talked to Darrell. They're just outside of Birmingham. He said he'd have her pick up the dog."

"Great. Oh, what does he know?" My stomach swirls at the notion that Jack might've mentioned the whole fake-relationship thing to Hannah's dad.

"Not much, just that y'all are on a break and you want to see her."

"Cool, you did good, Jack."

"I hope so. If not, you can borrow Bianca's deer."

"No way, that's my gift!" Bianca scolds him in the background.

I laugh. "Thanks, but tell Bianca she can keep the deer. I don't need something named after me with bullet holes in its head."

"Come on, I told you the whole Tanner thing was something I came up with last minute to make it through security."

"Whatever. Therapy deer my rear end."

"Seriously, I think this will work."

"Let's hope so. Talk later."

We both hang up, and I get back to work. Instead of playing poker last Sunday night, we morphed into planning how I can grovel to Hannah and win her back. For real this time.

Jack offered me the lodge to re-create the scene of our kiss. That whole kiss-scene re-creation was surprisingly Jonah's idea. He said that sort of thing happens a lot in movies. That led to us making fun of him for watching romantic comedies, even though we all do. Lucky for me, I have a sister who stays with me frequently as my excuse for watching them.

Since Hannah was at the beach, I had the week to hash everything out. Mary agreed to make a meal for us with the same foods from Jack's engagement party, including the small pecan pies.

Carolina had helped decorate the lodge that night, so I had her get the table we sat at under the big tree. She and Jonah also restrung lights in the tree. And for the final touch, I downloaded "Bubba Shot the Jukebox" on my phone.

So I'm not the most romantic person, but I know how to bring back a memory. And with any luck, all of this will lead to another toe-curling kiss.

The sun starts to set as I straighten the pillows on Jack's couch. Skip has made himself at home on the leather cushions. I jump at the sound of the doorbell and rush to open it. Either Hannah's early or . . .

"Mrs. Mary, come in."

"Hey, sugar. I usually come through the kitchen, but I only have the two dinners this time."

"Perfect." I accept the box from her arms. If heaven has a smell, this would be it. "How much do I owe you?"

She waves her plump hand in front of her face. "Nothing, nothing at all. I like to think of myself as your fairy godmother in this situation."

I chuckle. "I hope you are. You fit the bill better than Ms. Ethel."

Mary laughs and shakes her head. "Ain't that the truth."

"Thanks again."

"My pleasure. You let me know how it goes, all right?"

"Yes, ma'am."

She smiles, revealing the slight gap in her teeth, then retreats down the porch steps. I close the door with my foot and hold the box high when Skip comes sniffing. "Not for you, boy."

I place the box on the kitchen counter and start unpacking the contents. Beside the foil-covered plates is a note and a large candle from Daisy's.

Tanner,

Every southern woman loves a candlelit dinner. Trust me on this. Best of luck, sugar.

Mrs. Mary

I smile at the receipt paper covered with grease stains and solid advice from a woman I trust. "A candlelit dinner it is, then." I set the candle beside the plates and pull out drawers in the kitchen until I find Jack's grill lighter. Of course, it was buried under a hideous fish mitt.

The sun starts to set as I pace around the room and make sure everything is in place. When Hannah's had plenty of time to get back from the beach, I take the food outside, along with the candle. Then I turn on the lights hanging from the tree branches.

Now all that's left to do is wait and pray everything works out the way I planned. I join Skip on the couch and turn on the TV. We sit in silence for a few minutes until the doorbell rings. I exhale and get to my feet.

This is it.

CHAPTER TWENTY-TWO

Hannah

The last thing I wanted after a five-hour ride home with my family was to go pick up a dog. But Daddy missed Skip and said he'd told Jack he would get him tonight. He also asked if I'd pick him up so he could unpack all the suitcases and check the oil and tires on Mama's car.

I agreed, and Taylor offered to come with me. She claimed it was because she missed Skip, but I'm quite certain it was to prolong bedtime. Daddy must've agreed with me, because he promised to let her eat a cookie if she stayed back.

The adventure continued when I went to Jack's place and found a sign on the door that read, "At the lodge." I'd noticed some lights shining in the backyard on the way down to his house. I guess they're setting up to host an event tomorrow.

So now I'm on the front porch, waiting for Jack to answer so I can get the dog and go home. The door swings open and Tanner's standing behind it. My mouth goes dry. He's dressed in nice jeans and a button-down, hair in place, with those dimples that make me loopy as a cross-eyed cowboy.

"Tanner?" I run a hand across my messy bun and regret not slapping on some makeup and changing out of my gym shorts before coming. But in my defense, I assumed I'd be getting a dog from Jack. Not coming face to face with my knight in shining armor. I gulp.

"You look great."

I laugh so hard I snort. "Stop lying."

"I'm not lying. You always look great, and you're tan."

I hold out my arm and grin. "I am tan." At least that's one point in my favor.

"Come in."

I hesitate. This isn't how I pictured running into Tanner again. Can't he simply let me get the dog and leave? Take a rain check once I've showered and combed my hair?

An awkward moment passes as he smiles down at me. If he's mad, he's doing a good job hiding it. Despite my wavering mind, my body wants to join him, since I absent-mindedly wipe my flip-flops on the mat and step over the threshold. Skip notices me and runs, tail wagging. "Hey, buddy." I bend down and rub his ears, then stand. "Where's Jack?"

"Atlanta. He had some wedding stuff, so I offered to stay here with the dog last night and today."

"Huh." I want to ask if anyone else is here, but I refrain.

"Hope you don't mind."

I shake my head. "No, thanks for taking care of him." I slap my knees. "Here, Skip." He bounds back toward me from prancing around the living room furniture. I grab his collar and turn to leave. I'm sure Tanner wasn't expecting me tonight either.

"Hannah?" I twist my head, and Tanner's eyes lock on mine. He rubs his lips together as if he's got something to say, or as if he's about to kiss me. I'm not sure which, but my feet turn and take a step toward him.

"Yeah?"

"Can you come with me a minute?" He hooks a thumb over his shoulder toward the kitchen.

"Sure." I close the front door and let Skip loose again. He seems content with hopping on the couch and rooting around. Maybe Jack won't mind.

My heart picks up another notch with each step as I follow Tanner into the kitchen. What is going on? He opens the glass door leading to the patio. My eyes widen when I step outside. I fully expected to find his sister, or anyone else, back here decorating. Instead, the yard is void of anything besides the lights I saw when driving by earlier.

Tanner holds out his hand and smiles. I take it and lift the corners of my mouth into a slight smile as well. I have no idea where we're going or where any of this is going. But my hand relaxes in his. Oh, how I've missed his touch.

We walk hand in hand down the hill toward the same large tree we sat beneath at Bianca and Jack's party. As we get closer, I notice the same lights hanging from it and the same iron table and chairs beneath it. And there's a candle in the center of two place settings filled with food.

Tanner lets go of my hand and motions for me to sit. "You haven't eaten supper, have you?"

I grin and shake my head. "Just candied nuts from Bucky's. Daddy refused to stop, and I think I know why now." Which would also explain why he was so adamant that I go get Skip tonight, and why Jack happened to go out of town.

A laugh trickles out as I realize three redneck men have schemed against me. Or *for* me, in this case.

I glance down at the food in front of us. "This looks like the same meal from the party."

Tanner gestures around us. "Same meal, same table, same lights. I added a candle for ambiance."

I laugh harder.

"Oh." He holds up a finger. "But wait, there's more." He takes his phone from his pocket and hits a few buttons. "Bubba Shot the Jukebox" starts playing.

Now we're both laughing. My side starts to hurt as I double over. Never in my life would I have dreamed such a silly song would hold such meaning to me. After we finally settle down and catch our breaths, Tanner offers to pray.

I stare at my lap, smiling to myself as he thanks God for the food and for finally sharing another meal with me. All the while, stupid Bubba is shooting the jukebox in the background.

Once Tanner says, "Amen," I lift my head and meet his eyes. We sit in silence for a second, staring at one another. Then we both blurt out at the same time, "Jonah knows."

"What?" Tanner's eyes widen.

I sigh and shrug. "Jonah knows we were faking it."

He nods. "I know, I told him."

I narrow my eyes. "You told him?"

Tanner scratches his head and frowns. "Yeah, and Jack, and Ms. Ethel. All in a moment of weakness. I needed someone to talk to about it. I'm so sorry, Hannah."

"That's fine. I get Jack and Jonah, but Ms. Ethel?" I wrinkle my nose.

"She cornered me in the office. It was more to make her feel bad about pressuring us and every other single young adult in Apple Cart County."

I nod. "It doesn't matter. I told Jonah."

He wrinkles his forehead. "Really? He didn't tell me you told him."

"I told him not to say anything."

Tanner nods, then grins. "Good to know he can be trusted. When did you tell him?"

"In the Pig. The day you came in hunting me."

"Oh. Did he find you after I asked about you?"

I cringe. "Not exactly. I was squatted behind the register, tugging on his pant leg, asking him to lie for me."

"That little . . ." Tanner seethes.

"Tanner, don't get mad at Jonah. As soon as you left, he followed me and made me tell him what was going on. He didn't like lying to you. I guess he felt sorry for me."

"What did he say when you told him?"

"He was in shock. He thought we were really together."

Tanner nods.

"Sorry. I guess we both broke the deal by not keeping the secret."

He reaches across the table and takes my hand in his. "Hannah, it's fine. I broke the deal more than you."

I shake my head. "You may have told more people, but I told one of your best friends, and asked him to lie to you!"

Tanner lifts the corner of his mouth. "That's not what I'm talking about." He wraps his other hand around mine. "I broke the deal by not faking it."

"What do you mean?"

He peers around the space before meeting my eyes again. "That night, when we were here in this scene, I fell for you, hard. When I kissed you, I wasn't pretending or faking anything. It was the best kiss of my life."

The tension I didn't know I was carrying leaves my shoulders as a stray tear dances down my cheek. Still holding onto my hand, Tanner reaches up and wipes it away with his thumb. To hear him say that the kiss meant as much to him as it did me means everything.

"Hannah, that day in the park, I'd planned on asking you if you'd want to forget the whole deal and date me for real."

My vision blurs with tears. Tanner moves his chair closer to mine and wipes them away. "You did?"

He nods. "But you started all that talk about seeing other people, and I decided to let myself down easy. Suggest going along with the fake thing a little longer in hopes you'd come around."

I sniffle and blot the corners of my eyes, now thankful I didn't wear makeup. If I had, I'd look like Lady Gaga at a waterpark. "Tanner, I'm sorry."

He pats my hand. "It's okay. You can't help how you feel or don't feel."

"You're right." I suck in a breath and shake my head. "I felt jealous."

He blinks. "Jealous? Of what?"

I pull in my shoulders, almost ashamed to bring up what I've been avoiding. The blonde in Tuscaloosa is sure to make me sound like some desperate divorcée, but there's no turning back now.

"Some college girl came in Adrianne's the day I was getting my hair done. She started talking about seeing you in Tuscaloosa joking around with a beautiful blonde at the sushi place."

Tanner squints his eyes at the sky as if thinking. Then he widens them and drops his head toward me. "It had to be Bianca."

"What?"

"Last time I went to eat sushi in Tuscaloosa was a few weeks back with Jack and Bianca. He went to the restroom, and this girl from Auburn came up messing with me."

"Was she a redhead?"

"Yeah." He lets go of my hand and snaps his fingers. "That's her. I helped her out when she was drunk one night in Auburn. She flirted with me then and tried to again at the restaurant. But Bianca started teasing me about her, then whispered to me how you were so much better. I guess she thought we were together."

Groaning, I rake my hands down my face. "Ugh, I'm so embarrassed."

Tanner laughs. "Don't be embarrassed. I'm flattered you were jealous."

I peek through my fingers and shake my head before lowering my hands. "No, that's pathetic. I was jealous of your best friend's fiancée. How stupid."

He reaches for my hand again. "Hannah, it's not stupid. I just wish you'd have told me so I could've explained."

I sigh. "Our deal was to not be seen in Apple Cart with other people. I didn't want to interfere with your personal life in case you really did want to date someone."

"I do. *You!*"

What's left of me melts in a puddle. "Still?"

He grins wider, making those dimples pop in place. "If the offer's still on the table. And if Taylor approves, of course."

"Oh, she approves. Day one at the beach, she said she wished you were there to help her build sandcastles."

He laughs. "Glad to know someone missed me."

I frown. "I missed you, too, Tanner. More than you can know."

He strokes the back of my hand and drops his head. After awkwardly staring at his feet, he says, "I have one more question."

"Yeah?"

His eyes lift to mine, his face now serious as a heart attack. "I need to know if there's anything between you and Dalton." His Adam's apple bobs as he waits for my reply.

I wrinkle my brow. "Dalton? Why would you ask that?"

Tanner takes a breath before continuing. "A few Saturdays ago, I went to your Mama's to talk to you. I couldn't stand how we left things, and regardless of how you felt, I had to find out. Dalton answered the door."

I grab the edge of the table to keep from falling off my chair. "He did what?" I grit my teeth. It had to be the few minutes I walked down to the blueberry bushes to give him some alone time with Taylor. That didn't mean he had permission to answer his ex-mother-in-law's house calls.

Tanner raises his palms, then slaps the table. "He was at y'all's house. Said he was back in your life."

I toss my head back and inhale a huge gulp of air. "No, he did not."

"Is it true?"

I straighten my head and frown. "Not in the way he suggested. He asked to come back, and I pretty much let him know I'd moved on. We talked, and I agreed it would be good for both him and Taylor to have a relationship." I waver my head. "So the only way he's in my life is in the form of visitation rights for Taylor."

Tanner lowers his head on the table. "Oh, thank God."

I laugh. "I can't believe you thought I'd go back to him."

He raises his head and laughs. "Kinda how you thought I had the hots for Bianca?"

I slap his arm, and we both laugh harder. "We're both crazy."

"I'm crazy for you." He wiggles his eyebrows, making me laugh even more. "I even brought you flowers, but there was no way I was giving them to him."

I tilt my head. Flowers? "Wait, did they have a green zip tie around the stems?"

"Yep. That's all I could find in a pinch to hold them together."

"That rat."

"What?"

"Mama had them in a vase. She said Dalton brought them for Taylor."

Tanner rolls his eyes. "Of course he'd take credit for them. I dropped them in the driveway while I was getting out of dodge."

"I should've known something was off when he didn't bring them to the door right away."

"Doesn't matter now."

"Guess not."

Tanner stands and offers me his hand. I take it, and he wraps his other arm around my lower back, then spins me. "What matters now is we're here together, dancing in the . . . " He stares up at the tree above us. "Christmas lights Carol and Jonah so graciously hung this afternoon."

I giggle. "Sounds like you had a lot of people in on this little dinner date."

"We have a lot of people rooting for us, Hannah. Ms. Ethel included."

I smirk. "Well, we may as well give them something to talk about."

"For real." Tanner cups his hands around my face and brings it to his. Time stands still as his lips cover mine.

I'm not wearing a cute dress or an Adrianne makeover for my hair and face. Instead, I'm in old Nike shorts, a wrinkled T-shirt, and no makeup. But somehow, this kiss is even better than the last. Because unlike the last kiss, this kiss is meant to last. No more playing around or putting on a show for all of Apple Cart.

This kiss is for us.

After fireworks ignite inside me and a million fairy tales come true, we finally pull away. Tanner leans his forehead to mine and grins with those mesmerizing dimples.

"So are we doing this for real?" he asks.

I nod. "For real." Then I scrunch my brow and glance down at his phone. "Have you been playing 'Bubba Shot the Jukebox' this whole time?"

He bites his bottom lip. "Well, it is kinda our song."

I shake my head. "We need a new song."

Tanner bends and reaches his arm behind my knees, hoisting me into his arms. "We have our whole lives to find a new song."

I smile. "I hope so."

"I know so. As long as Taylor approves, of course."

"Of course." I smile.

He reaches across the table and hands me two mini pies. "What do you say we start with dessert on the front-porch rockers?"

I grin. "I've missed rocking-chair dessert time with you."

He kisses the top of my head and does his best to jog up the hill with me. I laugh hysterically as I try to balance the two small tins. Life with Tanner Nash is going to be fun.

Tanner

I gaze around in awe of how little the elementary school gym has changed in twenty years. The walls are still a weird beige yellow, and there's still a few dodgeballs caught in the rafters. Probably some on my account. While the flooring looks updated, and they've added a stage, the same metal bleachers that pinch your pants line the walls.

Hannah inhales and wrinkles her nose. Still smells like dust.

I laugh. "Brings back memories, huh?"

She cocks a smile. "Yeah. It's kind of cool Taylor gets to go to our old school."

I nod. "Emphasis on the old."

Hannah taps a tall formation of balloons. "They decorate cuter than when we were here. I'm sure Pinterest is to thank for that."

"For the giant balloon banana?" I wrinkle my forehead at the odd structure standing tall as me.

Hannah giggles. "No silly, that's a pencil."

I cock my head. "It is?"

"See, the top part's the lead."

"Oh, I thought that was the banana stem." I take a step back and form a square with my hands, then turn them. "If it was straighter, I might could see a pencil."

Laughing harder, she rolls her eyes and focuses on Taylor. "Are you ready to meet your teacher?"

Taylor nods wilder than a hula girl on a dashboard. She's wearing a cute dress with apples all over it and a red ribbon in her hair. Several other kids mill around with their parents, and it's easy to pick out which ones are ready for school and which ones aren't.

I'm neither a parent nor a stepparent . . . *yet*. However, Taylor asked me to come, and I couldn't turn her down. It's a big week for both my girls. Taylor starts school, and Hannah starts her new job at Apple Cart Community College. I'm excited for both of them, and super pumped that I no longer have to face Samuel when I want to see Hannah at work.

Hannah points toward a table filled with clipboards and candy. A big sign on the front reads, "Mrs. Haynes's Kindergarten." She smiles at Taylor. "There's your teacher."

Taylor grabs both of us by the hand and leads the way. Hannah and I nod or greet other adults along the way, many of whom grew up here like us. Apple Cart doesn't get a lot of new residents. Families just recycle. Occasionally, someone like Bianca will marry a local and move in. I snicker at the idea of her moving here full time, but it should happen soon enough.

"What's funny?"

I turn to Hannah. "Oh, just imagining Bianca moving here."

She smiles. "It'll be fun."

"Yeah, for us."

My head bobs as Taylor jerks us. "Come on." We shuffle through people to the table. "There's my teacher. She's pretty."

A young woman, most likely straight out of college, smiles at us. Between her perfect teeth and petite frame, she could moonlight as a Disney princess. Very fitting to teach kindergarten. Unlike the beastly old hag I had. I shudder at the memory of my first year. No wonder I didn't like school.

Mrs. Haynes bends toward Taylor. "Hello, I'm Mrs. Haynes. Your new teacher."

Taylor doesn't miss a beat. She drops our hands and extends hers to the teacher. "Nice to meet you. I'm Taylor Abner. This is my mama and my Tanner."

A warmth gushes across my chest. She just referred to me as "my Tanner." That's the most adorable thing I've ever heard. Hannah grins at me, then introduces herself to the teacher. I do the same, but everything the teacher says after that is muffled. I'm still in shock that Taylor thinks so much of me after a few months. Much less, after only two weeks of officially dating her mother. Of course, she doesn't know that.

Aside from the handful of confidantes we told, everyone in town, our families included, assumes we were dating, took a break, and then got back together. I'm sure we'll tell her parents the truth one day, but I doubt I'll let my parents in on my scheme.

I worried about Ms. Ethel letting the cat out of the bag. Then I overheard her bragging to some women in the office that she knew all along we would work things out. She even went as far as to suggest that she set us up. I started to step in and correct her, but better to let it go than out myself as an eavesdropper like the rest of them.

I wait while Hannah fills out the paperwork for Mrs. Haynes, then follow her and Taylor to a makeshift photo booth. We take a round of photos, both silly and serious, before heading out of the gym.

"Whew." I roll up my sleeves and fan my face. "We had to break some sort of fire code with the amount of people packed in that gym."

"This is a big kindergarten class for Apple Cart."

"Much bigger than when we went through." I turn to Taylor. "Hey, since this is your last day off work, how about we go get ice cream to cool off?"

"Work?" Her face sours.

"Yeah, school is your new job."

She shakes her head. "No, it isn't. They're not paying me."

I look at Hannah, and we both laugh. I shake my head at Taylor. "Kid, you won't do."

"How about ice cream for you starting school and us starting back to work, then?" Hannah raises her eyebrows at Taylor.

"That's more accurate. I'm in." She grabs both of our hands again.

The three of us walk toward my truck. A funny sensation of satisfaction runs through me. For the first time since I can remember, I feel complete.

No more casual dates to throw the grannies off my trail or to fill a mundane Saturday night. No more finding my full identity in a job or playing the fun one around all my friends. I'm free to just live my life and actually look forward to a future with Hannah—and Taylor.

Best of all, I no longer have to pretend. This is real life. They've welcomed me into their lives, and one day, I'm quite certain we'll form our own little family.

EPILOGUE

Four Months Later

Hannah

I lean back against Tanner and pull the blanket over my legs. Taylor came back from her dad's house late last night, which meant she went to bed way past her bedtime. That also meant I had to stay up extra late playing Santa.

However, her excitement at a new dollhouse by the tree and the half-eaten cookies made it all worth it. Tanner blinks beside me. As my righthand elf, he snuck in and clocked at least two hours on the dollhouse before going home to sleep himself. He was the one who insisted he get here early to see her reaction, though.

Mama videos Taylor on her phone, while Daddy has his pocket knife ready to slice the tape and ties from any toy she brings his way.

"I thought she'd be done opening gifts by now," Tanner comments.

I yawn. "Nope. Mama bought at least half of this. You just knew what I got her."

"Well, she's getting even more from my family tonight." He laughs. "And I'm not responsible for all the weird souvenirs my parents might have bought y'all on their RV trips."

I laugh. "I can't wait."

"Trust me, you can. But for what my mama messes up with gifts, she makes up for with food."

"Speaking of food, we get to eat Grinch pancakes once we're done with gifts," Mama chimes in.

I press my lips together. I'd forgotten she was videoing for a moment. Our comments about Tanner's mama's gifts will be on the video. Oh well, part of family Christmas memories. At least he complimented her cooking.

"What are Grinch pancakes?" Tanner asks.

Mama's face lights up. "They're green pancakes with sprinkles and whipped cream."

Daddy frowns. "You don't have to add the sprinkles and whipped cream."

Mama stops videoing and swats at Daddy's arm. "Darrell, you're such a Grinch."

He shrugs. "I like my pancakes with syrup only."

Taylor rips into her last gift and takes it to Daddy to cut open. "Nana, now I can have Grinch pancakes?"

"Yes." Mama stands, and so does Tanner.

"Wait a minute. I have one more gift." Tanner goes to the tree and pulls a box from behind one of the branches. He brings it to me and grins. "Here. This is from me."

We've only been together four months, and it's not small enough for a ring. Although I'd gladly say "yes" in a heartbeat, we both agreed to take things slow because of Taylor. I pull the ribbon loose, curious as to what he's giving me.

When I lift the box, my eyebrows lift with it. "Uh, okay . . ." I hold up a white lace garter.

"Is that lingerie?" Daddy leaps from his recliner as if he's ready to tackle Tanner.

Tanner turns red and holds up his palms in protest. "No, sir. It's a garter, and I don't intend on Hannah wearing it. Let me explain."

Both my parents stare at Tanner for an explanation, while Taylor is thankfully preoccupied with a pile of Barbies.

Tanner takes the garter from my hand. "This is a symbol of our love." A bit of confusion clouds the anger on my parents' faces. "I caught this at my friend Lacie's wedding not long before I met Hannah again. Everyone teased me, saying I would be the last person to get married. At the time, I caught it just to be funny, then stuffed it in the glove box of my truck and forgot about it. I didn't have anyone in my life then I would consider marrying, and my friends weren't far off on their assumption."

Tanner sits by me before continuing. "But then Hannah came back, and we started hanging out. She was unlike anyone else I've ever known, and I fell in love with her. Now, I know I'm still a little immature at times and rough around the edges, but I love Hannah, and Taylor." He holds up the garter, then puts it back in my hand. "So I'm giving her this as a promise. One day, I plan on proposing, when the time is right. But this garter symbolizes that I will one day get married to Hannah."

Mama moans and wipes tears from her eyes. "That's the sweetest thing I've ever heard!" She rushes over and engulfs Tanner and me in a huge hug. She cries against us, "And I don't have it on video!"

"Sheila, forget about the camera. Some things you just remember." Daddy is standing behind Mama when she pulls away from us. She goes from my arms to his and continues to cry.

He pats her back with one hand and extends the other to Tanner. "Sorry about the confusion. As far as I'm concerned, you're already a part of our family."

"Thank you, sir." Tanner shakes Daddy's hand.

I sit up straighter on the couch and stare at the tree. "I guess we can hang this on the tree as Tanner's ornament."

Tanner shrugs. "Sounds good to me."

Mama sniffles some, then goes to the tree. "But I already bought him that porcelain chicken."

Daddy and I simultaneously shake our heads at the ugly chicken from the General Store.

"Oh, right. I guess the garter has more meaning." Mama removes the hideous chicken from the tree. I stand and hang the garter in its place.

Tanner comes and puts his arm around my shoulder, admiring the new addition to the tree. "This garter will make for a good story every Christmas."

I smile. "Yeah, and to think all this started with a fake relationship."

"Fake relationship?" both my parents ask in bewilderment.

"Did I say that aloud?" I grit my teeth at Tanner, and he laughs.

"Looks like we've got another story to tell over Grinch pancakes." He bends down and kisses me as we continue to laugh.

Want to read Jonah and Carolina's friends to lovers story? Check out *Hammered by Love*.

If you enjoyed *Chicken about Love*, I'd love it if you left a review to help other readers find my books.

ACKNOWLEDGMENTS

First, I would like to thank God for giving me creative ideas and placing the right people in my path to help see them to fruition.

My husband, Blake, gets credit next for always supporting my writing endeavors, even if he finds my stories a little too "girly and Hallmarkish." But this one wasn't too bad.

Thanks to my friend, Chad Gilreath, for answering some random questions I had about the chicken business.

I also want to thank my friend, Sandy, who is great at reading my books and pointing out anything I missed. The same goes for editor, Joanne, and my ARC team. I couldn't pull this off without all of your help! Each of you is appreciated so much!

ABOUT THE AUTHOR

Kaci Lane is a journalist turned fiction writer who believes all stories should have a happy ending. While unsuccessfully trying to learn Spanish for a decade, she has become fluent in sarcasm, Southern belle and movie quotes. She is married to a Southern Gentleman and has two young children who help keep her humility in check. Connect with her on kacilane.com or follow her on Amazon for upcoming releases.

BOOKS BY KACI LANE

Schooled on Love Series

Taco Truck Takedown

Side Hustle

Buggy List

Off-Season

No Brides Club Series*

No Time for Traditions

Silver Leaf Falls Novellas Series*

A Perfect Match in Silver Leaf Falls

Bama Boys Series

Hunting for Love

Chicken about Love

Hammered by Love

Guilty of Love

Bama Boys related stand alone:

Christmas in Dixie**

*Shared series with other authors

**If you enjoyed *Hunting for Love*, you will enjoy *Christmas in Dixie*, which features some of the same characters during the holiday season in Apple Cart County.

www.ingramcontent.com/pod-product-compliance
Lightning Source LLC
LaVergne TN
LVHW041624060526
838200LV00040B/1426